Mikhail addressed the three crew members. "The mission to Kythe-Correy involves taking along five or six scientists, to be observers. They're going to study every phase of the cataclysm, from the orbital paths of the asteroids to the spread of the—"

"Cataclysm?" Taviella asked in a tight voice. "What cataclysm?"

Mikhail's shoulders slumped. He took a deep breath. "Kythe-Correy is a world, not far from here, with a full, lush biosphere. Plants, animals, the works. A complete and highly evolved chain of life.

"The mission is to kill it."

VOYAGE
OF THE
PLANETSLAYER

by Jefferson Swycaffer

Book 2
Tales of the Concordat

Cover illustration by
Mario Macari

New Infinities Productions, Inc.
P.O. Box 657
Delavan WI 53115

VOYAGE OF THE PLANETSLAYER

The New Infinities Productions logo is a trademark
owned by New Infinities Productions, Inc.

The "BSM" logo is a trademark belonging to Berkley
Publishing Corporation.

First Printing, October 1988

Printed in the United States of America

Distributed to the book trade by Berkley Sales & Mar-
keting, a division of the Berkley Publishing Group, 200
Madison Avenue, New York, New York 10016

9 8 7 6 5 4 3 2 1

I S B N : 0-425-11341-8

New Infinities Productions, Inc.
P.O. Box 657
Delavan WI 53115

Acknowledgment

Several of the concepts and nomenclatures used in this story are taken from the *Imperium*™ and *Traveller*® games, published by Game Designers' Workshop and designed by Marc W. Miller, to whom all my thanks for his kind permission regarding this use.

Loyalty, more than sunlight, makes the crops to grow.

— Achorus,
The Skeleton and the Chaffinch

1

We have created a situation in which there is an uncertain death penalty in force, which I hold is far worse than the certainty of a judge telling you the date on which you will die.

John Bradley, *The Undealt Hand*

Stasileus was the only one aboard the *Coinroader* when the Commerce Branch messenger arrived. Alien and man regarded one another with wide-eyed interest, the messenger pausing to survey Stasileus's towering, fur-bearing figure from crown to toe. Stasileus, for his part, was still unaccustomed to the varieties of mankind and gazed in rapt, innocent fascination at the young, red-haired messenger.

"Are you able to sign for your new orders?" the human asked, afraid for a moment that some subtle error on his part might elicit a snarl of attack from the white-furred alien.

Stasileus cocked his head curiously to one side and thought for a moment. "Yes." His voice was high and resonant and echoed strangely in the grounded ship's cramped airlock.

"Take them," the messenger said with a gulp. He thrust forth an unsteady hand gripping a loose sheaf of papers. Stasileus reached out and took the papers gently in his huge, four-fingered hand and held them as if they possessed an innate, if unknown, relevance.

Loath as he was to press his luck, orders were orders for the messenger. "Now sign here." He held out a clipboard and pencil.

Stasileus accepted them and looked them over with interest, but he seemed unprepared to apply the pencil to the forms. After a moment, however, he realized what was required and indited a mechanically perfect rendition of his name in thick, blunt block letters. He returned the items and smiled happily.

The messenger tipped his cap briefly and fled across the landing field. Stasileus watched him go.

Two races, tied to one another by destiny and in origin, had inherited the star-spanning jump drive from the downfall of a calamitously energetic precursor civilization. Having recently discovered one another, they seemed unable, still, to understand how to begin to cooperate.

Stasileus, the Verna, turned and padded back into the ship, shaking his large head in puzzlement. His thick, clumsy fingers turned the papers one by one as he speed-skimmed them. The small pointed ears atop his head were perked forward in interest, and his eyes, normally huge, grew even wider in astonishment.

Commerce Branch Relocation Order (the cover form read):

You are hereby ordered to proceed to Marterly/Environ, where you will report to Treasury Branch local division head.

The note, Stasileus saw with some relief, was addressed to the captain and crew of the *Coinroader*, and not to him alone. For a moment, caught up in his instinctive need to obey, he had been troubled with several doubts and concerns, not the least of which involved the fact that he didn't know how to fly the *Coinroader* by himself.

The orders involved him, however, as a member of the crew; he promptly set about preparing the ship for lift-off. He closed up all the auxiliary hull ports, took an inventory of fuel and other supply stocks, then hurried back to the engine room and patiently ran through the engine warm-up checklist. The work relaxed him, and the close walls of the engine room comforted him. He felt better in the tight quarters; he could ignore his loneliness.

Remington Bose was the first of the rest of the crew to arrive back at the small ship. He tromped aboard with heavy footfalls, stretching and yawning so loudly that Stasileus heard him the length of the ship away.

"Stacey?"

"Yes, Remington?"

"Why's the reactor all heated up? You tuning the engines, or are we going somewhere?" Remington was a large man, beefy and thick, with powerfully muscled forearms. He moved briefly to the cargo bay and looked around, confirming that it was still empty, seeing nothing that indicated the ship was ready to set out. He returned to the engine room, ran his hand through his short dark hair, and looked suspiciously at Stasileus.

"We have to go to Marterly," Stasileus answered. He held up the sheaf of relocation orders.

"Damn," Remington muttered as he began picking his way through the papers. "Damn and double damn," he said after a while. He looked up at Stasileus. "Do you know what these are?"

"No."

"Reactivation orders to go with the relocation ones. They're calling us out of reserve."

"Is that bad?" The words meant little to Stasileus, but he understood the lines of worry that edged Remington's eyes.

"Bad?" Remington thought it over. "It could be. Could be. . . ." He shook his head and thumped back into the cargo bay. "Got a thousand things to do before we boost out of here. . . ." he mumbled.

Stasileus felt better for having him aboard.

The next to arrive was Eric Fuller, the ship's engineer and Stasileus's immediate superior. He was relaxed and happy as he stepped through the lock — then stiff, tense, and alert the moment he was aboard. He charged back through the ship and dove virtually headfirst into the engine room, there to halt and cast his gaze about. His neck was unnaturally rigid and his eyes intense as he stared at Stasileus with suspicious anger. His neat blond hair was in sudden disarray; his dark eyes blazed.

His stance was that of a fighter encountering a sudden emergency.

"Why are the reactors cooking?" he demanded in a foghorn voice.

Stasileus shrank a little from Eric's wrath. Remington poked his head in through the door, but said nothing for the moment.

"We're warming up for takeoff," Stasileus said mildly. "We have orders."

"Orders? What—" He sensed Remington behind him and whirled. "What orders?" he repeated. He was relieved, at least, at being able to ask his stupid questions of someone who didn't *always* give stupid answers.

"Commerce Branch relocation orders." Remington handed Eric the papers.

Eric's anger grew more intense as he paged through the packet. "They can do this. Oh, yes, they've got the authority." His eyes blazed. "But I never thought they'd stoop to meddling with us. Us! What are we to them?"

"They want us all."

"They've *got* to stop interfering with us. Having Stacey aboard is bad enough. What are they going to want next?"

Stasileus, who couldn't have helped but overhear, said nothing and continued with the warm-up checklist.

"Remember, we don't own the ship," Remington said mildly.

"They don't own me, either," Eric fumed. "I could quit. I've got a surplus balance in my account. I don't have to put up with their damned pushy attitude. Look — these orders don't even say what we'll be carrying! I don't like it."

"It's too early not to like it."

"It's never too early not to like something," Eric concluded grimly. "Stacey! Stop that! Stop what you're doing!"

Stasileus left off with his double-checking of systems indicators and stepped back. His wide shoulders were straight and back, his head high, his hands at his sides. He might have been a statue, carved from a slab of cold, obedient granite.

Eric could feel Remington's disapproving gaze boring a hole in his back. He swallowed and continued in a milder tone, "You ought to have waited for me. Let's . . . uh . . . let's go through the checklist together, okay?"

While waiting for the other two crew members to return, the three of them puttered about, making things shipshape and bantering idly among themselves. This last was restricted mostly to Remington and Eric: Stasileus was too literal-minded to be any good at jocularity.

It was a dull and heavy three hours later before Maravic Slijvos arrived. The ship's navigator and copilot, she was a good-natured soul of generous mien and gentle temperament. The crew liked to joke that she had never lost her temper in her life.

"Are we going somewhere?" she asked sweetly, with a quiet little dart of sarcasm, as she strolled unannounced into the engine room.

Eric looked up in alarm, then relaxed. "Marterly. A nice planet, by most accounts. I looked up its stats in the gazetteer."

14

Maravic frowned very slightly. "Was this your idea?"

"Nope. Stacey's."

Maravic greeted the flip answer with a small sigh — which was, she immediately thought, more recognition than it deserved. Then, for the same reason that Eric had sought Remington for answers, she backed away and looked about for the cargo chief. Stasileus was sad to see her go: with her nearby, the engine room had been quite comfortably crowded. He looked down and wished, once more, that humans liked to stand a little more closely together.

"Remington?" Maravic found him in the deeper recesses of the cargo hold, fastening down loose items that had long since been very securely tied.

"Yes'm?"

"Marterly? Why?"

"Oh, right." He looked about, trying to recall where he'd last seen the package of orders. "Ah. Here we are." He pulled the stack of papers from a low shelf and handed it to her. Already it had become slightly dog-eared and the worse for wear; she read it over quickly. Looking about the mostly empty cargo bay, she thought about the profit-and-loss statement that such a wasted trip would generate. She sighed, this time long and deep.

"Taviella's going to be upset. . . ."

∞

Taviella-i-Tel, the ship's pilot and owner (under some Commerce Branch restrictions) fought her way through the crowd of eagerly milling speculators until she reached a place where she could see the scratchboard. Here in the crowded market gallery, wading through the crush, she sought to find a cargo that might offer a hope of a profit.

The high-vaulted room rang with the clamor of half a thousand voices, as half a thousand men and women vied for control of the commodities listed on the board. Cargo brokers scuttled back and forth, often stopping to bellow into their headsets. A wall-mounted bank of telephones was in constant use by buyers and sellers trying to get their orders through. The phones connected them to patient data-entry operators behind a large glass partition, whose job it was to register sales and opportunities for sales upon the scratchboard. Everywhere Taviella looked, people ran, rushed, and scurried — all of them, it seemed, shouting without the least trace of decorum.

She elbowed aside a large, fast-moving man who would have knocked her flat if she hadn't known how to lean into the impact. He staggered, gave her a momentary and uninterested glance, and sped on. It amused Taviella to note that he wasn't even annoyed. She didn't know how the regulars here could get through even a single day without accumulating enough bruises to hobble them for life. She sighed, a weary but good-natured sigh of anticipation. It was here that she'd find a cargo, and with it, a destination. Shipping was tight, and that was good: the competition for carriers would drive the tonnage price a bit higher. The way to profit, she knew, was always to take advantage of local fluctuations of shipping and cargo, and then to be gone away to some other spaceport before the word got around.

The high ceiling was vaulted and domed, a style favored in spaceport architecture perhaps two hundred years ago. The walls were bland and sterile, high domes and arches of pale sky blue, lacking murals or other decoration. She compared its austere grandeur with the vibrant colors and glittering decor of other ports, some quite close to Conops' World, where different planets had passed through different phases of art and style. At least the scratchboard here was up to date, displaying the offers and demands in a clear, tokenized shorthand that saved space and was very quickly comprehensible. She had learned to despise boards that depended on scrolling messages specifically spelled out in common language, although she knew that some notices could be publicized in no other way.

No one paid Taviella any real attention: she could have been any of a hundred spaceship captains searching for a cargo. Her long blond hair might have set her apart, or her high cheekbones and pale face; people might have noticed her amber eyes or her tall, long-legged stance. But her uniform was plain enough: a battered yellow and black jumpsuit, with pockets everywhere and notepads and chronometers clipped to belt and wrists. She was just one more Commerce Branch free-lancer, trying to smooth out the wrinkles in the economy with a small transport ship.

The scratchboard changed character, and Taviella shifted through the crowd for a better view. No one paid her any heed. That amused her; she was as different from most of them as a person could be.

They had grown to adulthood in the cities and schools of civilized planets, while she had fought her way up from savagery, having been rescued in her late adolescence from the primitive world of her birth. They were descendants of the revolutionaries, who had risen up in a tide of foment and slain their sultans and their emperor; she was a descendant, through several lines and over many years, of that very same emperor. They were little more than pieces of a great machine; she had the capability of taking sovereign command and ordering the stars into a new Empire. But, for all that, she only yearned to be more like the others — particularly, more like Eric and Remington, and especially like Maravic. She laughed: yes, even more like Stasileus. Her crew was composed of the most wonderful people she had ever known, and it was to them that she owed her complete loyalty.

A new series of listings popped onto the board, appearing like mushrooms on a lawn, or as the stars do at night: one here, one there, then another, until the once-blank board was crammed with them.

There were shipments, transshipments, cargos lost, cargos found, cargos to be split up, cargos to be combined. There were foodstuffs, radioactives, genetic encapsulations, machine parts, industrial chemicals, storage information registers, treasury shipments, military support supplies, and bales and bundles of unknown and unlabeled goods, most licit, some illicit.

There was also a corner of the board that listed Commerce Branch reactivations from reserve. She ordinarily would never have noted it, but her gaze happened to pass that way, and she saw the name *Coinroader* in bold print.

The first deep breath she took was of surprise; the second, of anger. And by the third, she was back in control of herself. *The ship isn't mine. It belongs to the Concordat of Archive; it belongs to the Commerce Branch. They only lent it to me with the understanding that they could order its recall at any time.* She wasn't any happier about it after this reflection, but she knew enough not to start a fight she couldn't possibly win.

The busy bank of sales-order phones had people stacked up in long lines waiting for a connection with the scratchboard. Another bank of phones was less used; it tied in to the Commerce Branch's services directly. Taviella found an unused phone-stand and coded for help. A recorded message came over the handset, stating matter-of-factly what ships were recalled to what service. "The *River Vapor,* Commerce Branch Reserve, Stonager's World; The *Off Pace Ace,* Military Transport, Volpla; The *Roasted Swan,* Commerce Branch Reserve, Perrin; The *Coinroader,* Treasury Branch Reserve, Marterly; The *Impassionate Distorter,* Commerce Branch Reserve, Corbo . . ."

The list went on for some time, and Taviella, dumbstruck at the invasiveness of it, listened to it until it began to repeat.

Our service gains us little, she realized. *There is no security, no safety, no peace. What we earn, someone else can take away.* The quiet, efficient, mechanical way that she had been robbed of her ship still amazed her.

Okay. We're going to Marterly. There was no sense going with an empty cargo hold. Shaking her head, she strolled back through the press of anxiously shouting traders and scanned the scratchboard until she found a shipment with the same destination that had been imposed upon her.

∞

She arrived back at the *Coinroader* at about the same time the sun was setting at the edge of the spaceport's landing field. The cargo she'd signed for had already begun to be carted out. Remington stood on the bare concrete, swearing furiously, directing a team of lift operators as they clumsily shifted cluster after cluster of shining stainless steel cylinders from their low carts. Beyond him, the cargo door of the *Coinroader* gaped, level with the surface of the field.

Remington's language got cleaner quickly, the moment he saw her. "Hello, Taviella. We got some bad news."

"The hijacking to Marterly? Or something else?" Distressed as she was, she still remembered to give him a smile. "You doing okay with these nitwits?"

"Um, yeah." Remington tugged at his jumpsuit belt and stamped his feet meaninglessly a couple of times. "I can get this all loaded, don't you worry. You already heard about our new orders?"

"I heard. How long until you're loaded up?"

Remington gazed expertly over the cylinders, then ran his thumb down a list of figures on his cargo manifest. "Less'n an hour."

"Stay with it." Taviella gave him a cheery thumbs-up sign, then went quietly away to circle the ship and inspect what she could see of it. It was snuggled down in its landing pit, so that only half of its bulk was visible. What she could see of it resembled a large, blunt wedge, a huge axe blade, flat on its side, thickest at the rear where the engines and engine vents were. She leaned over the edge of the landing pit, bracing one hand out against the *Coinroader's* rough flank. Peering down at the fuel umbilici and landing restraints, she assured herself that all was well, to a visual inspection anyway.

Shrugging, she returned to the crewlock and crossed over into the ship. The open cargolock let in an unaccustomed breath of fresh evening air and the unexpected glowing colors of sunset. The normally stuffy cargo bay seemed even darker and more cavernlike, with partially stacked cylinders piled up like broad, rounded stalagmites; Taviella hurried back to the engine room. Outside the hatch, Maravic lounged, sitting comfortably crosslegged on the deck, trying to pay no attention to the fuss being raised within. She saw Taviella and waved in evident relief.

"What's up?" Taviella asked, already knowing full well. Eric's loud, bawling voice carried, even over the clanks and thumps of the cargo being loaded.

"Our two pets are spatting," Maravic said with a sigh. "Honestly, there are days I couldn't choose which of them to push overboard."

"Both," Taviella laughed.

Maravic's face fell. "Oh, there's something you've got to know—"

"Marterly? Our freedom's at an end?" She didn't mean to sound so bitter, but the call-up still rankled painfully. She had been the master of her own fate, and now . . .

"Did Remington tell you?"

"Yes. But I also found out back at the market gallery. They had it posted."

"Did Remington show you the papers?"

"Hmm? We got papers delivered, too?"

"You know the folks at the Commerce Branch. Do they ever miss a bet?" Sighing deeply, Maravic fumbled about her, looking for the sheaf of orders. "Oh, blast. . . . They were right around here. . . ." She stood swiftly and shot off on a search of the ship. "I'll be right back," she called over her shoulder. "I'm sure they're right nearby."

Taviella shook her head as she watched Maravic prod and pry among the fixtures and facilities of the cargo bay and the tiny crew rest area. Then, from inside the engine room, Eric's voice rose to a full-throated cry, and Taviella knew she couldn't ignore it any longer.

"You lop-eared, fur-bearing, useless piece of garbage!" Eric swore. "Don't you hold *me* accountable to my own checklist!"

Trouble. Taviella ducked into the cramped engine room and pierced Eric with a sharp gaze.

Behind him, Stasileus had gone into his most cata-
tonic obedience-trance, standing stiffly erect, his
arms at his sides, his eyes wide — too wide — and
blankly staring.

"Don't yell at the Verna," she told Eric coolly but
firmly. "He's not like us."

"You can say that again," Eric grumbled. The
two of them turned to Stasileus.

"Stacey?" Taviella called softly. "You can relax.
Eric was just letting off steam."

Slowly, trembling minutely, Stasileus relaxed,
his stance easing into a more comfortable position.
His eyes recovered also, until his normally cheerful
personality showed again in his still wide-eyed,
foolish expression.

"You were right to call me off against my checklist, Stacey," Eric said a bit sourly. "That's what
checklists are for." Eyeing Taviella sidelong, he
muttered, "I apologize."

"I knew I was doing the right thing," Stasileus
said in his soft, echoing voice. "I *am* an engineer."

"Less than an hour until we're loaded, guys,"
Taviella said, happy to have yet another crisis over
with. "Will you be ready to take off?"

"Yeah. Say, did Maravic show you—"

"Our new orders? She's looking for them."

"Did she tell you who signed for them?"

Taviella looked up. "No. Who?"

Eric jerked a thumb at his outsized companion.
"Stacey did."

Taviella thought about that. "Well," she said at
last, "I'm glad he's showing a bit more initiative
these days."

She backed out of the engine room and nearly bumped into Maravic, who was hurrying over with the papers fluttering in her hand. "Here we are. I left them by your pilot's couch and then forgot. They're in order."

Paging through them, Taviella had to agree. They were caught. The only consolation was that the gas cylinders now being loaded would still be good for a moderate profit when they arrived at Marterly.

Less than an hour later they boosted clear of the spaceport of Conops' World, crashing up through the atmosphere and into the cool night of space. The sun rose again as they orbited once; then they drove directly outward. Four hours later, to Taviella's and Eric's command, the engines boomed, a huge noise like the echoing of a vast drum head, and the ship fell through a glowing rift into the red-shadowed realm of jumpspace.

2

The world's law is torture followed by murder, it is devastation and violence followed by thorough destruction. Why am I held to be the madman for wanting only to move ahead of the prelude to death and into the utter death itself?

Trinopus, *The Chiming Day*

Coasting through the burning red glare of jumpspace, the *Coinroader* grew warm, and warmer, until its outer hull was soon baking hot. Within, recycling air kept the crew comfortable, and shipboard routine kept them from contemplating too deeply the infinite menace and infinite promise of the unexplored cosmos.

The crew polarized, with Eric and Remington sharing their rough jests in the back, where they kept their hidden supply of beer, while Taviella and Maravic stayed forward most of the time, overseeing the ship's controls.

Stasileus wandered back and forth, never quite daring to feel comfortable with either of the two pairs of his masters. His training was as an engineer, and his expertise with both maneuver drives and jump drives was considerable. His experience with humankind, however, was far less, and Eric's territoriality left him bewildered. He suffered several rude shocks, all while doing no more than performing his duty.

"Hands off, there!" Eric snapped at him one morning during the lengthy trip. "It takes both of us to adjust those."

"These?" Stasileus stammered. He pointed a thick, blunt finger at the controls. "I've seen you adjust them by yourself." He brought himself up to his full height. "I am no less expert than you." He paused, letting pass an uncomfortable moment of silence. "And the reactor is burning too hot."

"Is it?" Eric rushed past him, edging him aside. He peered carefully at the data displays. "Hmm. Maybe." Without further consultation, and without intentionally belying his earlier statement, he began to switch the controls around, adjusting the fuel feed.

Stasileus watched him with troubled eyes, then exited silently. Unable to complain, built only to obey, he was discovering the agony of second-class freedom. One may free a slave, but it sometimes takes longer to free the masters.

When Stasileus wandered into the cargo area, Remington cast him a suspicious glare. Then, shaking his head, the cargo chief leaned back and tried to smile. He, too, knew what it was to be outcast. Nodding, he determined to include the assistant engineer in the sense of unity that he and

Eric shared. He put away the video magazine he'd been reading and rummaged behind a seemingly solid partial bulkhead.

"Care for a beer?"

"Thank you, yes."

Remington tossed him a can; Stasileus caught it easily, his muscles rippling smoothly beneath his huge, furred shoulders. But Remington noticed, as Eric had, that Stasileus's agility was not matched by his dexterity; it took him two careful tries to open the lid of the beer can.

They drank wordlessly.

"You've probably been wondering about our cargo," Remington said at last, to break the silence.

Stasileus's face was eager and excited. "Yes, please."

"Each one of these" — Remington indicated the stacks and stacks of metal cylinders occupying slightly less than half of the cargo bay — "is full of sodium cyanide, in solution, under pressure." He grinned wickedly, waiting for Stasileus to come to the same conclusion any human would.

But Stasileus thought differently; he was an engineer. "It has several industrial uses," he said, nodding his head. "I think it's used in annealing the surfaces of certain ceramics."

Remington's face fell. "Yeah, but it's also deadly poison." He pronounced the last two words ominously and harshly.

Stasileus blinked and tilted his head to one side in puzzlement. "Many industrial processes involve the use of toxic chemicals. That's why we have such strict safety standards." He smiled proudly. "I've worked with safety engineering teams, back at home, with the weights and measures volunteers."

"Aren't you worried that any of these cylinders might leak?"

Taken aback, Stasileus thought for a second. "I didn't think you would accept them on board unless they were properly sealed. Would you like me to help you inspect them?"

"No need for that," Remington grunted. He moodily sipped the rest of his beer. *I like the furry little airhead, but damn, he's sure got a lot to learn about people.* He shook his head and picked up his magazine.

Stasileus understood dismissal in all its forms. His race would have been useless to its makers without some skills in this regard. A blunt dismissal called for a prompt exit; a cool dismissal was best served by a careful exit, avoiding any incitement of full anger; a dismissal that was only hinted at called for a lingering exit, in which the precise measurement of the delay presented a tricky calculation and interpersonal evaluation. Remington's tacit dismissal called for a matter-of-fact departure, and Stasileus silently turned and moved away, instinctively setting his tread, his stance, and the tilt of his head in such a way as to elicit the least amount of notice.

Being unnoticed was also a trait highly valued in slaves.

Forward, Taviella and Maravic chatted gaily, their gossip running from the scurrilous to the dire and back again. They complained to each other about the Commerce Branch's recall, speculating over possible reasons for it. They dissected the sheaf of orders, going over and over it like augurs through the entrails of a sacrifice, seeking portents. The legal phrasing was sufficiently opaque to prevent them from finding any real hints of what their duty would eventually be.

"Did this ever happen to you?" Taviella asked bluntly. Maravic had been the custodian of the ship before its use was awarded to Taviella, and the first thing Taviella did was to give her the opportunity to remain aboard as copilot and navigator. Maravic had accepted readily, and to her credit had never seemed to resent Taviella for unseating her. Taviella was a leader type, where she was not; perhaps, Maravic had convinced herself, everything had worked out for the best.

Maravic breathed in deeply as she thought about the only two similar impositions she could remember. The first was the time they had taken the ship out of her hands and given it to a young, newly trained barbarian girl from a newly discovered world. She smiled inside, thinking about how shy and frightened Taviella had been then . . . and how bold she had become since. The second was when Stasileus had been given into the care of *Coinroader*'s crew, without any regard to their opinions on the matter.

"Can't think of anything," she finally said, deliberately untruthful. Both of those changes had been compulsory, but they had improved the quality of Maravic's life. Not for the world would she contest them now. It was Taviella's innocence she admired, she decided, more than anything else;

Taviella hadn't once today given a single self-conscious thought to the circumstances behind her own inheritance of command of the *Coinroader*.

"Well, they want all of us," Taviella muttered, scanning the orders closely. "But you know, it doesn't say anything specifically about the ship."

Maravic, surprised, would have commented, except that Stasileus chose that moment to knock diffidently upon the side of the open hatchway.

"Oh, hi, Stacey," Taviella said, turning her face momentarily toward him. Maravic's gaze made a more direct contact and lingered longer. She compared the confused and eager child that Taviella had been to Stasileus, an incurably forlorn waif. Taviella had grown to become a person of strength and confidence, but Stasileus was only the slave of his nature. His species had been programmed seven hundred years ago. His ancestors had been the slaves of the Empire.

She looked up again, but Stasileus had gone. She writhed in her seat, preparing to unstrap and go back to talk to him, but Taviella, not noticing, cried out in a voice of triumph and pointed to a clause of the orders.

"We're assigned as 'interim crew,' it says here. Now . . ."

She went on, but Maravic, wondering about Stasileus, scarcely heard her.

∞

Stasileus retired to the cramped shelf that served him for a bunk and, eyes wide, dreamed about his home. Somewhere, there was a critical difference between his species and these catastrophic humans. The external differences, great as they seemed, were obviously insignificant. In their very structure of mind, they were as alien to him as were the tree-leaping insects of his home world.

He flew, in his mind, to that distant world, not yet visited by humankind. Invernahaven it was named, and a warm and comfortable world it was. He floated down upon it, seeing the boiling gray clouds reflecting gold glints of polished sunlight. His earliest memory was of seeing those foamy, round-surfaced clouds above him in the vast blue sky as his authoritar lectured him on the origin of his species.

She had been called Musele, and he had loved her. She, however, yearned for the impossible. The last warrior-heroes had died centuries before, and yet she dreamed of finding love and satisfaction from one. Young Stasileus's attentions endeared him to her, however, and she finally assented to become his authoritar. His lessons proceeded apace; she guided his motivations well.

"We were not born here," she had said in her deep, echoing voice. "We come from the world of Archive, the world of humans."

How different she was from the human women he had encountered since. Stasileus remembered Musele's touch, her scent, her soft, textured brown fur that so pleasantly contrasted with his own white. He remembered love in her arms, and his utter bewildered astonishment at the sight of his son, a curled-up ball of damp, mewing fur, eyes

31

closed against the sight of the universe that had created it.

The years had passed, years measured against the clock-kept standard of lost Archive rather than the distorted years of Invernahaven's gold sun. Musele and he had grown close, and she had arranged his higher education. Then was his patience rewarded. Closed away for the rest of his life to the mysteries of sexuality that Musele and the females knew as both reward and torment, Stasileus was instead given the universes of abstraction and practicality: physics and engineering sciences. The work was hard, harder than any manual labor he had ever devoted himself to.

He achieved his full growth in his ninth year, the same year that he was given the powerful tool and infinitely pleasurable toy of mathematical analysis. The cosmos could be contained in unbreakable laws; machines could be made to demonstrate those laws, to practical effect.

He was, however, still a Verna.

In his seventeenth year, Musele came to where he took his schooling and regarded him appraisingly. "You are well formed, in mind and in body," she told him. A crowd of chattering comrades, schoolmates of both sexes, surrounded them, but it was as if they stood apart from Musele and Stasileus.

He looked at her and remembered his love of her, but it was a distant, warm memory. His love had matured into a sense of obedience; she was now — perhaps she had always been — his only law. "I have held myself responsible to the precepts of health."

She smiled, her huge eyes jovial and obscurely sad at the same time. "Come with me. We shall talk."

She led him away from the crowd, away from the warmth and the contact of the others. He walked close by her side, his arm tight about her. They passed beneath the elevated sluices and hanging gardens that an appointed leader had ordained as beautiful. They left the buildings and hangars behind and approached the small fane that framed the entrance to deep, secure caverns. Musele let him in, and they left the sunlit sky behind. They progressed downward among limestone galleries and intricate traceries of dripstone.

At last, far beneath the surface of the planet, in a hall untouched by time, they stood amid the neatly stacked bones of twenty generations of Vernae. Stasileus walked slowly, regarding the tight bundles of bones with quiet reverence. Each individual's long bones — the bones of legs and arms — had been bound together, and the skull fastened at one end; four skeletons thus prepared could be fixed into a flat rectangular solid, an open brick that was roughly thirty centimeters by sixty by ninety. Thousands of these had been stacked high against the walls, and the empty eye sockets of thousands of skulls looked out into the cavern with identical expressions of forlorn bewilderment.

"Stasileus, the masters have come back."

"Humankind?" Stasileus's heart leaped within him. Would his skills now be put to good service? "Yes."

"The prophecy of old is fulfilled. Is it not?" He

33

hesitated. The disturbed look on Musele's face troubled him.

"They have forgotten us," she said. "And they have forgotten honor. They have no emperor, and have even forgotten how to revere his name."

Stasileus blinked. "I don't understand."

"They worship no gods; they revere no traditions. Their systems are based on universality and upon compulsory economic equality."

"No emperor?" Stasileus was stunned.

"They are ruled by a praesidium of six."

"No gods?"

"They will have none."

"Can they still be men?"

"I do not know."

Stasileus saw her face go harsh and cold. Never had she been so lovely, never so forbidding. He backed away from her until he came to rest against a wall of cool, comforting bones.

"I am your authoritar. I have a final command."

"Final?" Stasileus looked at her.

She smiled, walked toward him, and embraced him with a gentle, loving touch. "Yesterday, my left kidney failed. Tomorrow I will be dead."

Holding her with all the careful tenderness in his great soul, Stasileus nestled his cheek close to hers. "I will honor your bones here."

She breathed deeply, and he could feel her pain. Her body was breaking down even as she stood. Perhaps she would not live until tomorrow; perhaps . . . The members of his species, he knew, had short life spans, and death came suddenly and unexpectedly.

"I am sending you to the humans. They have asked for five hundred of us, to take among them and introduce to their populace."

Stasileus held her, his large hands massaging her shoulders very carefully. He loved her, but far more than that, he obeyed her. She was the source of law in his life; it was her right to enforce that law in whatever way she saw fit. His voice did not tremble when he spoke next, and he pulled back to meet her gaze when he did.

"Yes."

∞

A series of misadventures had led him to the Commerce Branch of the Concordat of Archive. How inelegant were humans; how poorly they coordinated their efforts. Even their cross-purposes had cross-purposes. He already knew how to wait patiently, and so his endless trek through the bureaucratic labyrinth caused him no trouble of the spirit. It did, however, annoy his sense of efficiency that paperwork operations proceeded at such a leisurely pace.

In time, he was assigned to the Commerce Branch's Department of Small Traders, where an effort was made to indoctrinate him in an interminably recomplicated system of economic ideology. As a mathematician, he was offended by the nonsense; as a Verna, he strove to master the facts, figures, and doctrines.

As uneasy as he was around the humans, it took him some time to notice that the humans were equally disturbed by him. But they were disturbed by one another also: he watched them fight and feud, and he watched carefully.

Eventually, he ended up as an assistant engineer aboard the *Coinroader*. Taviella and Maravic were unlike any other humans he had met. Remington and Eric were also entirely new types of people. During a dangerous salvage expedition on a long-lost communications station in deep space, he learned to trust them, even to love them. And they learned to respect him.

∞

In his long bunk aboard the *Coinroader*, Stasileus mused, his thoughts wandering among memories of all the humans he'd ever met. They seemed so diverse. . . .

They are a population with a great variability in temperament. Unusual. . . . He stared blankly into space, digesting this observation. His own species had a large variation of fur colors — from black through a spectrum of browns to creams and whites — and this was taken as a meaningless mode of identification. Psychologically, the Vernae were so similar as to be identical to one another. Humans, even more physically diverse than his species, were also emotionally and mentally dissimilar. There was a full spectrum of anger and an entire continuum of courage. . . .

I can categorize this! I can isolate the components and plot humankind on a graph. The thought galvanized him. He leaped up and dug about for a record pad and stylus. Then, quietly and without fanfare, he began to jot down his notes.

His first subject was Eric. He found the engineer on station as usual, nursing the engines to greater and greater efficiency.

"Hello, Eric."

Eric eyed him suspiciously. "Hi."

"How courageous are you?"

Eric frowned quizzically. "Why do you want to know?"

That response left Stasileus at a loss. He was clever enough to know that it would never do to explain what his project actually involved. A subject who was aware of the nature of the experiment would naturally behave in such a way as to optimize the outcome of the tests.

"I just wanted to get to know you better."

"By asking me about courage?"

"Would you prefer that I ask another question instead?"

Eric waved that aside. "It's just that I don't normally go bragging about my courage. Courage is a kind of quiet thing."

"In what way?"

"Well, I've been in danger of losing my life, you know. But it wasn't courage that saw me through it. It was reason."

"Reason?" Stasileus busied himself taking notes. Eric squinted at him sidelong, but made no objection.

"Sure. Look, have I ever told you about the ship I served with before this one? The *Starsweeper*? I was fourth engineer in an engineering division of five. It was my watch. The others were forward, jousting at knucklebones." Eric warmed to his story. "The engines had been bothering me all day. Something wasn't right, and I couldn't pin down in my mind what it was. All the readings were within normal range, but we were getting little static charges building up on all the exposed metal surfaces. The bigwigs didn't seem to care, but it was driving me frantic.

"Half an hour before my watch was supposed to be over, things got hot. I couldn't touch anything without getting blasted by sparks big enough to knock me over on my backside."

Stasileus thought about it. "The reactor had built up a resonant wave in the plasma."

Eric gave him a sour glance. "Yeah." He took a moment to reconsider Stasileus's qualifications. "Well, that's what it was, all right. I figured it out later. At that moment, I knew I had to act quickly, but I didn't know what to do." He held up a hand to forestall Stasileus's suggestion. "I can't explain it exactly, but I changed then. For about half a second, I was scared, deathly scared, and I just drew my arms in and cowered. Then I got over it and became a kind of machine. I was still scared, but that didn't seem important any longer. There was just the job to do, and I didn't know how much time I had to do it."

"You would already have been dead, if it had happened on this ship," Stasileus estimated.

"Yep. I was on a much bigger tub, however. The old *Starsweeper* was a ten-thousand-ton fuel tanker. We only used it for short jumps, shuttling back and forth between two close systems. I know now that I had about a minute before the thing went supercritical. Before that, of course, the electricity would have killed everyone aboard. Then — bang! — goes the engine and scatters us and our cargo into jumpspace, with the compensator fields collapsed. We'd have been a drifting powder of monatomic elements, gone to bits in a picosecond." He paused. "I didn't know what was wrong at the time, of course. So I gritted my teeth and opened up the access port."

"Your courage was automatic, then? You didn't choose to be brave?"

"Well, that's my point. If I would have been able to choose, I'd have probably done something foolish like shouting for help, or just running away. I wasn't what you'd call courageous; I just did what had to be done."

"What did you do?"

"Oh, the right thing, of course. Flushed the reactor out with neon and vented the whole mess. Then dropped us out into normal space as fast as I could."

"Then what?"

Eric smiled. "The rest was really the worst. I had to sit and take a sound chewing-out from the rest of the crew, the captain, the chief engineer, everyone, for leaving them stranded. It took two weeks for a rescue ship to find our beacon . . . about average, really, but that was a hellish two weeks."

"Thank you," Stasileus said quietly, then turned to leave.

Eric blinked. "Hey! Where are you going? We

were just getting started." His face held the most honestly friendly expression that Stasileus had ever seen from the man.

"I'm sorry. I have to reduce some data."

"Some . . . ?" Eric shrugged. "Okay. But some time, you've got to tell me about your narrowest escape."

"I will," Stasileus promised.

∞

In his notes, he recorded the first entry in his new experimental science of psychology: Eric Fuller: Courage, 15 per cent.

Now he had to make Remington angry. . . .

3

Slay them; death to all; slay them; death
to you; slay them; death to Arcadian.
> Basil, *the War-Chant*
> from *Revolutionaries' Common*

The *Coinroader* flipped out of jumpspace awkwardly, tumbling end over end. While Taviella
wrestled it back into a normal orientation, Maravic
sat in her couch, clinging to her webbing, and in the
rear of the ship Remington, Eric, and Stasileus
grabbed for support to avoid falling headlong to the
rear bulkheads.

Eric's grip loosened and he slid helplessly along
the deck plates, scrabbling desperately for pur-
chase. Remington, holding on tightly, could do
nothing to help. Gravity shifted again, flipping
Eric up off the deck and tossing him into the open
air. Stasileus reached quickly out from his own
handhold and caught Eric to his chest, then
wrapped a thick arm tightly around him to keep
him from falling farther.

Gravity had gone topsy-turvy; in the control

room, Taviella applied thrust with precision and care.

"You caught me," Eric said to Stasileus, his astonishment showing in his face. "I thought I was going to fall right through into the cargo."

"You would have," Remington said from nearby. He breathlessly held on against the shifting acceleration, clinging to a wall bracket, and anguish was clear in his voice. The direction of "down" swung somewhere below and behind him. "You would have landed in the midst of all that metal, and you'd have been knocked senseless. Maybe killed. I couldn't get to you in time."

"That would be one for the books. I knew a guy once who was crippled by cargo falling on top of him, but . . ." Eric looked down at the furry arm that gripped him. The Verna's strength was incredible; he could never have fought his way free.

"Thanks, Stacey."

"You're welcome." The acceleration faded, until interior gravitic compensators could restore a semblance of normal gravity. Stasileus released Eric, who staggered to his feet with a gust of expelled breath.

"What say we wear our restraints next time?" Remington said, looking around. "You know, the way we're supposed to?"

"C'mon, Stacey," Eric snapped, back in control of himself. He ignored Remington's suggestion. "We've got to check the engines *now*, after a fractional misjump like that one."

"Yes, sir." Stasileus darted after him, through the hatch and into the engine room. He wished he

could have seen and heard Taviella and Maravic
during the action: it would have provided him with
useful information for his notes on human emotional mentality.

∞

Forward, Taviella swore, venting herself of a few
rich profanities. The expressions, words she had
overheard and didn't entirely understand, cleared
away her anger and fear. She lifted her head and
combed back her hair.

"You can say that again . . . but please don't."
Maravic had already run through the emergency
postbreakout checklist, and found the ship whole
and fully operational.

Taviella clenched and unclenched her fists.
"You just can't be prepared for that kind of thing,"
she said ruefully.

"It's no reflection on your piloting. I understand
it's a probabilistic effect, unpredictable even in
theory."

"It was my fault," Taviella announced firmly.
"Even though I couldn't anticipate it, I should have
known how to react to it."

Maravic looked to the side and reviewed the
computer summary of the maneuvers Taviella had
used to correct the tumble. "You did just fine."

Looking at her copilot, Taviella shook her head.
"It wasn't good enough."

"We're alive, aren't we?" Maravic shrugged.
"Remington, at least, did his job properly: no shifting of the cargo. And I see that Eric and Stacey have

got the drives cooled. We'll have headway in a few minutes."

The gravity pulse of their jumpspace exit had reached the nearby planet of Marterly approximately five seconds after their breakout; soon thereafter an indicator tone sounded to let them know that planet-based scanners were tracking them. Shortly thereafter, radio communication was established.

"The *Coinroader*, from Conops' World," Maravic said in a gentle, professional voice. "Requesting permission to approach and land."

After a ten-second lightspeed lag, a mellow-voiced controller confirmed their message with friendly informality. "C'mon down, *Coinroader*. The weather's fine, and it's six-eighteen in the evening local time. We saw your exit — a bit bumpy, wouldn't you say?"

Taviella sighed, but Maravic merely drawled in response, "A space puppy took us by the scruff of our neck and gave us a shaking. But we got away, and we're fine."

"And we're glad to have you with us. There's a spot reserved for you in the VIP section of the port. See you in about nine hours."

"*Coinroader* out." Maravic looked up to meet Taviella's amused gaze.

"A 'space puppy'?"

Maravic smiled. "Sure. About a hundred kilometers long, frisky and playful, no manners . . ."

Taviella breathed heavily in and out. "Okay." She smiled weakly. "You're a whimsical woman, Maravic."

Nodding in agreement, Maravic returned to her instruments, plotting a course down to Marterly's only spaceport. "Phooey. On days like this, my sense of whimsy is all that keeps me going."

"Was my breakout that bad?"

"You said it yourself: you simply can't be prepared for something like that."

Below them, the planet swelled, a pearly blue-and-white bubble that appeared incongruously dull against the magnificent starry background. Their course swung them neatly past a small moon, through a belt of biocontained satellite settlements, and over and around the night side of the world. Only a few cities were visible, as soft, glowing shapes that lay like gentle phosphorescent splotches on the flat black landscape.

They soon arrived over the spaceport, as they maintained their steep descent. The port's landing-and-boost grid detected them, analyzed their course, and focused in on them with concentrated gravitic energy. Taviella cut the engines and let the grid handle their landing. Softly, gently, the grid's controlled gravity fields levitated the ship toward the landing surface.

Darkness covered the city, but in its midst the port was a blazing sea of light. Taviella saw landing lights, set flush in the concrete surface of the field, and saw by their colors and patterns that the landing was properly under control. Maravic saw the brighter lights, high atop poles, that floodlit the field for the convenience of cargo crews and maintenance workers. In their glare, she could even see the shining glints reflected from the boost grid's wide expanse of metal rails. The ship soon hovered low, sliding gently above the surface of the grid, then dropping toward a series of holding pits.

Watching attentively, Maravic began to see the port in finer, sharper detail. She saw massive fuel tanks, bulking against the city lights, eclipsing them. She saw the spaceport buildings, a low, out-flung terminal sheltering in the lee of a towering office complex. She saw other ships, some as small as the *Coinroader* and others that were vast buildings, almost cities in their own right, all hunkered down in blast pits that fitted them snugly.

She saw the spaceport rise up to engulf them, as the horizon closed in, until the ship was grounded, half submerged in a pit of its own. Under Eric's control, the engines whirred down, a descending scale of atonal power. At Taviella's command, the ship accepted the several service umbilici that the pit extended to mate with the hull. Maravic's control board flowered with new data: fuel availability at fluid pressure, electrical power, outside hull temperature as sensed by thermocouples inside the pit, and a data link. From the last, she read the local time and adjusted the ship's local clock to match it. It was four twenty-six in the morning, a figure almost eleven hours out of synchronization with the ship's internal clock, which could never be set either forward or back.

It'll take a bit of getting used to, she thought. *Night is going to seem like day*. But already the suggestion of the clock time conspired with the evident night that covered them; she yawned hugely and blinked.

Two hours later, she and Taviella had finished the postflight checklist. Eric had the engines shut down and cooling off, ready for maintenance. Remington checked in with the good word that the cargo was secure, having come through the flight without shifting. And Stasileus, oddly inquisitive, had asked Maravic a series of questions that were nosy, if not downright invasive.

Now Maravic staggered back to her bunk, determined to catch a hefty nine-hour sleep before taking her first breath of Marterly's fresh and wintry air. She tried to recall what her answers had been to Stasileus's questions, and found that she could not easily do so.

I hope I wasn't too flippant with him, she thought as sleep claimed her. *He's a kindly, if naive, alien, and he can't learn if he doesn't ask questions.*

∞

Eric's duty shift during the trip had been more closely aligned with Marterly's day-night cycle. He took advantage of his coincidental acclimatization to get out of the ship early in the morning. He put in a brief social call at the portmaster's office, snooped about a bit for a purchaser for Taviella's load of chemicals, drew approximately a tenth of his accumulated license cash, and went out in search of a high-stakes gambling house.

Not long after he'd found one, Remington wandered into the same game room, spotted him, and quickly walked out. That was one of the rules they'd made for themselves, to preserve their peaceful working relationship: the two could never, ever be found in the same gaming establishment on their free time.

Our new assignment will be coming up soon, Eric thought, while facing down a stranger in a complicated bluff. *We haven't got more than a week's worth of freedom, if even that long. I intend some heavy dice-playing to while away the time. Win, lose, or draw — I don't care. I only want to play a couple of dozen hard-fought games before I have to look at another engine.*

He won that round, lost the next, and after a time, as usually happened, he stopped keeping count of just how much he had lost. He saw Remington later and paused with him in a crowded meal bar to compare notes.

"Winning any?"

"Yep." Remington gave his most rapacious grin.

Eric hoped his own smile didn't look as insincere as his companion's. "Me too."

They parted, going back to the wars of skedge, blackmurray, and wheel, their fortunes rising and falling at the whim of chance.

∞

Taviella combed out her hair and dressed herself in fur-lined cold-weather wear. Maravic, more hesitantly, tossed on an outerwrap and joined her as they exited the ship. Stasileus, wearing his yellow and white ship's coveralls, padded along behind them.

"Time to see what it's all about, I guess," Taviella sighed.

"I guess," Maravic seconded. Before them, over the flat expanse of the landing field, the spaceport office annex loomed. A high, pale sun sent out weak tendrils of warmth, which an icy wind swept away in chill gusts. The field was active this time of day, just past noon, with cargo movers and equipment carts running seemingly at random back and forth between ships in their access pits. Stasileus took it all in with open-eyed fascination; spaceports were still new to him.

They neared the office complex and passed inside, moving through high blue-glass doors emblazoned with the Commerce Branch seal. Through another set of doors, Taviella could see the gallery where the scratchboard announced cargos and markets: a hive of economic opportunity. She yearned to look in and sample the atmosphere, but duty interfered.

They rode an elevator to the ninth floor and asked to be announced to the Treasury Branch representative. Taviella and Maravic took seats in the comfortably furnished waiting room, while Stasileus stood and swept the room with a curious gaze.

By the time the receptionist called for them, Stacey was the only one of the three not utterly dejected by the boredom of the wait. He followed the women through double doors of thick wood and looked with fascination at Hens Sargent, Concordat Treasury Legate to the world of Marterly. Then his attention was caught forcefully by the sight of Sargent's aide, who stood silently by his side.

Sargent gazed tolerantly at Taviella and Maravic. The latter two stared for a moment at Sargent's aide, a tall female Verna with deep, dark blue-black fur. Stasileus's surprised stare lasted much longer, as did the other Verna's.

"Welcome to Marterly," Sargent said, his voice deep and gruff, a voice that was foreboding but which carried a note of lightness, a hint of good-natured humor. He was a big man, thick in the waist and chest. His gnarled hand looked like a workman's rather than like a bureaucrat's. His face was broad and tanned, and he had a wide, smiling mouth. His eyes were ice blue; his hairline had fallen back, leaving his high, domed forehead bare.

"Thank you, sir," Maravic said, slightly anticipating and trying to stem Taviella's outburst of protests.

Her attempt at subtlety failed, however, when Taviella leaped right ahead and began asking her pointed questions. "Why were we brought here against our will? What kind of mission are we being sent on? And what's this about bringing us up from standby reserve?"

Sargent spread his hands. "Sit down, won't you?" He smiled disarmingly. "Can I have some coffee sent for? My Verna, Roxolane, will be glad to bring it."

"Thank you, none for us." Maravic's soft voice still seemed inadequate to compensate for Taviella's anger.

"I see you have one of your own. Handy beasts, I suppose. Roxolane was foisted off on me by a direct order from Secretary Wallace. Damnedest thing . . ."

"Treasury Secretary Wallace? Himself?" Maravic's astonishment was profound.

"Hmm? Why, yes. And yours?"

"Stasileus. Commerce Branch orders. He's our ship's assistant engineer."

The three humans went on making small talk while Stasileus stood by, observing them. He and Roxolane shared a brief exchange of glances and assured each other, wordlessly, that all was well. Neither of them was free, but their slavery was comfortable, and for more than that, no Verna had ever been able to ask. Stasileus and Roxolane waited in silence, allowing the humans to speak of them as if they weren't present, and neither was irked in the least by this slight.

They couldn't be even slightly perturbed; it wasn't in their nature.

Taviella, by her nature impetuous and strong-willed, didn't wait long before she began again to demand answers. "This is all very well and good. But, Mr. Sargent, what is our mission?"

Sargent regarded her with a smile. "Well, yes, that. Ahem. You'll be given command of a new ship, a fairly large ship, in fact, and—"

"What? What about the *Coinroader?*" Taviella was on her feet, her fists balled at her hips. "You're not taking my ship away from me!"

Maravic was appalled and shrank back in her chair in alarm. Sargent gaped, unprepared for Taviella's violence.

Stasileus's eyes went very wide and his spine

went unnaturally stiff; deep within his mind, however, he gauged Taviella's wrath and tried to categorize her words and actions in his system of human behavioral charting. Roxolane's eyes, too, grew extraordinarily wide, and she stepped back involuntarily.

"No, no!" Sargent hurried to say. "You'll have command of the — the *Coinroader*, did you say? — again as soon as you return from this temporary mission."

"The *Coinroader* will wait here in the meantime, safe and unmolested?"

Sargent shook his head. "Good heavens, no. We'll be using it for a temporary transshipment of our own. But only for the duration of—"

"No." Taviella stepped closer to the desk behind which Sargent sheltered and leaned heavily over it. "Not even a possibility. That ship stays here, and no one — *no one* — sets foot on it. That's my ship, and I'm not letting some useless pack of idiots get their handprints all over its controls. *I* fly that ship. Do you understand?"

"This is most unusual—"

"It's the only way I'll work things."

Sargent looked to the side as if appealing for help. Only Roxolane stood there, unable to help him in any way. Taking a deep breath, Sargent began to suggest a compromise. "Now if—"

"The ship is mine."

"Technically," Maravic put in, her soft voice gently penetrating the unpleasant silence, "the ship is the property of the Commerce Branch, and we're only operating it under a long-term lease." To

52

forestall Taviella's anger, she continued swiftly, "But the orders we received didn't call the *ship* back from standby reserve — only us, its crew. I think . . ."

Sargent leaned back in his chair, and a relaxed expression came over him. "I had only planned to use your ship to fill a few holes in my schedule. Other vehicles will serve as well." He eyed Taviella sidelong and gestured her back to her seat with little shooing motions. Taviella turned sideways and sat leaning against the edge of his desk.

"We're agreed, then? The *Coinroader* waits in its cradle? No one goes aboard? The duration of the mission . . ." She paused. "How long is the mission? *What* is the mission?"

"Um . . . Let me begin again, then." Sargent took a deep breath. "You'll be given temporary command of the *Indagator*, a five-hundred-thousand-ton tanker. You'll fly it to Kythe-Correy, a world only a jump or two from here, and you'll execute a rather complex flight plan. Now—"

"How complex? What kind of complexity?"

Sargent was clearly approaching the limit of his patience. "Bear with me, young woman. I'm not a mission briefing specialist. The whole of it is in the flight-plan papers that I'll be handing you in just a moment." He brought himself under control. "The mission is something in the nature of a terraforming task. You'll be moving asteroids around — the *Indagator* has a fairly substantial set of bay repulsors — and then comes the trickiest part of the job: you'll have to fly this large tanker quite low into the world's atmosphere and dump the entire cargo of pressurized liquid over a wide area of the surface."

Taviella looked at him suspiciously. "That's it? That's the mission?"

"In a nutshell. Do you think you can handle it?" He sneered. "I heard about your somewhat flamboyant exit from jumpspace when arriving over Marterly. If you're not the pilot for this job, then perhaps I should look somewhere else."

Taviella's eyes narrowed. "Perhaps you should. Come on, Maravic. Let's go."

"No, not so fast. I can't afford to wait any longer than necessary. The *Indagator* must fly soon. I need you, *and* I have a legal claim on you."

"Why us?"

"I'd settle for someone else. I'd settle right now for anyone else." He grimaced. "But I haven't any time to waste. You're flying for me."

"And if we refuse?"

He met her gaze squarely. "You lose the *Coinroader*." He shrugged. "The mission is not a particularly odious one."

"We shift some asteroids around and we dump some chemicals. Is that all?"

"No. There's more. I'm going to send for Mr. Petrov; he'll explain about the passengers." Sargent turned to Roxolane and snapped his fingers. "Find Mr. Petrov."

"Yes, sir." Roxolane's echoing, inhuman voice caught and held the humans' attention. On her way out, she passed close by Stasileus, so closely that their hips rubbed beneath the fur.

"Tell us more about the *Indagator*," Maravic urged, hoping to get Sargent and Taviella talking about something mutually agreeable. In this, she both succeeded and failed.

"To begin with, it's huge. Five hundred thousand tons, mostly pressure compartments, automated right down the line. It can't land, of course, but it has launches and boats. Now—"

"Wait," Taviella said, holding up her hand. "Automated? How?"

"Your crew of four—"

"Five."

"Um, five, will have no difficulty in piloting and controlling it. Everything on it is fully checked out and adequately maintained, and several systems have levels of redundancy built in. It's an extension of the highly successful Block class: more mass, more cargo space—"

"What do you mean, 'automated'?"

"Well, it won't fly itself, if that's what you're asking," Sargent said sarcastically. "We can't do this without you and your crew."

"That's why we were dragooned into service?"

"Yes!" Sargent's face grew hot. "Now look here, Ms. . . . Ms. . . ."

"Call me Taviella."

"See here—"

His outburst was interrupted by a gentle voice from the doorway. "Mr. Sargent? May I come in?"

Roxolane had returned, and before her she ushered a small man, young and strong, with luxuriant black hair atop his large head. His expression was pleasant and inquiring; his eyes, polite and mild. Roxolane towered over him, but his stance was the more assured and dignified of the two.

"Ah, Petrov. Come in."

"Thank you." He turned and shut the door. Turning about again, he regarded Taviella and Maravic with open warmth. "Hello. You're going to be the pilots of the *Planetslayer*?"

"Petrov!" Sargent snapped. "We agreed that you were not to use that name."

Petrov gave him a glance that might be interpreted as a polite reminder that Sargent's demands had not, in point of fact, been agreed to. He looked back to Taviella and Maravic. "I'm Mikhail Petrov. Head of the Mathematics Department at the University of Marterly." His voice dropped conspiratorially. "Actually, I'm just an astronomy professor who got kicked upstairs."

Maravic found herself quite taken with the fellow. "Hello, Mikhail. I'm Maravic Slijvos, and this is Taviella. She's the captain, and I'm copilot and navigator. And this" — she gestured toward Stasileus — "is our assistant engineer, Stasileus. You can call him Stacey."

Mikhail faced Stasileus squarely and looked up at the alien's face. He held out a hand. "I'm most pleased to make your acquaintance, sir."

Stasileus blinked in surprise, but nevertheless took Mikhail's hand and shook it gently. "Hello," he said softly.

"I'm going to have a thousand things to ask you about once we're aboard ship." Mikhail looked at him slyly. "Do you play chess?"

"No."

Sighing in long-suffering despair, Mikhail lowered his gaze. "No one does these days."

"Mr. Petrov," Sargent said icily, "if we could get along with our business . . ."

"Oh, yes." Mikhail turned slowly about. "Whatever you say, Mr. Sargent."

"I was just describing the ship — the *Indagator* — to its new captain and first officer. Now, to continue, the ship has a three-G gravitic drive, a standard jump drive, a very sizable computer that was recently retrofitted, cabin space for thirty-two—"

"Thank goodness we won't be needing that!" Taviella laughed.

Mikhail Petrov looked at Sargent, and Sargent coughed delicately.

"Well, actually—"

"Mr. Sargent, didn't you tell them *anything*?"

Sargent glared at him. "No, Petrov. It seems that I didn't. Why don't you go ahead and handle this, if you're so much more capable than I?"

Mikhail ignored the sarcasm and addressed the three crew members. "The mission to Kythe-Correy involves taking along five or six scientists, to be observers. They're going to want to study every phase of the cataclysm, from the orbital paths of the asteroids to the spread of the—"

"Cataclysm?" Taviella asked in a tight voice. "What cataclysm?"

Mikhail's shoulders slumped. "Mr. Sargent didn't tell you anything at all, did he? Not even the first little details." He took a deep breath. "Kythe-Correy is a world, not far from here, with a full, lush biosphere. Plants, animals, the works. A complete and highly evolved chain of life.

"The mission is to kill it."

"Kill it?" This time it was Maravic who echoed Petrov's words.

"Yes," Mikhail said, a hint of embarrassment in his voice. "Kill it. The *Indagator* — the *Planet-slayer* — will bombard the world with asteroids, then spray the land masses with a herbicide. The dust raised from the asteroid impacts will join with the herbicide to kill all off all the plants, and with the plants dead, don't you see . . . ?"

Maravic and Taviella stared at him in wide-eyed, speechless dismay.

"I wish Mr. Sargent had told you that part earlier." Petrov paced the length of the room twice, then threw himself into a chair. "This is going to take a bit of explaining. . . ."

Stasileus alone of the *Coinroader*'s crew did not look at Mikhail as if the scientist were a madman. To Stasileus, *all* humans were somewhat mad, and this was just more data for his new studies. He listened attentively.

4

I know the answer to your question, and I won't tell you it.

Trinopus, *All Works Wounded*

"The planet known as Kythe-Correy could be a twin for Archive," Mikhail explained carefully, aware of Taviella's and Maravic's distress. "It orbits right in the heart of the habitable zone of its main-sequence G3 star, in a region of space relatively free from orbital distorters. The whole region, in fact, is anomaly-free, to the degree of being anomalous for that reason alone. The star has a sixteen-year magnetic cycle, driven by a harmonic pulsation in its jumpspace counterstar, so that—"

Sargent cleared his throat portentously. "To the point, Petrov."

Abashed, Mikhail started afresh. "Kythe-Correy is just the kind of world that we would want to colonize and settle. It's rich — simply and squarely rich — and its resources could unlock this whole sector's potential. You don't often find Archive-class worlds in such convenient locations. And its location is exceptionally suitable. A spaceport there is more than highly desirable: it could well be vital."

"Why kill away all of its native life, then?" Maravic demanded. "What aren't you telling us?"

Mikhail waved his hand aside, dismissing her implication of a conspiracy. "I'm not a biochemist, so I don't have this all clear, but it seems that the native life is built around an antagonistic protein. The planet is poisonous to us — and we to it, I daresay." His eyes were troubled as he explained further. "A biosphere is a very intricate thing — and that's an understatement for the record books." He smiled. "You know, like: 'Space is a big place,' or 'A billion years isn't much time if you're not in a hurry.' "

Maravic smiled, but Taviella and Sargent did not. The two Vernae stood by like statues, the conversation flowing past their pliable minds like words across a transcription device. It was impossible to determine how much attention they paid: None? A little? Total?

"Well," Mikhail went on, a trifle too quickly, "a complete and highly evolved biosphere cannot be destroyed easily. The unwelcome protein is involved in every phase of life. It's dissolved in the soil, it's borne in the seas, you can't crack open a rock without finding traces of it. If we're going to introduce a life-supporting biosphere that we can live with, we'll have to kill the native one completely. And life is tenacious. There are so many redundancies. . . . You know that natural patterns of mass extinctions are fairly common on most life-bearing worlds. And you can have up to ninety-five percent of the *families* of life die away completely, without losing much evolutionary momentum. Life is redundant; it's going to take competition from a technological species armed with impressive weapons of biochemical warfare before Kythe-Correy goes down to defeat."

Taviella stirred and shook her head. "I can't believe I'm hearing this. I don't want any part of it."

"You're stuck with it," Sargent said brusquely. "You buck me on this, and I'll take the *Coinroader* away from you."

Taviella rose from her perch on his desk, turned, and leaned forward to face him, her eyes dangerous.

"Fine," Sargent muttered, spreading his hands. "If you want to make things worse for yourself, you know how." He leaned forward. "I've been hit before. You want to hit me? I know you pilots; you're all the same." He stuck out his chin. "Go ahead. Go ahead." He smiled, and when Taviella made no further threats, he leaned back.

"You're on edge," he said, breathing heavily. "You're on edge, and you don't know what to do about it. You don't want the mission, but neither you nor I have any choice. I need the *Indagator* flown, and you're drafted. Now, do you want to talk terms?"

"Later," Taviella snapped. "Maravic, Stacey — time to go." She swept out of the office, her crew members following closely. Moving swiftly, Mikhail joined them.

In the broad, uncrowded hallways of the port

annex, Taviella strode furiously along, looking over her shoulder to check on Stasileus and Maravic. Seeing Mikhail, she whirled about, walking backward, her anger expressed in her motion. "You go away. I don't want to talk about it now."

"I'm not your enemy," Mikhail said to Taviella as he kept pace with Maravic. "I'm just an astronomer who gets easily distracted by interesting stellar features."

"You want to kill a world."

"I *don't* want to kill it. I don't want to kill *anything*." Mikhail's protests were earnest.

Taviella slowed. Maravic cast a forlorn glance at Stasileus, who watched the spectacle with wide, interested eyes.

"This project isn't your idea?"

"Mine? Good grief, no. I don't like it any more than you do. But they put me in charge, and what can I do?"

"Quit. Have nothing to do with it. Resign."

Mikhail stopped, and his arms, with which he had been gesturing, dropped to his sides. Taviella stopped also and challenged him with her eyes. The sparse pedestrian traffic in the hallway passed them by on both sides without seeming to notice.

Maravic spoke then, her voice soft and reasonable. "Taviella, you don't want to lose your ship. What is it, then, that Mr. Petrov stands to lose?"

Mikhail looked at her in surprise; he opened his mouth to speak, but held his peace.

Taviella's taut shoulders slumped and her face relaxed. "This mission is wrong."

"Not entirely," Mikhail said quietly. "The planet has been visited by scouting expeditions and by a substantial collection mission. They took away some two million tons of plant and animal specimens for preservation in simulated planetary environments. Not everything needs to die." He paused. "And the human benefits outweigh the costs."

"*Do* they?"

Mikhail bent his head and looked very small and very forlorn. "I really don't know. An entire world . . ."

In silence, the three humans and one alien walked back to the *Coinroader*.

∞

"Take the job, Taviella," Eric said, his normally loud voice moderated for once. His initial outrage had abated — helped along by the fact that his financial situation had recently taken a turn for the worse. "Once you figure how much they have to pay us for this mission—"

"The pay? Is that all that matters?" Taviella regarded her crew unhappily as they sat about the ship's kitchen in various attitudes of repose. Maravic lay on her back beneath the small table, while Eric and Remington sat on the floor, their legs out before them.

Stasileus stood with his huge arms crossed upon his chest, his head bent in rapt attention. Mikhail leaned against the doorway, very much an outsider to the group's discussion, yet already feeling as if he knew these people. His eyes were upon

Maravic; he was fascinated by her equipoise and by her unswerving gentleness.

"What do you care for a weed-patch world?" Eric grumbled. "Plants and animals: big deal."

"And what about the way they're forcing us to accept the job?" Taviella's voice was harsh.

"I don't like it. So what? There are a lot of things I don't like, and I can't always do anything about them."

"Are we slaves to the system? Can they order us here and there without any compunctions?"

Maravic interjected an observation, quickly derailing the trend of Taviella's objections. "We'll be paid hazardous flight pay, and reserve pay on top of that. We won't get rich, Taviella, but the flight is going to be worth it."

Remington looked around and put in his own opinion. "I looked up our contract, the one we all signed back when Maravic was in charge. We're guaranteed about half a million in license cash, less the operating percentage, just for accepting any one special mission. It costs them a lot of money to activate us like this. Split five ways . . . well, I'm with Eric: how many plants and animals can you buy with that kind of money?"

"Right," Eric growled. "We joined the Commerce Branch for profit, not for our freedom. We knew they'd send us places we didn't want to go."

"I'm not prepared to argue with all of you," Taviella said, evidently unhappy with her crew's acceptance of the situation. "If you're agreed, then I guess we'll do it."

"Taviella," Maravic said softly.

"Yes?"

"You're still our leader. We're only giving you our opinions."

Remington and Eric nodded at that. "Whatever you say, we'll follow," Eric pronounced firmly.

"After all, where would we find a pilot good enough to replace you?" Remington asked bluntly.

"But we do want to take the mission," Maravic concluded gently but firmly.

Mikhail stood by, watching Maravic's gentle handling of the emotional balance of the crew. Without her, the team would be split along lines of temperament and anger. He smiled thinly and resolved to get to know Maravic better during the mission.

"Now what?" Eric asked of the room in general.

"We go back to Sargent and talk terms," Taviella sighed.

She and Maravic had no sooner stepped out of the *Coinroader* and onto the hard surface of the landing field, however, than Roxolane arrived in a ground skimmer. The tall, black Verna came out of the car and fearlessly strode up to the two humans.

"Sargent sent me to see if you needed anything," she said, her high, inhuman voice resonant.

Taviella sighed. "Did you bring the contracts and mission briefings?"

"Yes." Roxolane reached back inside the skimmer and handed a bundle of papers across.

"Contract . . . flight plan . . . storage agreement for the *Coinroader* . . ." Taviella flipped through the papers carefully. "Everything's in order." She looked back at Roxolane. "That's all, then."

Roxolane looked back at Taviella. "He asked me to see to one more thing."

"Yes?"

"He wanted me to give you your first tour of the *Indagator*."

Helplessly, Taviella looked at Maravic. "Now?"

Maravic shrugged. "Why not?"

Roxolane observed the two, her eyes huge and wide and watchful.

"Let's round up the crew, then," Taviella said sourly. "We're going up again."

∞

The orbits about Marterly were clear and open; no great amount of shipping came to or through the lonesome world. Roxolane piloted a ground-to-orbit shuttle with expertise and carefully brought Taviella and her crew on an efficient approach to the *Indagator*.

"It's fueled and ready for departure," Mikhail announced. "The viral agent is already mixed in the storage tanks. I've seen to just about everything. And just before we left, I notified the university that the other scientists can start getting ready."

"Viral agent?" Taviella asked. "Is that the herbicide that Sargent mentioned?"

"Yes. It's an aerosol-supported virus that attacks only the chloroplasts — chlorophores, actually — of Kythe-Correy's native plant life. It has no effect whatever on the forms of plant life more familiar to us."

"But it might mutate, or something, couldn't it?" Eric suggested.

"That's not completely impossible, but it isn't at all likely." Mikhail spread his hands. "You haven't yet seen how different these plants and animals are from the biochemical patterns we're used to."

Eric shrugged.

"I don't see it yet," Maravic said. "Or is that it?" She pointed out a viewscreen toward a tiny point of light. Far below, Marterly shone as a crescent, a lovely thing of sea glints and cloud lusters.

The point of light swelled in the screens until it could be seen as a spacecraft.

"The *Indagator*," Mikhail said as he pointed. "The *Planetslayer*."

"That isn't all it does, is it?" Eric's voice was incredulous. "A ship of that tonnage, just for killing worlds?"

Mikhail smiled inoffensively. "Oh, no. Its normal duty is for bulk tankerage." He paused. "But it has killed before."

"Where? When?"

"About eight years ago. A bit of a way from here, in the Penander Sector. They used it to sterilize Catalart."

In silence, they neared the *Indagator*. Maravic got the first clear view of it as they rounded its sunlit side and prepared to dock with it. "A nose!" She giggled childishly. "It looks like a giant, space-going nose!"

The group's gloom was dispelled instantly as everyone crowded forward for a better view. Across the intervening miles, the ship could, in this lighting, be seen to resemble a gigantic, swollen cartoon of a nose. The bulk of it was long and roundedly conical, a sealed tank for carrying fluids through space. Two vast pods swelled out from the sides and below, merging back again with the heavier rear portion of the ship.

Seen in this perspective, the ship seemed less deadly. Even Taviella laughed when she finally was able to see the resemblance. "Take us closer in, Roxolane," she ordered needlessly, and the Verna pilot brought the shuttle up to the tanker.

From a nearer viewpoint, the swelling of the tanks filled out and the welded plates of chainplastic hull metal showed clearly. Forward, the crew section and control housings could be seen, projecting from the tanker's curves as if glued onto the surface as an afterthought.

The shuttle slid up to the supertanker, and the airlocks mated with a hissing of seals. Roxolane powered down the shuttle and rose with grace and agility to guide her charges through their new ship.

Taviella was the first to step across, and she paused for a long moment on the threshold. The interior of the *Indagator* was darkened, and the entryway corridor seemed cold and threatening. Shaking her head, pushing her hair back with a self-conscious gesture, Taviella crossed over. She found the light switches without difficulty and brought the temperature controls up also. The *Indagator* had a cold, unpleasant scent, somewhat moldy, somewhat acidic.

Eric pushed ahead and rushed down the first cross-corridor, heading for the control room.

68

"All the controls and cabins are on this one deck," Roxolane said softly. "There are sixteen double-occupancy cabins—"

"We'll be spreading out, of course," Taviella said, forcing her voice to sound cheerful. She had been aboard less than a minute, and already she hated this ship.

"There's no reason not to," Roxolane agreed.

Remington plunged ahead next and was lost in the brief maze of corridors and cabins. Soon he found the pump rooms and was absorbed in the task of sorting out the controls and dials that measured the fluid cargo. The temperature was maintained at seven degrees, so that the viral herbicide would keep without freezing. Everything else seemed satisfactory to him: fluid volume; antislosh and vibration safeguards; the pumping mechanisms and hull-fitted spray devices. He wandered for a bit, looking for the others.

Maravic and Mikhail strolled at random, discussing features of the ship's flight plan. "Will this old wreck handle the stresses of an atmospheric dive?" she wondered.

"Well enough. The thing is partially streamlined, and the dive is a shallow, steady one. You can see, however, why we needed a slightly more than competent pilot."

"You needed an expert?"

"And Taviella is one." Mikhail paused. "You're another."

"Was that why Sargent put so much pressure on us? He wanted a crew with a backup pilot?"

"He needed one."

"And where exactly do you fit into all of this?"

Mikhail sighed. "I'm the reluctant project coordinator. I'm to oversee the actual destruction of the world, while making sure that the scientists and observers get an unimpeded view of the devastation. I'm also the one who files all the paperwork afterward."

Looking at him carefully, Maravic asked him bluntly, "What do you think, morally, about killing all life on a world?"

"I'm against it, of course. Here, on Marterly, we were able to come to a peaceful coexistence with most of the native species. But, you know, we had to kill a few. And several are only found in simulated environments — zoos and preserve ranges."

"Does being compelled to oversee the matter cause you any difficulties?"

"The way it bothers Taviella?" Mikhail smiled. "I'm a department head at a large university; I'm quite used to being ordered around." He leaned closer to Maravic. "I merely prefer to keep my dignity while under these kinds of orders."

"Dignity is important to you?" A cheerful glint showed in Maravic's eye.

"Oh, absolutely," Mikhail said with a grin, his voice so lugubrious and solemn that Maravic had to laugh.

Forward, Taviella and Eric looked over the controls. The bridge was semicircular, ringed with viewscreens beneath which control boards governed the various matters of flight. A special board controlled the gravitic repulsors hidden away in their weapons bay.

70

"We don't need to worry about midflight collisions," Eric commented sardonically.

"The repulsors?" Taviella asked. "How good are they?"

"We'll be shifting around a lot of kinetic energy. The flight plan calls for us to go out and start tossing asteroids at that poor damn world. With these repulsors, we'll knock them around like billiards. These are full-scale military-grade weapons."

"What parameters?"

Eric bent over the board. "Straight push-pull. No tangential acceleration. But we can funnel nearly all of the ship's power through them." He straightened. "I'm going to want to look at the power buses. They must be as thick as tree trunks."

"What else do we have here?"

"A hell of a lot of automation equipment. There isn't really an engine room as such, so I'll get to fly up front with the aristocrats."

"Watch your language."

Eric shrugged. "Still, it'll be kind of relaxing for me. All the nasty stuff — fuel feed, power plant vessel pressure, jumpspace springboard — is automated. I just sit back and press switches."

Taviella laughed. "I should think that would annoy you more than relax you. You usually prefer to keep direct control over events."

"Well, you can bet that I'm going to give these controls a good looking-over before I trust my life to them. Automation is fine, until you start to depend on it."

In a more serious voice, Taviella concurred. "Be sure of it. I feel just the same way."

"I'll go aft, then, and start getting my hands dirty. Do you know where my assistant has disappeared to?"

Taviella lifted her head. "Stacey? No. He can't have gone far."

Eric nodded and went back to the engine access shaft.

∞

Stasileus and Roxolane stood face to face, their arms about one another. Their touch was not erotic, but it was very comforting. Each inhaled deeply of the comforting smell of the other.

"Does Mr. Sargent treat you fairly?" Stasileus's heart hammered with a joy he hadn't felt since he left his home: the joy of close contact with another — any other — of his species.

"He disdains most of my skills," Roxolane said softly. "I was trained to be a pilot, but he prefers to keep me as a file clerk and factotum." She held him tightly. "I think that he would like to have sex with me, but he is afraid. He looks at me with disgust at other times. And sometimes with fear. The humans are so much like the gods; we can do nothing but obey."

"We must obey," Stasileus agreed. "But sometimes . . . how?"

"People sometimes think one thing, but truly believe differently. This makes their whims dangerous to obey."

Stasileus held her tightly. "How can someone not know his own mind?"

"I don't understand it," Roxolane admitted. "It perplexes me."

They spoke swiftly, their words tumbling from them with clumsy haste. But they spoke softly; it was bred into them from the creation of their species that gossip about the masters was to be kept circumspect.

"I am an engineer," Stasileus said, "but they prefer me to keep out of the way of the other engineer, Eric."

"What world are you from?"

"Invernahaven."

Roxolane shook her head. "My world didn't have spaceflight after . . . after the breakup. We were contacted by others of our own kind shortly before the human rediscovery. My world was called Winter, because its seasons were only variations of the bitter cold."

"Do you think that there are others yet undiscovered?" His world had kept spaceflight, but had used it only sparingly, colonizing two nearby worlds, then stopping.

"I'm certain there are." Roxolane clung to him. "And worlds where we have died away, having lost the technology to maintain our life span."

"The humans don't understand us," Stasileus said, and added bravely, "I'm going to change that, I hope. I will begin by understanding them."

"*Can* you understand them?" She looked deeply into his eyes. "They are scions of the gods. Is understanding possible?"

"It is," Stasileus said, "if one looks at them scientifically. They are not gods; they are only masters. It is not forbidden for us to study them. I have begun to do so. I will continue by investigating how someone can be ignorant of his own knowledge."

Roxolane was fascinated. She wanted to ask more, but just then they were interrupted by the cycling of the airlock.

"Hello? Hello? Is anyone here?" A small, fiery human woman stamped in through the lock and threw puzzled glances all around. "Oh! Vernae! What are you doing? Well, stop it at once."

Stasileus and Roxolane sprang apart and came to attention.

"You. The black one." The woman gestured rudely with her thumb. "Come and help me with my luggage. My ferryman had to dock with your other airlock, and I just came straight through." Short, flighty, middle-aged, the woman had short black hair, gray nearsighted eyes, and a forward-stooping posture. "I just dropped my stuff inside. Hello!" she called again. "Is anyone here?"

"Do you want me to bring the captain?" Stasileus asked softly.

"Hmm? Yes. Yes, certainly. That will do fine."

Stasileus went off swiftly to find Taviella. It took him only a few moments to discover her in the control room.

"Someone has arrived and is asking for you," he announced.

"Okay. I'm coming." Taviella sighed and put aside her examination of the controls.

Back in the entryway, Roxolane stood, burdened with the woman's belongings. Remington arrived at the same time Taviella did, drawn by the

74

sound of the woman's breathless instructions to the two Vernae.

"Hello," Taviella began. The woman cut her off.

"Hello, dear. I'm Bea Chapman. I'm professor of medicine and xenology at Perrin University. It's about time they dredged up a pilot for this run; I've been cooling my heels for two months. Quickly, then — assign me a stateroom and hook me into the ship's computer. And be sure to notify me when we're about to leave; jumpspace makes me intensely uncomfortable."

Shocked, Taviella shook her head to clear it. "Remington, help the woman. Stasileus, help Roxolane with those packages. Ms. Chapman, welcome to the—"

"Yes, yes, enough of that. Who are you?"

"I'm Taviella-i-Tel. The commander of the ship on this mission."

Chapman bent close to Taviella and looked up at her face. "You're the pilot? Very good. Now, as I said, I'll need a room and a lot of computer time. Be good and hurry, lad." This last was to Remington, who stood in astonishment, not knowing whether to laugh or snarl. Shaking his head, he turned and led her to the nearest cabin, staying only long enough to be certain her packages would all fit. He then fled back to the pump room.

Roxolane's heart hammered in instinctive fear. She and Stasileus set Bea Chapman's luggage and equipment on the bunk and shelves with extreme care, Roxolane staying as close to Stasileus as she could through the completion of the task.

"Good, good. You two may go. Thank you both."

Chapman whirled and began spilling the contents of her packages all across the cabin.

Outside, in the peace of a silent corridor, Roxolane hugged Stasileus tightly. "You hope to understand such as them? Can you dream of it? They are the gods reborn."

Stasileus felt extreme doubt just then, but he would not abandon hope.

"Scientific observation," he said dogmatically, "solves all riddles." His heart hammered also, and he trembled the entire length of his body.

5

They told me that the law followed a "legal code," but I didn't know it was a black-book triple-substitution trap-door random-cipher non-mnemonic *enigma*.
Kelki Hume, *Personal Journal*

Shortly, the *Indagator*'s corridors became the entryways and scurry-runs of yammering scientists by the score. Only a few of them would be accompanying the ship and its crew on the mission to murder a world, but every life scientist on the world had at least one observation he insisted be made on his behalf.

In accordance with Sargent's orders, a streamlined pod was welded to the outside of the tanker's hull, just forward of the control room. Inside the pod, cameras, light sensors, IR sensors, and other remote measuring devices were crammed, each device competing for view space through narrow, shielded ports. On the underside of the hull, workers in vacuum suits attached a launcher equipped with three remote drones, and Taviella was instructed firmly how and when they were to be launched.

Throughout this period of preparation, with scientists and technicians stamping through the ship, Eric and Remington found themselves shuffled about, constantly being asked to move somewhere else.

"This is going to drive me insane," Eric complained. He made a face at a technician who insisted on running a hand over his preset engineering instruments. The control room was evidently not the haven he hoped it would be.

"I've got a still working in the pump room," Remington whispered in his ear. "It's just about the only place we'll have any privacy."

Eric rolled his eyes. "Not your crummy vacuum-distilled grain mash, I hope. If Taviella ever finds out . . ."

"There's nothing wrong with my grain mash," Remington insisted, speaking almost too loudly. Forward, in the copilot's seat, Maravic lifted her head as though she had overheard, but then she was distracted by a technician's insistent tug at her sleeve.

"Okay." Eric nodded. "Let's get out of here."

They exited the control room with elaborate nonchalance and made their way back to the pump room. No one was in sight as they slipped within.

Around them, large masses of pumping machinery loomed, casting odd shadows in the uncertain light. The room was larger than Eric had imagined it would be, and it did offer a substantial amount of privacy.

"You've got it nice here." He looked around. "How far does this go?"

"Just around that corner, and that's it. You can see how low the ceiling gets." Remington gestured past the pumps and pipes. "That's the hull, curving down."

"Is that where you drilled your vacuum feed?"

"Right around there."

"It's sealed, right? No danger of a blowout?"

Remington looked pained. "How careless do you think I am?"

"No offense. Just asking." Eric looked significantly at his friend. "I've worked with some mighty careless folks in my time."

"Well, not me. I've got it wrapped in packing. Besides, the hole I drilled isn't big enough to blow, and I'd be able to detect a slow leak."

"Okay, then. Let's have a drink on it."

They turned the corner — and discovered that Stasileus had found both the hiding place and the still. Humans and Verna gazed unhappily at each other.

"Hello, Stacey," Remington said at last.

"I needed to hide from the crowd of people." Stasileus looked at them with raw misery in his eyes. "I wish they wouldn't shout so."

"You can stay here with us."

"But you will place a condition on my remaining. You will insist that I keep your secret. And how can I?"

"Stacey . . ." Eric began, his voice beginning to rise.

"No, Eric." Remington took him by the shoulder. "Wait." He met Stasileus's gaze. "We're breaking the rules . . . but only a little. Taviella knows that this is something we like to do, and she doesn't object. But even so, you can't tell her about it." He sighed and shrugged, frustrated by trying to explain the inexplicable. "It's an unspoken agreement. Do you understand?"

Stasileus looked down. "I think so. Before she left, Roxolane gave me a very powerful hint."

"Roxolane?"

"The other Verna." Stasileus looked past Eric and Remington, the light of discovery in his huge eyes. "She told me how people sometimes know things, but don't realize or don't want to admit that they know them. Human minds work on different operating levels, and the thought patterns are partially independent."

Eric stared and Remington gaped.

"Thought," Stasileus continued, "seems to be self-referential. It seems obvious that there would be an amplified feedback effect. Different levels of thought provide a safety precaution: the feedback is prevented from uncontrolled variability."

"You sound like an engineer," Eric muttered.

"I *am* an engineer," Stasileus said, surprised.

"But you're studying psychology."

"Is that the name for it? The study of the human mind?"

"Yes."

"Is there a term that pertains to the fact that people are unaware of their own thoughts, drives, and motivations?"

"Yes. The unconscious."

Stasileus thought about that for some time, then nodded. "Yes, the unconscious. I think that describes humanity very well. Thank you."

"Um . . ." Eric was perplexed, and for once at a loss for words.

Stasileus looked at the humans, his expression very serious. "Taviella knows that you have an improper distillation unit here, but she does not know that she knows. It would be improper for me to awaken her to the fact." He gestured to the mass of tubing and receivers that Remington had constructed. "I've examined this carefully, and you're right: it poses no threat to the vacuum integrity of the hull. You could increase efficiency by using a crystal filter instead of a distillation coil, you know."

Remington blinked, then began to stutter. "Well, yeah, I suppose . . ."

Stasileus blinked. "I see. You knew this, but you didn't know that you knew it. I apologize for bringing it to your attention."

Remington swallowed, looked over at Eric, then pushed past Stasileus to check on the fluid level in the reservoir. About a five-centimeter depth of murky brown liquid had been generated. "Do you want any?" he asked of his two friends. "Because I sure as hell do."

"Pour for me, too," Eric said. "I don't know what to think about this guy."

"I'd better not," Stasileus said softly. "But . . ."

"Yes?"

"Do you have any beer hidden here?"

Remington nodded, poured whiskey for himself

and Eric, and pulled a cold container of beer from a small chest to toss to Stasileus.

∞

During the comings and goings of technicians and installation workers, the next of the passengers came aboard: an urgent, hasty young man, with wavy dark hair above a shy and desperately emotional face. Maravic was trying to direct the operations of a group of clamoring technicians when he arrived.

"Welcome aboard," she smiled, pushing free of the cluster of people. Behind her, Mikhail breathed deeply and took over working with the technicians, trying to answer the thousand questions that so suddenly needed answering.

"Why all the furor?" the newcomer asked Maravic. "Hasn't this mission been in the works for over two months?" Despite the sharpness of his words, he seemed to have difficulty in working up the courage to speak them.

Maravic shrugged. "Things always need doing at the last minute. Right now, we're trying to get an atmosphere tester installed forward." She aimed a thumb over her shoulder, narrowly missing a technician's eye. "Half of these fellows want a pitot-tube arrangement, and the other half are dead set on having a diffusion trap."

"I'm not sure I . . ."

"You don't understand? Good. Neither do I." Maravic took his hand and pulled him out of the entryway, clearing a space for a worker who bore a complex mechanical apparatus upon his shoulder. "I'd lead you to a quieter space, except that there aren't any. Who are you, anyway?"

"Oh, excuse me." The young man stood formally straight and introduced himself. "I'm Gerald Wilson, professor of biology at Perrin University. We — our planet — we're the co-sponsors of the observation part of this tour."

"But not of the project itself?"

"No!" He blushed and stammered. "That is to say, the eradication of all life on Kythe-Correy is a Concordat Treasury Branch operation. We're just hitchhiking."

"Knowledge marches ever forward," Maravic laughed. "But the footing is sometimes slippery. Come on; I'll get you installed." The stateroom she assigned him to was one of a block of six. Even inside it, he found little privacy.

"How can they be working even here?" he asked.

A green-uniformed technician turned him a lazy eye. "We're putting in a computer link," she said in a toneless yet insolent voice. "They tell us everybody on board's going to want a lot of computer time."

"Well, yes, of course," Wilson muttered. He lifted his hand as if to gesture with something he carried, then realized that his hands were empty. "I — ah — left my own computer and terminal back on my shuttle."

Maravic smiled indulgently and shooed him away. "Go get it. We'll be needing the entryway clear soon, and they're already stacking the shuttles up three deep against our crewlock."

Wilson smiled. "Only two deep right now. I passed through one to get in." His eyes went wide. "I hope my pilot doesn't leave without waiting for me to get my bags. . . ." He turned and fled.

Maravic looked after him until he was out of sight, then frowned at the technician. "Computer link? Into this ship's computer?"

"Yeah."

"But the computer isn't particularly powerful. It's downright minuscule, compared to the size of the ship. I don't see how it can service four remote terminals and balance jumpspace tensions also."

"It can do it just fine," the technician drawled. "Operations will be slow, that's all." She pierced Maravic with a cold glance. "You in the control room will have foreground priority, of course, but you'd better not abuse the privilege: you'll get an allocation snarl-up if you do. Okay?"

Maravic could only shrug. Normal-space flight operations were maintained by smaller, dedicated computer systems, leaving the ship's primary computer free to calculate the field stresses involved in faster-than-light jump. If these people wanted to jeopardize that with their petty calculations, she was willing to let them.

In only a few moments Wilson returned, burdened with such a load of baggage, cases, boxes, and bundles that she wondered how one person could carry it all. When he set one bag down, two more slipped from his arms, and he dropped the rest while trying to catch those.

Maravic eyed him sidelong, while the technician glared at him in disgust.

"Sorry," Wilson said weakly.

Maravic shook her head. "Welcome aboard the *Planetslayer*."

∞

Mikhail soon proved his expertise in administrative judgment, getting the technicians to finish their finagling projects at last. For the final half-hour, the corridors of the ship looked like electronics factories opened up inside out: heavy cables snaked along the floor plates; computer terminal plugs appeared inside cabins and in holes in walls; the peculiar hissing sound of laser welders permeated the suddenly too warm air. The projects, however, now proceeded according to Mikhail's time schedule and not by happenstance. When the workers finally left, they left together, their projects completed.

The scientists and other observers who had sponsored the data-gathering experiments were more persistent nuisances.

"You understand," repeated one older woman, a white-haired and unrelenting vision of energy, "that these containers must not be unsealed before they are filled, and they must be filled from a still, sunlit pond."

"I'll be going onto the planet's surface with the EVA," Mikhail said softly, "and I'll collect the samples personally. Just write out the instructions plainly and attach them to the bottles. Number the bottles, too; that'll help me keep records."

"One more thing," the woman said, placing a

hand gently on Mikhail's shoulder. "The temperature of the water—"

"Please," Mikhail said, his voice firm but his expression gentle. "Write it all down for me. I can't remember this all, you have to understand."

"Oh, very well. . . ."

Mikhail exited, a trifle too swiftly, with a secret dread that if he didn't hurry, the woman would ask him for a pen to borrow. The corridors had been cleaned up, he was pleased to see, and most of the scientists aboard were finishing up last-minute adjustments of their instruments. Through one open door he saw Bea Chapman in her stateroom, and he paused and gaped in dismay.

The room was a dismal mess. Packing materials lay strewn around, sliding underfoot, and Bea's unpacked clothes had been put into service as cushioning for her instruments. Her computer terminal had been set out on the floor, and the small room's floor space was completely taken over by it and by a lumpy nest of clothes that the scientist was obviously using as a seat. Her desk was rendered useless by a gigantic crate labeled "Supplies." The bed was piled high with measuring instruments, medical bags, and a jumbled collection of bottles, jars, and jugs of various chemicals. The shelves over the bed and across the room were also jammed with odd bits of equipment: Mikhail recognized a stellar neighborhood projection, a musical entertainment center, a quick numerical integrator, and — his eyes widened in amazement — an ancient eight-stringed cittern. The whole mess was so precariously balanced that Mikhail doubted it could survive a sneeze, let alone the stresses of the ship's acceleration. He reminded himself to speak to Taviella about this as soon as possible.

His dismay was taken to new depths when, as he passed another entryway, the sharp, loud voice of Fortuna DeVries suddenly blasted his eardrums: "Well, Mikhail!"

He wheeled, his eyes wide. "Fortuna! I never thought I'd see you again."

Fortuna was a large woman, built around huge bones and muscled like a wrestler. Her hair was straight and blond, cut shorter than anyone would have thought fashionable. A mouth built for shouting split her face from cheek to cheek beneath her small nose — her only delicate feature. Her eyes were greedy and sly, shocking blue; the eyes of a gossip, missing nothing; the eyes of a morals division censor, approving of little that they saw.

"And I never doubted that I'd be back someday." Her voice was as large and raw as she was. "I consider it my life's ambition to hound you to misery." She smiled. "It's not that I don't like you, either. This is just the way it turns out. It is fate. It is—"

"May I see your papers, please, Fortuna?" Mikhail shuddered and held out his hand.

"All perfectly in order. You drove me out of one university, but I got just as good a post with another." Her papers identified her as a professor of computer science at Perrin University.

Mikhail shook his head. "I never meant you any personal harm or ill will, Fortuna."

"Then why did you have me bounced out on my ear?"

"I had no choice. You sold university projects to corporate purchasers, in violation of university rules of ethical behavior."

"Rules? *Rules?*" Her expression was wild. "Mikhail, darling, you fried me, you butchered me, you got me run out of town, just for violating a few ethics committee rules?"

"Well . . ." Mikhail began.

"No. Don't apologize." She smiled fiercely at him. "All is forgiven . . . if not quite forgotten. Now show me to a room, and I'll begin to unpack."

"Did you bring a very large amount of belongings?" Mikhail's fertile imagination painted a picture for him of another stateroom in the same shape as Bea Chapman's.

"A very large amount?" Fortuna looked at him blankly. "For heaven's sake, no. Not a lot at all. Clothing and supplies — sundries, really. I will want to make notes, however, so I brought a computer terminal. Really, though, which of us would be without one?"

"Not I," Mikhail admitted.

"Good. Now do we call a truce, my little one, or do we have to fight our fights all over again?"

Mikhail, having no illusions about the upcoming fights that he and she would be having, quietly and hopelessly agreed to her truce. "Peace, Fortuna. I'll get you to a stateroom."

"Very good, Mikhail. I think that amity is much better than our prior continual warring. And if it makes you feel any happier, I'd like to make you a promise."

"Indeed?"

"You just tell me what the rules are here, and I promise I won't break them. We'll be able to get along then, won't we?" Her large blue eyes seemed serious, yet Mikhail couldn't escape the feeling that she had a sly, hidden motive behind what she was saying.

"The most important rule is to do whatever the crew — you'll meet them soon — tells you to do. They're the ship's leadership, and we're completely subordinate to them."

"How quaint. How military. They're Navy fly-boys, then, sent to oversee us in our civilian role?"

"No. Actually, they're Commerce Branch pilots, serving in the reserve."

"So? How much real authority do they have?"

"Enough, Fortuna. Enough. Please don't cause any trouble with them."

"Any other rules?" Her voice was sardonic, almost mocking.

"Just that I'm in charge of the research project, and that among us passengers, my word goes."

"We seem to have a regular little chain of command here, don't we? Very efficient. Very firm." She looked at him, her eyes still wide. "I don't have to approve, do I? I can always disagree with the way things are run and exercise my freedom to say so?"

"We can't stop that, Fortuna," Mikhail said tiredly. "Express your opinions any time you think it will help."

Soon, leaving from the draining encounter, Mikhail sighed sadly. Not a moment of peace and quiet would be given to a single one of the passengers or crew. He knew Fortuna; he knew her well.

And he would have given anything he owned to be free of her.

∞

Last aboard the ship was a grotesquely fat man wearing a thick growth of curly red beard. He wore dark glasses to protect his eyes from even the mild shipboard lights; his hair was slick and plastered tightly to his skull. His face was heavily sunburned. His voice was raspy and sharp, and he spoke haltingly in a heavy accent.

"I am Van Wyck Henson. Not my real name. My real name would be unpronounceable to you."

Taviella, after hearing this proclamation exhaled toward the world at large, nodded. "Greetings." She tried not to stare at him. Obesity was not at all current among the worlds of Archive, nor was personal uncleanliness. Van Wyck Henson, extraordinarily fat and unignorably unwashed, would have been a wondrous sight on any world in the Concordat; aboard a ship already crowded with strong and argumentative personalities, he was one more threat to peace.

"What is your real name? Where are you from?"

"I am—" He spat forth a collection of vocables, gnashing sounds, and throat-tearing noises, completely bewildering Taviella.

"That is your real name?"

"Yes. It means — is a long name, and says my history." He evidently had difficulty speaking, and fumbled often for words to express concepts. "The first part means that I killed a shag-wolf in single combat when I became a man. The rest explains things about what else I have done."

"You're from a newly contacted world!" Taviella said, excited by the thought. "So am I!"

He peered at her, a deep, hidden gaze that made her feel small and nervous. "What name is your world?"

"Well," she said, suddenly a bit shy, "I was the first person they took away from the world — I volunteered to go — and so they named it for me. Taviella's World. I am Taviella, and I'm happy to meet you."

"Ach! We are sister and brother, then!" He evinced a strange unease, which he quickly overmastered. "I, too, am from 'Taviella's World,' and I have heard of you. They call us 'barbarians.' I come from shores of Sea of the Moon's Shame, where my tribe lived. I came out into the Concordat when a young man."

"We must have lived far, far apart," she said, unable to think of anything more astute. Taviella's mind reeled. She hadn't known of other tribes living on her home world. "My family lived on a grassy plainsland in the middle north latitudes."

"Hmm. You have adapted well to the Concordat's society. I am still seen as fat and ugly. You will help me, then? You will help me to be seen as less of a barbarian?"

"If I can."

"You owe me this, by the bond we share as natives of the same world."

I owe you nothing, Taviella thought in a flash of anger. *But wait: he's right. I left at a much earlier*

91

age, and I was able to learn social customs more readily.

"I'll be glad to help you in every way I can."

"Good!" Henson burst into a fit of coughing. "Good."

"To begin with, are you part of the scientific mission?"

"Yes. Am representing the DuPres Academy of Sciences. They rescued me from home — from 'Taviella's World.'" He grinned. "They taught me science, biochemistry. I am a teacher there — Pah! Students hate me. Hate being taught by 'barbarian.' I show them: I learn subject better than they ever will."

He went on after pausing scarcely long enough to take a breath, and his tone changed abruptly from dark to light. "And subject is fasc-in-a-ting! I never tire of it! Do you know how many worlds have evolved life on their own in this part of space? Just over one dozen! Unlikely? I don't know. All other worlds with life are worlds seeded by precursors: Empire of Archive. Your and my ancestors." He spat.

Taviella gasped. Quickly, she controlled herself. "Please, Mr. Henson. No spitting aboard ship."

"Okay. First lesson. You tell me more?" He bent and wiped up the spittle with his bare hand.

No doubt. "I'll help you; I promise. Come with me. I'll show you your stateroom."

"I only spit when I name the Empire. But not now. Save it for dinner."

With that alarming remark, he bowed slightly and followed Taviella to the stateroom she had assigned him. Soon he was set up in comfort and style and had begun to take advantage of the computer link. He, too, she noticed with amusement, was attached, symbiotically, to his computer terminal.

∞

The preparations were completed. After one pile of her crates and boxes had collapsed, Bea Chapman was persuaded to anchor her goods. Van Wyck Henson was shown where he was and was not permitted to go. Eric and Remington were given time to run the ship and its cargo through a last-minute checklist.

Then, responding to Taviella's deft handling, the ship turned and began to accelerate gently. Internal gravitic compensators corrected for the motion, and Taviella's touch was sure.

Three hours later, the red rifts of jumpspace gaped to receive them; the ship fell through the hole and into the ovenlike heat. The voyage was under way.

6

The true evil isn't in failure, of course,
nor is it in not trying. The true evil is in
stopping others from trying.

Szentellos, *Regrets*

Aboard the *Indagator*, what had seemed a crowded
coterie of bustling researchers quickly devolved
into a generally orderly society. It took Taviella little time to put together a mental map of the friend-
ships and antagonisms among her four crew members and the five scientists. Most pleasing to her
was that she could honestly consider Mikhail Petrov more as a crew member than a passenger, and
certainly as more of a friend than a foe. He and
Maravic sat near her in the control room, speaking
of matters more and less technical. While Taviella
could hear every word, she had to admit that she
understood little.

What she did understand, she approved of. She
sat back in her control couch and smiled lazily
while watching the two. Maravic, always at ease,
relaxed in a happy, absorbed pose, leaning on one

elbow upon her control board. Data display visuals and status telltales shone in reflected highlights from her dark red hair. Beyond her, his face animated with the glory of the storyteller, Mikhail spoke, waving his hands, waggling his eyebrows, and smiling all the time.

Taviella smiled likewise and shook her head. The room was filled with buzzwords — "counterstar," "jumpspace leakpoint," "poles without residue," and, sounding fairly ominous to Taviella's mind, "crumbling space." The words meant nothing to her, but Maravic both nodded in comprehension and made cogent comments, countersigns in the coded language of physics. Watching them, Taviella thought she saw another kind of communication unfolding, and her smile became softer and happier. She lost herself in a daydream involving "crumbling space" as a vast landscape of tumbling boulders, through which no ship could pass unscathed. What wonders might lie beyond?

The intercom chimed, and Taviella caught it on the first tone, instantly awake. She'd learned, in her years of piloting, the trick of coming awake in a moment. "Yes?"

"Eric here." With the increased size of the ship's complement, identification of the speaker had become a new form of intercom courtesy. "Remington and I have got things laid out for a get-together dinner. I'll bet you didn't know Stacey can cook."

Taviella laughed. "Of course I did. He's cooked for us before."

"Not like this." Eric signed off, leaving Taviella to wonder. About her, about them all, the huge ship, the *Planetslayer*, drummed its steady mechanical throb and drone of power. Above each ceiling, beyond the piping and wiring and air ducts, separated from the living spaces by only a thin shield of hull metal, a deadly viral agent lay waiting. Just abaft the control room, a battery of gravitic repulsors stood passively ready for their task of hurling asteroids like falling stars at a defenseless world. By impact and by poison, the world was to be bombarded with death from the skies.

Taviella shook her head again and straightened in her seat. True to Sargent's word, the ship virtually flew itself . . . out here in jumpspace. How it would handle when hurtling through an atmosphere? Even as she asked the question, Taviella knew herself to be equal to the task.

With a happy glance at Maravic and Mikhail, she left the control room. The corridors were mostly vacant, although she glimpsed Fortuna DeVries pacing a cross-corridor with a swift, stamping gait. She might have followed, but the sudden scent of food tickled her curiosity, and she turned instead toward the ship's lounge.

Roughly triangular in shape, squeezed between the galley and the control room, the lounge was actually too small for a banquet for ten people. Eric looked up and waved to Taviella as she squeezed in. Remington and Stasileus carried a small table into the room and unfolded it. The rich, ripe scent of a meal in preparation wafted from the galley.

"Everyone will be here," Eric said cheerfully. His face immediately twisted into a wry, sardonic grin. "That'll be a sight, now won't it?"

"They've got to get to know one another, and this is the way to do it." Taviella's certainty showed in the set of her jaw. People ought to like each other, and that was that.

"Do you know what Vernae eat on their home world?" Eric asked. Stasileus paused while setting up the table and blinked at him watchfully.

"Fish?" Taviella guessed. "Bread? Dried fruit?" She laughed. "We ate all of those on my home world. Why should the Vernae be any different?"

"Rotten cabbages. Decaying fruit . . . fruit ripe past bursting. Vegetables boiled so long they've dissolved into paste."

Taviella screwed up her face. "Sounds rather unappetizing."

Bea Chapman flounced in just then, her earlier anger gone. "The Vernae? I heard you talking about their filthy habits. Good reasons, though, you know."

Taviella opened her mouth to welcome the scientist, but was interrupted by Bea's next words.

"The poor dears are involuntary vegetarians. Animal proteins give them the runs. But, you know, they were made with carnivores' teeth."

Stasileus cocked his head to one side, fascinated by this human woman and her apparent knowledge of his species. Not for the world would he have interrupted.

"A poor adaption, evolutionarily speaking." Bea's sprightly tone and nearsighted stance took the sting from her comments. "But then, they didn't evolve. Left to themselves, after the Empire dropped the ball, they had to find ways of feeding.

How do beings with carnivores' teeth eat vegetables? Their teeth would be ground down to nothing in no time if they tried to eat fruits or grains. But they're not stupid: they learned how to cook with microorganisms: a rotten habit, but necessary."

Taviella spoke up more quickly this time. "How do you know so much about them? They were only discovered recently."

Bea peered at her. "Oh, I was with the contact team that followed up the first discovery. I got to dissect a clump of cadavers; I know more about Verna internal organs than anyone else." She squinted up at Stasileus. "I know more than you do, youngster, about your own guts." She smiled in self-satisfaction.

"I studied engineering," Stasileus said with quiet dignity.

"And cooking. Hmm. I can smell it." Bea turned to Taviella. Eric and Remington stood back and watched the exchange resignedly. The more scientists who showed up, the worse the evening would become.

"That's rotten food you smell. Garbage. Bacterial composts. You should never have let him cook."

Taviella faced Stasileus. "Is it safe for us to eat the food you've prepared?"

"Yes."

"Bea? Is that true?"

"Oh, it won't make us ill. We won't be spewing it all up. But doesn't the thought of eating a bacterial culture just make you feel all wobbly?"

In truth, the thought of it did precisely that, supplying Taviella's imagination with horrid no-tions of rot and decay. But the scents coming from the galley were appetizing: rich, savory, redolent of spice and flavor.

"I'll eat anything once," she said gamely.

"As you will," Bea chortled. "I'll make do with canned stuff from your larder, if that's acceptable to you." She seated herself and began to read and make notes in a binder full of papers.

Taviella followed Remington and Stasileus into the small galley, leaving Eric to finish setting up.

"There's one rude woman," Remington muttered. "But they're all that way — surly, and rude, and innately vicious." He looked at Taviella with sad eyes. "I wish we'd never taken this mission."

"She is not innately vicious," Stasileus said. Remington and Taviella turned to him, hearing the complex overtones and echoes of his voice. The oversized alien virtually filled the galley; his huge feet took up a great portion of the floor space. "She is providing a personality structure for us to perceive, in hopes that we will overlook the basic shyness that is underlying. As opposed to vicious, it would be more fair to say that she is very, very lonely. She only wants someone to talk to."

Taviella and Remington blinked. Stasileus tilted his head to the side and tried to explain. "I've been watching her and learning what to look for."

Remington objected weakly. "I've been watching her too, and she's the most standoffish snob I've ever seen. She doesn't want companionship. She just wants to annoy everyone."

"No," Stasileus said firmly. "No one hurts others without feeling hurt themselves."

Remington and Stasileus tossed the idea back and forth for a few more minutes, but Taviella scarcely heard them. She moved to the doorway and watched Bea at work. Stasileus's observations made sense. . . .

She squeezed through the door and sat near Bea. "Doctor Chapman," she said softly, "do you think we're doing the right thing?"

Bea looked up slowly. She glanced at Taviella, then at Eric, who was busy laying out the table settings. "What do you mean?" she asked.

"This mission. It makes me very uneasy."

Bea looked at her long and hard. Her eyes crinkled about the edges, little lines of personality coming out on her face. "Uneasy, eh? What about it upsets you?"

Taviella groped for words, suddenly aware that she was not merely making idle conversation but that this issue was centrally disturbing to her. "The taking of life on that scale . . . it seems wrong. Entire herds of grazing animals wiped out in almost no time. . . ."

Speaking with unusual gentleness, Bea met Taviella's gaze. "You came from one of the lost worlds, didn't you? I seem to remember reading about you in the mission briefing. You were raised with hunters and gatherers." She sighed heavily. "Primitive people understand how intimately tied they are to their world's life cycles. Wiping out an entire herd of meat animals means starvation the next winter."

"Yes," Taviella admitted, "but it works on a larger scale in the same way, doesn't it?"

Bea's voice harshened. "Scale? You only perceive the difference in scale?"

"No. . . ." Taviella tried to explain. "It's wrong because there can be no recovery, whereas a herd can always replenish itself, given time."

"Oh, very good," Bea sniffed. "You don't perceive the loss of the unique rhythms of interlocking predator-prey cycles. You don't perceive the chemical balances reestablished on a moment-by-moment basis. You can't see the way the whole balances the parts, and the way the entire biosphere represents a single membrane." Her voice became shrill. "Would you cram mice's lungs into fishes' bodies? Would you force a shark to eat vegetables?"

Eric threw Taviella a significant glance, as if to remark ironically on Bea's emotional outburst. Taviella tried to pretend she hadn't seen it, but Bea saw her distraction, and her face froze.

"You think it's funny, don't you?"

"Please," Taviella said, desperately seeking a way to pull the conversation back onto a safe track. "I don't want to murder an entire world. But I must do it; I'm under orders. It's only . . ."

"Yes?" Bea looked at her with sharp disdain.

"I want to know what it is that I'm doing." Taviella felt small and alone. "We are responsible for our actions, are we not? But how can I be if I don't know what it is that I'm doing?"

"After dinner," Bea said, her voice reverting to normalcy, "I'll show you. I'll show everyone."

"Thank you."

Some minutes of silence passed. Bea scribbled furiously in her notebook, her ciphers and calculations and symbols all completely abstract and foreign to Taviella. Eric, his work done, sat and relaxed and smiled at Taviella, wordlessly communicating his disdain of the emotionally unbalanced Bea Chapman. In the galley, Remington and Stasileus puttered, arranging the meal. The odors were none the less appetizing for all of Bea's excoriation of Vernae home cooking.

Without warning, Van Wyck Henson stumbled in, breathing heavily. "What smells so awful?" he demanded. "I am not eating in with you."

Taviella, taken aback, stuttered an inquiry. "The food? But . . ."

"No. I eat alone. Please." Taking a deep breath, he began again. "I am afraid that if I ate with you — with all of you — I would in-ad-ver-tent-ly give offense. I know."

"No. Please . . ."

He beamed at her. "Thank you. But no. I am a barbarian, and not fit for civilized company. I spit where people should not. I am fat and ugly. I know."

"Mister Henson—"

"Oh, no. I am *Doctor* Henson. I have right to insist." He gazed at Taviella significantly through his thick-lensed glasses. "I eat alone. I would not want to give offense." He wheeled ponderously and stamped away. Just before he passed out of sight around a bend in the corridor, he spat hugely against the wall.

Taviella drew a deep breath, then let it out slowly. Bea, pretending a fine obliviousness, continued to write notes without pause. Eric shook his head and went to wipe up the spittle.

Soon Maravic, Mikhail, and Fortuna arrived. Not long after, Gerald Wilson followed. The seating was cramped even without Van Wyck Henson's enormous bulk; Remington chose to eat standing. Stasileus, as heavy as Van Wyck Henson but trimmer for being much, much taller, also stood, filling the galley doorway. The deep trays of food that he brought in sizzled and piped on the two tables.

"What have we here?" Fortuna demanded.

"Sludge," Bea said quietly. In accordance with her earlier demands, Remington had opened her a tray of stir-fried seafoods and bread-baked fruits. The meal that the Verna set before the rest seemed horribly sludgelike indeed: the pans contained puddings, gravies, and mashes, all soft foods to be ladled out with care.

Taviella tried some, out of politeness. The flavor was astonishing: the food was a mouth-watering nutty confection, a contrast of sweet and salt tastes. Eric and Maravic gingerly began to sample theirs, accepting the experiment for quite different reasons. They, too, nodded in surprised satisfaction. Soon, the passengers and crew, excepting only the fastidious Bea, began to eat in earnest, and the food was pronounced excellent by all.

∞

"Who is it," Gerald Wilson asked late in the meal, "that's using all the computer time?" He blushed a bit as everyone looked toward him. "It's only . . . it's only that my terminal is working quite slowly. I've timed it, and would you believe that I'm only getting half a million operations per second? I'd be better off with an abacus and sand table." He grinned weakly.

Fortuna raised one eyebrow and peered at him inquisitively. "You know, my young friend, that we must all compete for the same limited resources." Her look turned sly. "Although I, too, must admit to finding a pressure for computational efficiency. My project . . ." She waved her hand self-deprecatingly. "Well, my project can't be as important as all of yours." She returned to her meal, at which she picked and fidgeted.

Having spent more time in the control room than the others, Mikhail had become privy to the operations of the ship's computer. Fortuna herself was responsible for most of the tie-up, making incredible demands upon storage and processing resources. He frowned and determined to say nothing just yet. The problem would likely resolve itself, and he hated to intervene.

"Is there anything I can do?" Taviella asked, trying to help.

Fortuna turned to her, a crooked grin on her face. "Oh, no, darling. Your ship has done it all for you. In fact . . ." her voice sunk to a conspiratorial whisper, clearly audible to all present. "In fact, who, right now, is flying the ship?"

Taviella's shoulders tensed. "No one. The ship is self-contained and self-operating, here in jump-space. Once we hit atmosphere, I'll be in control."

Fortuna's smile grew wider. "Certainly. Of course. We mustn't forget the old human element, must we?"

At a loss, Taviella shook her head. The meal before her was too good to be ruined by Fortuna's blatant attempt to unsettle her, but the woman's motive was completely unclear.

Oblivious to Fortuna's machinations, Remington waved an eating utensil in the air like a lecturer's wand and began to expound upon the ship's automated features. "Human element? Hell, this ship could work more than half the mission without any human aboard. The computer acts like it's alive . . . and that's no joke, 'cause I've seen computers that were." His face was lit with a lively exuberance. "This ship has lesser computers, really nothing more than point processors, to handle everything from cargo weight to local jumpspace field density. Isn't that right, Eric?"

Eric gave him a sour grimace. "Right." He seemed unwilling to make the effort to get along with the passengers.

"A ship this big," Remington went on animatedly, "gets little gradients of the field strength at different places along the hull. We've got sensors aboard that measure this, and . . ."

"Do go on, my boy," Fortuna purred. "I assure you that we find this most interesting." She closed her eyes and stretched.

Remington lowered his gaze. "Oh, that's all I had to say." He glanced at Eric, who wore a tired, I-told-you-so expression. Remington smiled weakly at him; he didn't need to be hit with a hammer before he got the message.

Throughout dinner, Maravic, normally outgoing and cheerful, found nothing she wanted to say.

Even in silence, she was aware of the group, feeling them with tendrils of sympathy. Out of this many people, she felt certain that more ought to be openly and warmly friendly. Yet there was nothing here but hurt: bruised egos and aching loneliness.

Maravic then looked at Mikhail and instantly felt the warmth and cheer that normally sustained her. He, like she, ate in silence, searching for but not finding any way to crack the shells that the other passengers had erected about themselves.

At one point he looked up and met her gaze. The two smiled, honest and sincere smiles that signified true warmth. They, at least, were not alone, and even in silence would not be unhappy. They drew strength from one another and found peace.

Bea Chapman ate swiftly, making a bedraggled mess of her plate and her setting, and continued to write in her notebook, ignoring the food stains that marred the pages.

Stasileus, standing in the doorway, watched them all, seeing everything, missing nothing. His understanding of the deep ways of the human mind was becoming more thorough, and the information coming to his wide eyes and sharp ears was carefully sifted. He believed that he had identified three levels of human thought and five qualities of thought that could fit each of the levels. Of the one hundred twenty-five permutations thereof, only a very few made sense, and yet the eight humans before him had displayed, at various times, as many as thirty of the modes.

I'm thinking like an engineer, he suddenly realized; the thought shocked and intrigued him. *But is not this science different from engineering's formal precision?*

He blinked in distress and hurriedly scooped the last of his meal into his small mouth. The discrete and modular approach he'd invented had seduced him . . . although he realized happily that it might not all need to be scrapped. He would need a statistical method to accompany his observations, as a means of measuring and validating.

The depth of human complexity seemed unplumbable . . . but only for a second. These humans still followed stiff and regular rules of behavior, and the rules were discoverable. He watched and listened.

∞

After the meal, while Stasileus and Remington cleared the tables and bore away the empty pans, Bea spoke. "Who is against this thing? Who is in favor?" She looked up, as if to catch the facial expressions that people had thought secret from her.

"None of us is 'in favor' of every part of the mission," Mikhail said, after a long moment of silence. "I think we all have reservations."

"Reservations?" Bea craned her neck forward in an unpleasant fashion and looked at him. "But are you in favor of completing the mission?"

Taviella took a quick breath. Was the woman about to try to incite a mutiny? Almost as if sensing the thought, Bea fell back in her chair and closed her notebook.

"I don't know how many of you know the full

details of the fate of Catalart/Penander. I don't even know if any of you care. But I brought a projector with me. If everyone will do me the kindness of waiting here for just a few moments . . ." She abruptly got up and strode out of the dining area. In her absence, conversation was sparse.

Shortly Bea was back, holding a clumsy-looking image projector by one worn carrying strap. She dropped it heavily onto the table and retook her seat. From a flimsy bag she drew four or five cassettes, which she peered at nearsightedly. Finally she chose one, blew on it, and jammed it roughly into the projector's cassette port.

"This will work better if someone turns down the lights," she said bluntly.

Stasileus, by nature sensitive to orders even when they were disguised as suggestions, hastened to obey.

The projector, badly out of tune, sputtered and clanked in the darkness, and an image took shape above it.

7

I'd have to say that it's certainly interesting — and highly fallacious — to penalize someone for being too honest.

Justice Goto, *Collected Casebooks*

Bea's presentation was a collation of recordings made over a long time, interspersed with animation sequences. The first scene showed the world of Catalart. Bea's projector caused the image of the blue-and-white world to hover steadily over the table, in appearance the size of a large world globe, approximately one meter in diameter. The point of view was the same for everyone in the room, regardless of where they were seated.

"Catalart/Penander," Bea said quietly. "I was there."

The world turned silently beneath them.

With a brief flicker of multicolored light, the scene shifted. A view over a vast arid steppe was represented. White dots moved over red sands. The magnification increased slowly as the scene zoomed in on a cluster of the dots, which were revealed to be bandy-legged animals, cropping the skimpy grasses. One raised its head, twisted it in an awkward-seeming motion, and threw its mouth wide, showing sharp, flat teeth. In response to its alarm, if alarm it had been, the animals near it leaped nimbly into the air and sprinted off at an incredible speed. The point of view drew back again to show the entire plain alive with their motion.

"The sound portion of the recording won't come through," Bea said. "My projector isn't working just right."

"Bring it by later," Eric said softly. "I'll fix it."

"Thank you."

The next scene was of a grassy copse, a shadowed hollow sheltered beneath boulders towering overhead. Half-melted snow sprinkled the ground, and a tiny waterfall sparkled, running down a crack between two large rocks. Although the water fell free for about half a meter, it didn't splash normally, but simply drooled into a small basin. The point of view drew closer and closer, until everyone could see a thick mass of tendrils, thin and reed-like, suspended in midair inside the water's flow.

"Worms of some sort," Bea explained. "They move upstream and are capable of climbing higher waterfalls than this one. We don't know why they do it."

"A homing instinct?" Mikhail asked. "Part of a cyclic pattern?"

"We don't know."

"You never will," Fortuna said chattily.

"Correct."

The mysterious worms writhed, some serving

as a bridge for the others until it became their own turn to crawl upward.

Again the scene shifted, once more marked by a varicolored flash of light. This was not normal; Bea's projector was in sore need of maintenance. The next few scenes were of birds, or birdlike animals. The vivid plumage came in every color conceivable, and the birds showed every imaginable adaptation of fur and feather, of claw and bill. They ranged in size from quick-flitting little things only centimeters in length to a great and solitary animal of purest white whose wingspan could not have been less than four meters. The point of view followed this last creature for some time as it soared, wings motionless, in the sun. At last it was lost behind an upthrust crag.

"Birds," Bea said simply.

The final shot in the first sequence was a mobile viewpoint. The recording technician had sought to follow a long, lizardlike amphibian; the amphibian, with at least equal fervor, had sought to escape the human.

The chase took on a comic aspect as the frightened animal squeezed between rocks, trampled ferns in its haste, and climbed a tree only to fall back to the ground. The human was its equal in mobility, and the point of view of the recording kept pace with the scrambling lizard, although with some difficulty. Finally the lizard won its freedom by leaping from a low bank into a swift-moving stream. Its head quickly disappeared under the muddy ripples.

"For the next sequence of shots," Bea explained,

111

"we had to use a specially sensitive film. By this time, it had already gone quite dark."

The scene resolved in midair, and the crew and passengers of the *Indagator* studied it closely. It was a forest of broad-leafed trees, marching up from left to right until the trees at the extreme right edge of the image brushed their leaves virtually in the face of the audience.

"This part actually comes after some of what you'll see in a bit. Oh, and it's time-lapse."

A wave of motion began at the farthest left and swept slowly across the image. The trees were losing their leaves. By the time the effect had reached across to the nearest trees, most of the forest was denuded; the trees were bare and harsh and cold. In a flash, the leaves that were closest paled and shriveled and dropped away.

"That was when they dropped the virus. The earthquakes and things had already been taken care of; those are in the next part you'll see."

"This is a delightful appeal to the emotions," Fortuna said with a theatrical sigh. "If you're set on making us feel guilty, you're doing a marvelous job. A perfectly nice world, gone completely to ash, just so sinful mankind can make productive use of it."

"There will always be people who feel that way," Bea said. There was no anger in her voice.

"Well, come on, then. Complete the job. Show us your worst." Fortuna crossed her arms heroically, turning her defiant face to the projector.

"The worst is coming."

The image shifted abruptly to a combination of visual images and data displays. In the center of the viewing field a vast asteroid hovered, bulky and irregular. Cracks and rifts mapped out a pattern of impact and shear deformations over its surface; clearly its life in orbit had been marked by more than one major collision. Overlaid onto the picture was a series of graphic symbols, representing velocity and gravitational vectors. The scene lasted only for a few moments, long enough to show the asteroid's velocity vector changing rapidly due to acceleration applied from the ship's repulsors.

Another, even briefer, shot showed the ship — the *Planetslayer* — from the outside. The ship that Maravic had derided as a flying nose now moved backward and away, propelled in the opposite direction from the asteroid it was pushing.

Then the recording returned to a point of view on a hilltop on the surface of the world of Catalart. The scene was tranquil and lovely: a balmy afternoon overlooking a thick rain forest. The canopied forest dropped precipitously down a plunging hillside and ended against a thin, curved strip of beach. Warm, slow ocean rollers curled and broke over diamond-white sand.

A bright streak fell out of the sky and into the ocean somewhere beyond the horizon. For a while, nothing seemed to happen. The scene was as it had been: placid and welcoming.

Remington saw it first and drew in his breath. One by one, the others did also. A roiling disturbance churned over the surface of the ocean, moving swiftly toward a landfall. It covered the last few kilometers in a rush, whipping the breakers to foam, throwing up the beach's sands in gusts and gouts, and blasting the forest into a frantically waving chaos of tossing limbs.

"The first overpressure wave from the shock of the asteroid's impact." Bea's voice was strangely loud in the ship's lounge.

The recording continued. Soon the horizon darkened, but strange spokes of light and shadow seemed to radiate into the sky. The trees continued to whip and wave, many of them snapping off at the base and flinging themselves in unexpected directions. A long time seemed to pass, but the crew and passengers watched the play of light and dark with complete concentration.

Again, Remington was the first to see a new development: a dark line appearing on the horizon.

"That's gonna be a big wave," he muttered.

"A twenty-meter-high wall of water," Bea said calmly. "I don't remember its velocity."

Everyone watched and waited. Fortuna, who pretended not to care, never blinked. Eric mentally calculated the energy such a wave would carry and shook his head in nervous disbelief. Maravic bit her lip.

Silently, inexorably, the wave came closer in, until it looked as if it would strike in only a few seconds. The minutes dragged out, however, and the smaller breakers continued to roll: playful heralds of the leviathan approaching behind them. Silently, the sea dropped away, and the water swirled out, draining the beach and revealing a section of the muddy bottom. Then the monstrous wave smote the land.

Spume and spray shot up into the sky; the

water rose against the cliffs, gnawing away at their solidity. Ton after ton of dirt and rock slid into the white-foaming teeth of the sea. The forest was stripped away, submerged, ground into splinters in only seconds. The sea continued to rise, preceded by geysers and jets of agitated water. Finally, when it seemed that the highest point of the flood would swallow up the recording device, the waters swirled, eddied, and began to subside. With violence equal to its arrival, the wave was reflected out to sea, taking yet more of the cliffs and forests with it.

A tiny clinking noise broke the deathlike hush of the room, and the image faded.

"Oh, dear," Bea said, her voice disturbingly normal after the scene of such horrid abnormality. "My projector seems to be broken."

∞

Everyone was momentarily dazed when the lights came on. Mikhail turned around to see Stasileus's stubby fingers pulling back from the light switch. He smiled, obscurely relieved by the huge alien's thoughtfulness. Horror could come and horror could pass, but as long as one being remained in the universe with the common sense to turn on the lights when they were needed, civilization might be expected to endure. With that thought, he stood, moved past Stasileus into the galley, and began preparing an after-dinner tray of coffee and tea.

The uneasy silence was finally broken by Fortuna, who yawned hugely, then leaned forward,

115

her elbows perched on the table's edge. "That was truly remarkable," she said sweetly. "It displayed creative animation techniques. One would have almost thought it real."

"It was real," Gerald Wilson muttered.

Fortuna glanced at him, wryly amused. "I pity the cameraman they left behind, exposed to such elemental violence."

"I think," Maravic said gently, "that they used automated recording equipment."

Fortuna's lassitude would not be dispelled. "What a waste," was all she said.

"A waste?" Bea snapped. "The true waste . . ." She composed herself, but only with an effort. Across the table, Fortuna smiled a secret little smile of triumph.

"This ship?" Taviella asked in a small voice. All eyes swung to her. She met the gaze of her friends and her passengers, although her face had gone quite pale.

"Is it the same ship? This *Indagator*, this *Planetslayer*? Are we traveling along in the ship — the *weapon* — that did that?"

Bea's voice was soft. "Yes."

With a faint, mocking smile, Fortuna took Taviella's measure with her gaze. "Didn't you know?"

"Yes, I knew," Taviella said, her voice low and worried. "But I never fully grasped it. . . . The enormity of the task is staggering, and . . ." She shook her head. "Eric," she said unhappily, "can you fix Bea's projector? I want — I need to see the rest of the recording."

"Easiest thing in the world," Eric said, his voice

loud and self-assured. A bit of worry showed in his eyes, however: he didn't look forward to watching more scenes of widespread destruction.

Mikhail returned then with a salver of coffee mugs and tea cups. Stasileus stood out of the way and let him distribute them to the eager hands of the diners. The solid clank of the mugs against the table, and the delicious heat of the savory liquid, brought the assembly back to a comfortable sense of propriety. Even Fortuna's biting comments seemed excusable, and Taviella, watching her sip her tea contemplatively, thought she understood some of the woman's bitterness.

"Eight asteroids in all," Mikhail explained in a soft, casual tone. "They were scooped up from various parts of the system, which doesn't have an organized ring of them."

"Deposited directly upon diverging tectonic plate boundaries," Bea said, her voice flat and lifeless. Her coffee mug had been handled clumsily, and it left little rings of spilled coffee here and there upon the table before her. "You can't imagine the destruction. That strike — the one you saw on the recording — was the most successful of the operation. More than a hundred cubic miles of dust and water vapor went straight up into the atmosphere's highest, most stable levels. If my projector had held out, you would have seen a pair of truly incredible explosions, out at sea. That strike hit a shallow seamount volcano under no more than forty meters of water."

She grinned a tight, ironic grin. "Given another few thousand years, it would have become a nice little island, just like the one that was flooded in the recording."

Remington thought aloud. "The impact would be in the megaton range of explosive yield."

"A range of five hundred to five thousand megatons over the eight strikes." Bea sounded weary and unhappy. "The impacts did most of the damage themselves, creating large volumes of hot dust and ash. The vulcanism and other by-products didn't contribute too awfully much." She paused. "Although we did get some very widespread forest fires, and they had a significant effect."

"What was . . . What is the purpose?" Taviella needed to know.

Nearly everyone looked at her.

"Purpose?" Fortuna asked softly.

"No . . ." Taviella waved her hand in a gesture of frustrated communication. "The purpose is to clear a world to make more living room for people. I know that part. We can't live there, because . . ."

"Because of a particularly offensive amino acid produced by all native life forms," Bea responded when Taviella paused.

"Why the asteroid strikes? Why the mass destruction? Wasn't the sprayed virus sufficient? Couldn't you simply have poisoned the world, without battering it also?"

"Artificially induced virus plagues are tricky," Mikhail answered. "If the epidemic is too virulent, then pockets of forests will survive by isolation. If the plague isn't virulent enough, then immunities have time to develop. The airborne virus might have been enough. . . ." He shrugged. "But it might not have. The same thing is true for the atmospheric sunlight blocking: by itself, it was probably sufficient. But the operation was felt to be important enough to justify redundant approaches."

"The plants seem to have been the primary targets. Why?"

"Oh, they're the key to it all. Kill the plants—"

Fortuna interrupted cruelly. "Does she truly not understand?"

Mikhail continued, choosing not to acknowledge Fortuna's chill contribution to the group's unhappiness and tension. "The plant life feeds the animal life. With both dead, only the reducing agents — bacteria and some of the insects — remain alive. Then follow-up expeditions seed the world with algaes and tough grasses that follow our own pattern of life." He grinned at Taviella, his eyes crinkling happily at the thought of the life-giving to follow. "We're as poisonous to that world's original life as it is to us: it's just a matter of getting a foothold.

"Suppose," he continued, "that we had evolved on one island there, and the native plants and animals on another. There would be constant little invasions . . . seeds blown across the ocean by trade winds, or migrating birds that get stranded on the wrong land. Most invasions would die quickly, and the islands would be pure enclaves of different life chemicals. Some invasions — the toughest grasses, or certain chemically inventive bacteria and other microbes — could survive on the hostile island, but they'd never be able to go on to build up a life chain. The native arrangement would be too strong, too healthy. But if it was weak . . ." He shrugged his shoulders. "A local plague could have weakened the island, or maybe a typhoon torn it up a bit. Then the invasions would have had a better chance to compete."

Remington chuckled and drained his mug of coffee. "Your analogy is exact. The two islands are in space: planets. Our own and this alien one."

Mikhail nodded. "The best analogies are exact."

"So Catalart died." Taviella said, struggling to comprehend the right and wrong of it. "And it's now being settled by people?" She looked to Bea for an answer, but the older woman was staring down into the depths of her empty teacup, withdrawn and abstracted.

"Not for several years," Mikhail explained. "There's still a lot of biological engineering and world-forming to do there."

"And the life that we saw — it's all dead and gone?"

"Some was preserved," Mikhail said, "and some was taken away alive, to live in enclosures. The world of Anitra/Penander has a large, artificially maintained habitat, where they managed to save several breeding populations of herbivores."

Bea looked up slowly, her eyes squinting as if against a painful or unpleasant sight. "A whole world full of interlocking chains of life: an entire planetary surface covered with interacting molecules. We kept no more than two or three hectares of feeble grass and mangy grass-eaters. You can't pretend to believe that those things are representative of . . . of . . ." She faltered and fell silent.

120

Mikhail looked down in embarrassment. "No. I can't pretend that."

Maravic took his hand.

∞

Stasileus, an engineer from a culture long accustomed to mass extinctions, sensed the distress of the humans in the room. He also realized that his formative emotional calculus was completely inadequate in the face of the metamorphoses that he had watched unfold. The human mind worked on levels of more and less conscious awareness, certainly, but in what fashion did the activities reinforce one another?

With a pang, he admitted to himself that his entire body of earlier work had been incorrect and needed to be discarded. Just as the theories of impetus and inherent motion needed to be thrown away in favor of the unifying theories of simple mechanics, so too his intuitive and descriptive thoughts had to be thrown out to make room for a composite theory.

The human mind, he saw, was mechanical and driven by certain tropisms. Habits formed long ago came to be underlying structures of some permanence and inflexibility. Instincts came into play also, which explained the necessity for human gestures and expressions, for the loudness or softness and the pacing of words in speech.

Human reason, the pride of civilization, had to struggle to survive this morass of emotional obstructions that lurked beneath the surface of conscious thought, like entangling weeds and muck beneath the clean surface of a pond. Intellectual courage lay in avoiding becoming ensnared; productive thought was a challenge to the self-honesty of humans.

Stasileus repaired to the galley, to wash pans, clean and put away the foods and supplies, and to think more about the riddle of human intelligence.

∞

In the control room, Taviella sat in her command couch, leaning back and brooding over the death of a lovely world.

Intruding without a knock, Van Wyck Henson lurched in, his immense, obese bulk somehow alien and frightening.

"I came to talk," he said, his words coming thickly through his beard.

"Very well," Taviella answered. She sat up straighter in her chair.

"The meal that your alien brought me was very good. I thank you." He inclined his head in a ridiculously formal way.

"He cooks very well," Taviella agreed.

"I have come to apologize for the offense that I have given."

"You've given us no offense."

"I have. I have." Van Wyck Henson's voice was thick and strangled. He started to spit, but caught himself. "I am a fat, crude, vicious barbarian, and no one wants to be near me."

"That's not true," Taviella said. "In fact—"

"Did I miss any important conversation during dinner?"

"Doctor Henson, don't you think it would be a good idea to get to know your fellow passengers a little better?"

"Fah!" This time he spat a viscous stream at the decking. "With that Fortuna woman? With Bea Chapman, who is mindless? With Gerald Wilson, whose idiocy offends even me? Only Mikhail Petrov has a working brain in his head, and still he nauseates me. The whole group of them ought to be put alive into space!"

"Doctor Henson!" Taviella's rebuke was sharp.

Van Wyck Henson stepped back and folded his hands across his stomach. "Oh. I apologize. You see? I have again given offense. Fat, crude Van Wyck Henson, they say. . . ."

Taviella swiveled out of her chair and stood to face the man. Behind his dark glasses, his tiny pig eyes were wrinkled and squinted. "Doctor Henson, listen to me. Stop spitting. Listen with respect to your colleagues. Come and join the discussions at dinner. Do these things, and you will become accepted by the others."

"I understand."

"Will you do what I said?"

"No one wants fat, crude *Doctor* Henson to be near them." His voice sank to a low, self-pitying moan. "No one wants him near. The mission must progress whether he approves or disapproves. No one wants his opinion."

Taviella sighed. "*I* want your opinion. Tell me what you think of the mission."

123

Van Wyck Henson looked up at her. "Really? You want to know what I think? Me?"

"Yes."

He leaned forward and raked her with his foul breath. "The planet ought to die. All primitive planets ought to die. The uncleansed wilderness must give way to cities of men. Is that not our purpose here?"

Taviella gritted her teeth. "How old were you when you left your world?"

"Hmm? My world? Your world also. We never learned to count the seasons with any precision: I was between twenty-seven and thirty-one."

"How old are you now?"

He smiled hugely. "Between thirty-nine and forty-three."

"And you earned your doctorate in that time?"

Van Wyck Henson regarded Taviella's obvious and frank skepticism.

"Yes. At the DuPres Academy of Sciences. They were most helpful."

"I'm sure." She sighed. "The mission should go on, then?"

"Yes." He nodded his head with unswerving firmness. "The planet must be cleansed."

8

I think that they despise you because you
don't despise them. Jealousy is often thus
inelegant.

Achorus,
The Skeleton and the Chaffinch

John Bradley, looking about the courtroom wist-
fully, thought, as he often had before, that the universe could well have been constructed solely for
the purpose of measuring his patience. The more
he compelled himself to tolerate fools and condone
foolishness, the more blatant and offensive were
the shenanigans that people displayed before him.
Whenever a simple, straightforward situation
would arise, rare though such situations might be,
someone in his presence would find a new and
creative way to propel it into wanton chaos.

A big man, Bradley appreciated a big room. A
good deal taller than average, Bradley was long-
waisted and long-armed, and his face was comfortable and jovial in the way that frustrated men's
faces sometimes are. His eyes were dark and obser-

vant, and his long, sharp nose lengthened his face. His hair was a salt-and-pepper blend of silver and white, giving him the appearance of greater age and heightened dignity.

The courtroom on Marterly was well constructed: a high, soundproofed ceiling reflected the room's lights efficiently and cleanly. The room featured several stations for witnesses, for recorders, for a variable number of judges, plaintiff and defendant, and ancillary staff for large trials or small. White, textured walls encompassed the room with sensible grace, and even traffic flow had been carefully thought out before construction had begun. Attorneys tend to pace, Bradley knew, himself belonging to the wandering rather than the sedentary variety.

The three judges of the Tribunal were known to him. The legal machinery on Marterly was not widespread, and the planet didn't generate high-ranking cases in any great number. To the left, in gleaming black finery, Justice Edward Goto leaned forward, his cheek on his fist, his dark hair and thin moustache balancing his slightly forward-set chin. Heaving a sigh, Justice Goto shifted his balance on his high seat behind the bench and settled again to listen.

To the right, also in a tunic of shimmering black, Justice Sonia Lindstrom sat stiffly upright, her expression taut and glowering. Blond, long-faced, pale nearly to the point of albinism, she pierced Bradley and Bradley's opponent alternately with sharp, disapproving glances.

In the center, presiding over the Tribunal,

Justice Hamilton Venda leaned forward, fixed his gaze sharply upon Bradley's moustache or chin, and sat back again, not quite prepared to speak. A tremor of rage seemed to pass over him, and he pulled tightly with his hands at his fine tunic of judicial red. His dark brown hair was oily and unkempt, and his eyes were red from overwork. The man was obviously nearing collapse from exhaustion. Bradley tried not to sigh aloud.

"Your case . . ." Justice Venda began, and then he stopped, choking back either wrath or bile. "Your case . . ." Again he was unable to continue.

"Your honor," John Bradley began, his voice perfectly controlled, his expression polite although not deferential.

"Be still!" Venda snapped.

"Your honor . . ." Those soft-spoken words came from Kelki Hume, the attorney representing the Concordat's Treasury Branch in the matter at hand. Tall and slender and straight and serious, Hume wore her soft brown hair slightly longer than shoulder length. Bradley had worked with her before and had discerned her, at least, to be no fool. She seldom smiled, but she never whined, stammered, seethed, shouted, or threatened, and Bradley had never known her to use any demonstrably fallacious argument in debate.

If this case had been simply a contest between her and me, with Justice Goto presiding over it alone, Bradley thought, *things would have been immeasurably more controlled.*

"Councillor Hume?" Justice Goto said softly, when neither of his companions behind the bench seemed willing to do more to acknowledge the interruption than glare in hot and cold passivity.

"Treasury is willing to contest this case."

Bradley did sigh that time. He couldn't help himself. A hurried week of preparation and diligent research had enabled him to put a decent case together, but all of his facts and statements counted for less than one quixotic Treasury Branch factor and the frame of mind of two acerbic justices.

Justices Venda and Lindstrom glared their disdainful glances at him, and all he could do was shake his head in resignation. John Bradley was a patient man and had suffered far worse treatment from his fellows in previous cases. Was his patience inexhaustible? He honestly didn't know.

"Councillor Bradley has no case," Justice Lindstrom said sharply. "He has presented no convincing grounds for penetrating State Immunity." Her bitterness stemmed largely from her resentment at the hurried impaneling of the tribunal. Bradley wondered, however, if that was sufficient to explain her unhappiness now.

"The Treasury Branch does not wish to invoke State Immunity," Hume responded. "We think the case has sufficient merit to be contested openly."

"State Immunity," Venda ponderously informed her, "applies whether or not it is invoked. A case cannot be brought against any branch of government without clear and urgent grounds for penetration of such immunity."

Hume lifted her eyebrows. "Yes, sir. But the Treasury Branch elects to waive such immunity."

Bradley shook his head again. Had Hume accepted the immunity to prosecution that the Concordat afforded its branches, she and he could have left the courtroom, she in victory, he in defeat, and perhaps lunched together and discussed the case's merits in private.

A coalition of desperate college professors and their graduate students begged me to defend the planet Kythe-Correy from obliteration. The case makes fascinating law, and I accepted it in a hot second. I'd love nothing more than deciding the right and wrong of it in a public forum. I don't like Tribunals comprising two fire-eaters and one man who can't relax any more than he already is without going to sleep. And I mistrust opponents who waive any of their rights.

"I'm of a mind not to accept your waiver," Venda grated.

"You have that option, your honor," Hume acknowledged. "But the matter can then simply be renewed."

"I'm also of a mind to dismiss the case as irrelevant," Venda continued. "I understand that the mission to sterilize Kythe-Correy has already been dispatched, and that it can neither be recalled nor interrupted."

"That is the case, your honor," Hume said, nodding her head in complete seriousness.

Bradley stood by, wishing for the freedom to pace, and waited. It unnerved him to have his opponent present his arguments for him. He admired Hume's honesty and ethical commitment; he resolved to present an equally conscientious case. If the Tribunal would let him.

129

He caught Justice Goto's gaze, and for a second the two shared a wry, amused glance. The human contact reassured Bradley and helped him keep the matter in perspective. He couldn't save the planet, perhaps, but he could fight a clean and honest fight here, with at least one Justice on the Tribunal sympathetic to his style of legal debate: cool, calm, and reasonably factual.

"The case is moot, then," Justice Venda announced heatedly, and leaned back in his chair. Relief showed on his face now that he had an excuse to dismiss the case.

"Not so, your honor," Bradley said hurriedly. His voice was low and almost musical. He looked around; Hume returned his glance with a slight quirk of her mouth that might have been a secretive smile. "The time to decide the matter is obviously today, before the expedition of the *Indagator* to Kythe-Correy can be perceived as unambiguously approved. There are serious ramifications to actions such as this, and it is our intention to demonstrate that the costs outweigh the benefits."

"Whereas it is our contention that the benefits are the greater," Hume took up as Bradley paused. "Planets with Archive-like qualities are so rare in this region of space as to require development at all costs in order to maintain vital traffic linkages and economic avenues. The costs—"

"Stop," Justice Venda snapped. "We haven't yet agreed to hear this case."

"That's right," Justice Lindstrom seconded him. "The matter of immunity has to be clarified."

A long moment of silence filled the courtroom.

"It surely is an interesting case, though," Justice Goto said, very, very quietly.

"What do you mean by that?" demanded Justice Lindstrom.

"Why, nothing." Goto smiled a thin smile and leaned forward on one elbow. "But I do think I would like to hear opening arguments, at least, preferably today."

Venda heaved a sigh. "Very well. Councillor Hume, we will hear this case and decide it in accordance with all applicable laws and statutes. But understand this." He leaned forward, pointing at her with a long, rude forefinger. "This is a courtroom, not a forum for civic debate. I will not have you using either this Tribunal or its authority as a means of solidifying your public support.

"If this case is tried, our decision will be binding upon you. You will not be allowed to invoke State Immunity once you have waived it. You will not be able to back out of an unfavorable decision. You will be bound, in law and by law, to adhere to the exact terms of any decision we hand down. I disapprove of what you are doing, and I disapprove strongly. Your actions will not be permitted to devolve into political activities. State Immunity is the doctrine that protects the government from lawsuits, so that it may freely undertake the necessary tasks of coordination and regulation. The government — the Concordat of Archive — is above such considerations as petty defense against nuisance suits. By exposing the government to such vulnerability, you have, in effect, undermined the legitimacy of the government, and that is an action of which I am most direly suspicious. Do you understand all of that?"

Hume, her back stiff and her neck straight, answered him without visible emotion. "Yes, your honor."

"Do you choose to waive State Immunity at this time?"

"Yes, your honor."

"Councillor Bradley?"

"Yes, sir?"

"You've heard what I have to say. It also applies to you. I do not like to place the government on trial. There are proper channels for what you are intending, and this High Court is not one of them. Only extraordinary circumstances permit this. Any deviation from propriety, and you will find yourself met with the harshest of penalties. Do you also understand?"

"Yes, your honor." Bradley kept his face stiff and impassive, but inwardly, he couldn't help but observe what an unhappy man the judge became when angry.

"Then we will begin." Venda leaned back and folded his hands before him. "Gerald Wilson et al, H. vs. the Concordat of Archive, Treasury Branch, Development Division, D. Justices Venda, Lindstrom, and Goto, in Tribunal, K. Councillor Bradley, you may begin with an opening statement."

Whew, Bradley thought. *The hostile bastard is out for blood today. And he doesn't care whose.*

"Precisely twelve worlds have ever been known to have originated life," Bradley began. "Among them, our home, Archive, is in our minds paramount. Tenh Sonallae, the home of the race with whom we have only just concluded a series of wars, is perhaps the second most notable. And High Reynid, the home of the Reynid race, must be the third.

"Virtually every other world of the one hundred twenty thousand or so known planets that we have settled had its biosphere artificially generated, many centuries ago. Plant and animal life was brought from Archive by the now long-dead Empire and seeded throughout this region. We have fallen heir to the worlds. Our own world of Marterly was seeded and inhabited by the Empire, and now, seven hundred years after the Empire's fall, we still benefit from the rich farmlands and bountiful seas they bequeathed us."

He couldn't help himself: he began to pace.

"The world of Catalart, rather a long distance from here, was one of the nine worlds remaining that had evolved its own varieties of life. The actual process of origination is still largely a mystery to us. Billions of years of developmental processes took the world through different chemical stages, only the broadest outlines of which can now be detected. Plant and animal life developed, radiated, spread across continents, and raced through the steps of evolution until the richness of the many life structures there rivaled Archive."

He paced to the left, striding slowly and deliberately until he came nearly to the wall. He turned about and came slowly back, passing by the table and chair reserved for his use, until he approached as near to Hume as etiquette would allow. Then he spun on his heel and reversed the route. He could no more have spoken at length without pacing than he could have walked without swinging his arms. He was a big, physical man, and disliked any enforced motionlessness.

"The Treasury Branch sterilized Catalart." His voice became somber and funereal. "With an entire host of technological dooms, they vented their furies upon the surface of a green and pleasant sphere. And, ladies and gentlemen," he said, letting his voice sink even lower, "they made one hell of a mess."

Justice Goto smiled, as did Councillor Hume. Justices Venda and Lindstrom sat in stony silence, their faces icy, disdainful blocks.

"The plants died. The animals died. The entire living belt of microorganisms woven throughout the soil died. And why? Why? Just to make room for more people? More cities? A small spaceport?" Bradley timed his conclusion to coincide with the end of one of his tours of pacing. "The losses outweighed the gains. The loss of Catalart was unjustified. The loss of Kythe-Correy is also. I'll have specific scientific evidence to present to bolster that claim. Thank you."

He sat down quickly, ready to wait with long-suffering patience while Hume tried to demolish his contention.

Hume stood, straightened her clothing, moved her hands nervously through her hair, and smiled, without notable response, at the judges.

"It seems coldhearted," she began, "to compare the loss of scientific data that goes with the razing of a world to the human benefits that are gained

134

from one more inhabited planet. It seems that we already have so many. Can one more world make that much difference? But, you know, only one star system in every two or three has planets at all. Of those, only one in ten is suitable for human habitation, and that suitability includes a sizable degree of variability. There are worlds that are covered with deep drifts of snow year-round, where the seeded life has been tailored for conditions of extreme cold. There are worlds where the heat can drain the life out of an unprotected human except for narrow habitable zones near the poles. I myself was born on Pactolus, quite some distance from here — I doubt any of you will have even heard of it. It's metal-heavy. Almost but not quite poisonous. Our people tend to have short life spans unless they're lucky enough, as I was, to find passage away. Some worlds are metal-poor, and the inhabitants of those have a different set of problems to overcome."

She stood quite still, her feet planted. Bradley wondered how anyone could stand so still while speaking without going quite mad. He admired her, however, for being sensible and factual in her discourse.

"Every world is needed. There is no room that we can afford to waste. Space has a definite structure or terrain, a geography determined by the location of worlds in the void. Archive, for example, has only two avenues of approach or lanes of escape, due to its location in the middle of a small pocket of star-poor space. The Sopenstil and the Idesuto links are vital to Archive's commerce;

without them, our ships are incapable of traveling away from our home world without the accompaniment of auxiliary fuel tankers. And indeed there are several worlds that lack such approaches at all, and travel to and from them does require tankers. At a larger scale, lanes of easy jumps make some worlds often visited and leave others forlorn, seldom seen by freighters, tankers, or suppliers."

Her voice was serious and even, and her posture was forthright. She gestured, but not in such a way as to distract attention from the points she sought to make.

"Marterly is a world that could be the center of an economic sector of great strength. And it will be, now that the mission to Kythe-Correy is at last under way. And just as the spaceport on Catalart will open the entire Penander Sector to a developmental boom on a scale not seen since the early days of the Line Worlds shipyards, so will Marterly benefit. Jobs, commerce, contracts, transshipments, and cargo. These things spell wealth, and, although it seems tawdry to compare wealth with lives, and commerce with the existence of a biosphere on a planet, that's what the question comes down to. Marterly is currently a backwater. It can become a center of trade, fully deserving of being a Sector capital in fact as well as merely in name. Thank you."

∞

The rest of the morning and afternoon was taken up with presentations of factual evidence. Bradley's displays were typically technical ones, deeply rooted in the biological and biochemical sciences, while Hume's, as he had expected, were mostly economic testimonies. He had to admit that she presented a good, strong case. And — he smiled to himself — despite Justice Venda's demand that she not use this opportunity to present any sort of public case, she was speaking to the public nevertheless, knowing that recordings of her arguments would, in due course, become public record. Venda knew this as well, as did Lindstrom and Goto. The former two stewed in silent, helpless anger, while the latter listened more complacently.

Bradley, too, took care to keep his arguments plausible and accessible to the hypothetical public audience. He didn't dare let Hume win a victory among the populace by dint of a clearer argument or a nicer presentation. He felt secure, at least, in the knowledge that the visual record would show him to good advantage. Unlike most people who photographed differently from different angles, John Bradley didn't have a bad side. Even news photos of him came out looking well. Kelki Hume looked very good as well, and her steadiness was a strong asset.

What most irked Bradley about the entire situation was that Venda and Lindstrom were more alert for weaknesses in the two attorneys than they were for strong points of argument. They waited, impatiently and unhappily, for one of the two to make a mistake. Neither Bradley nor Hume had any intention of delivering them one.

Finally the day wore to its close, and the Justices departed from the courtroom. Bradley looked at Hume, and she smiled noncommittally.

"A very good showing," he said to her. "You argue well."

She nodded. "As do you, sir."

They looked at one another for a moment longer, still in the mind-set of antagonists. Then, as Bradley smiled and Hume laughed, the spell broke and they were able to relax.

"I don't expect this to take longer than tomorrow," she said, quite at ease.

"Right," Bradley said. "This is a clean and clearcut case. For us, that is. I'll tell you, I wouldn't want to be one of the Justices deciding this one."

"No? Why not?"

"We're both right," he said, then chuckled. "We're *both* right."

She smiled at him. "That's true."

∞

They ate a large dinner together in one of Marterly's choicest restaurants. Bradley feasted on fish steaks and flame-broiled greens, while Hume relaxed with a plate of whipped eggs and toast. Their conversation ranged from the stars to the seas, from the heavens to the hells, and from love to death. Only once did the subject of the case arise.

"Why," Bradley asked, speaking into a lengthening silence, "did you waive State Immunity?"

"Why not?" teased Hume.

"By not doing so, you could have avoided the case entirely."

138

"And miss this dinner with you?"

Bradley laughed. "You won't tell me?"

"What makes you think that it's anything other than what I said today in court?"

"That you want the case decided on its merits?"

"Correct."

"I've learned to mistrust people who don't fight dirty," he said, after thinking for a few moments. "I've grown accustomed to thinking of myself as the only fair-minded attorney left in practice."

"Oh, no," Hume protested. "I'm sure there are one or two others. Out of millions, you can't be the only mistake, can you?"

He laughed and let her win that one.

∞

When he arrived home, he discovered that a note had been neatly pinned to the pillow atop his bed, although his apartment door had been securely locked.

Stay home tomorrow, it read, *or dire happenings are inescapable. You are not expected to win your case.*

Bradley read it over and over again with growing dismay. A threatening note. It stunned him. He removed it, thought for a moment about phoning for the militia's constabulary office, then shook his head.

He didn't like being threatened, but so long as it was no more than a threat, he was willing to remain patient.

9

We will be contending with the collective
minds of some of the most dangerous and
desperate people on the planet.
        John Bradley, *The Undealt Hand*

Shimmering black against the hot glow of
jumpspace, the *Indagator* traveled steadily past
dangerous and hot X-ray stars. Each star was the
counterstar of another star in normal space, linked
to it by the naturally occurring jumpspace rift that
stars all generate. Aboard the safety of the ship,
five crew members maintained an uneasy living
arrangement with five energetically opinionated
scientists. The corridors rang with heated discussions, but seldom with laughter. A brooding truce
came into being, holding apart the two strong-
minded women who headed two differing ideologi-
cal factions.

    Fortuna DeVries continued to make use of the
greatest share of computer time, for purposes that
no one pretended to understand. Smiling with
broad, sarcastic derision, she made no explana-

tions. Van Wyck Henson, blunt, crass, bloated, and profane, supported her views whenever asked, seconding her opinion that the destruction of Kythe-Correy was a good and necessary undertaking.

Opposing them was Bea Chapman, whose brusque nature and sloppy habits drove away any would-be allies. She kept to herself almost as much as the retiring and reclusive Gerald Wilson. These four scientists, thus polarized, dominated the social life of the ship by their quirks, moods, and mutual disdain.

Forward, in the control room, Taviella shook her head and saw to the running of the ship. Aft, in the pump room, Eric and Remington held conspirators' council over their illicit brew and spoke of their disdain for the mission and the passengers. Alone together in the lounge, Maravic and Mikhail discovered their mutual fascination and interest, and love, under siege, blossomed.

Stasileus, seeing all, wondered often, but kept his silence.

Blinkered, bearing death, its hull hot and blazing, the *Indagator* moved on, wrapped in its protective blanket of space- and time-warping force field projections. Blunt, ungainly, the squat ship that had killed one world moved toward its rendezvous with another.

∞

"Secure for jumpspace breakout," Taviella announced nervously. All intercom stations echoed her order. Leaning aside to Maravic, she muttered,

"Nip aft and see that Bea's room is ready, this time, would you? And ask Fortuna to stop using her terminal. I'll need the extra processing speed here."

"Sure," Maravic said cheerfully as she started to unbuckle her restraints.

"No, I'll go instead." Mikhail put a hand tenderly on Maravic's shoulder and answered her smile with his own. Taviella nodded.

She and Maravic continued to run through the pre-breakout checklist. They were soon gratified to learn that the ship's condition was as good as Sargent had promised. The critical moment neared.

Mikhail popped his head in the doorway. "Bea's okay, but Fortuna refuses to strap in."

Maravic frowned, while Taviella looked up in consternation. The two looked at each other, and unspoken messages passed back and forth between them. Time was short. Breakout was imminent. Computer efficiency was invaluable. Maravic unbuckled herself and trotted quickly behind Mikhail out of the control room and into the deserted corridors.

Fortuna's door was shut and locked. Mikhail tapped politely on the thick plastic panel, then, receiving no response, thumped energetically.

"Do go away, little boy," Fortuna's weary voice came muffled through the door.

"I can't do that, Fortuna. Please let us in."

"Well, I won't."

Mikhail looked at Maravic, his eyes worried.

Maravic ran to the nearest open intercom, nearby in the lounge. "Taviella? Maravic here. No luck. Fortuna won't budge."

142

"Okay." Taviella's tense voice echoed throughout the ship, still being sent through all intercom stations. The passengers might become alarmed, but the ship needed to be ordered before attempting a jumpspace breakout. "Overriding her door lock now. Eric, to the control room, please."

Maravic and Mikhail ran back to Fortuna's door, to find it slowly opening. Dashing down the corridor toward them was Eric, his jaw set and his expression dire. He hurried past without a word or sign.

Mikhail and Maravic looked at each other, unhappiness mixed with irresolution in their expressions. Taviella had sent the two most gentle persons aboard to deal with the emergency.

"Four minutes." Taviella's voice issued from both inside and outside the room. Mikhail edged forward and saw Fortuna's stateroom. Maravic moved up beside him, ready to support him in whatever way might be needed.

Fortuna's room was kept scrupulously neat and tidy. Everything had been stowed with military precision in neat rows on shelves and in open-faced cupboards, and restraining straps had been fastened. Even the bunk's bedding was folded up neatly, so that the room looked more like a barracks room than a passenger's stateroom. Seated before her terminal, Fortuna ignored the intrusion and continued hammering away at her keyboard. She seemed ridiculous at the keypad there; her huge, long-limbed and muscular frame looked as if it belonged on skis, or racing along a track. Maravic hadn't realized how large the woman really was: a giantess who used a computer. Her face glowed softly in the light emitted by the data display screen, which sat on a small, fold-down desk.

Mikhail didn't recognize the data codes running rapidly up the screen, but Maravic did.

The operating system code for the ship's navigation computer, she realized with a shudder. She leaped forward, and things happened with astonishing rapidity thereafter.

∞

Arriving in the control room at a near run, Eric ground to a halt near Taviella. He didn't waste time announcing his presence; he merely stood, breathing heavily, and waited.

"Pull Fortuna DeVries out of the computer, without shutting the system down," Taviella snapped toward him. "There's less than three minutes to breakout."

Eric inhaled deeply, less a response than a gasp, and turned and ripped open the control circuitry panel. For a long moment he did nothing obvious, but merely stood and gazed intently at the connections. The switchbox combined circuit breakers, physical switches, and software loops to hook the various compartmented sections into the main computer. Finally, with nervous haste, Eric reached in and snapped a small green switch from left to right.

"Nobody on line but you, Captain."

"Breakout in two minutes," Taviella spoke into the intercom, her voice under tight control. She spared the attention and energy to look up at Eric and smile weakly. "Thanks."

"Sure." Eric closed the switchbox. His expression was again placid, and perhaps a bit sour. He looked as if a great deal of fuss were being made about nothing very important at all.

"Now strap in, and hurry."

"Strap in?" Eric's face was bemused. "Hey, I trust you."

"And last time that trust almost got you killed."

"Don't you want me to check in on Maravic and how she's doing with Fortuna?"

"I wish I could send you." Taviella's voice was tight and unhappy. "But I can't spare you and I can't risk you. Strap in."

Eric sighed. "Yeah." And, belying his apparent calm, he fell hurriedly into an acceleration couch and fumbled with the safety straps.

∞

"Stop her!" Maravic shouted, her aplomb utterly shattered. With speed and strength born of panic, she rushed in and yanked Fortuna's arms away from the keypad. A look of blank astonishment passed over Fortuna's face; then she began to fight determinedly. Mikhail, equally astonished, plunged into the room and caught at Fortuna's flailing arms.

Outside the door, his eyes impossibly wide, Stasileus arrived in time to watch the bucking, heaving fight. His expression was quiet and observant.

Thus they stood — Stasileus with his head cocked slightly to one side, and Maravic, Mikhail, and Fortuna piled in a struggling mass on the floor — when the ship fell through the jumpspace boundary and into normal space.

Fortuna, although the strongest of the three, stopped fighting first and lay on her side beneath her assailants. Breathing in gasps from the effort of the fight, her only words were obscenities. Mikhail and Maravic backed away slowly and got to their feet.

"You . . . *idiots!*" Fortuna snarled. "Do you have any justification for what you're doing?"

"You got greedy, Fortuna," Mikhail said, his voice sad but his eyes alert. He squinted at Fortuna in wary curiosity: this had been the first time in his life that he'd ever hit anyone, and he was astonished by the emotional cost of the exercise.

"I've always been greedy." Fortuna rose to her feet, as did Maravic. But Fortuna had no intention of renewing the confrontation and seated herself on her bunk, idly straightening her hair with her hands.

"You assigned yourself extra time slices on the computer," Maravic said, her own voice slightly less than steady. It had by no means been her first fight, but fights bothered her as much as the discovery of violence was bothering Mikhail. "We overlooked that, you know."

"Generosity is not the coin of civilization," Fortuna japed. "Opportunism is."

Maravic pretended not to have heard her. "But when you were working with the ship's navigation system, changing it, interfering with ship's operations, you had to be stopped."

Fortuna glared at her. "I was *not* changing it. I wasn't changing *anything*! What kind of sabotage are you accusing me of?"

"What kind were you perpetrating?"

Fortuna leaped to her feet. "Why, you . . . you buffoon! You leering clown! Do you think I'm utterly brainless?" Her gaze switched back and forth between Maravic and Mikhail, although once, for a moment, it lingered on Stasileus in the doorway. Stasileus watched, astonished by the play of human emotions displayed before him. He said nothing and observed carefully.

"Was it sabotage, or not?" Maravic pressed.

"It was nothing of the kind!"

Mikhail, knowing Fortuna of old, had quietly picked up one of her data cassettes and was reading its handwritten label.

"The computer's navigation operating system is copyrighted, you know, Fortuna," he said calmly.

She whipped about to face him. "What? Give me that!" She snatched the cassette from his hand. "What gives you the right to assume—"

"Your thefts in the past."

Fortuna reddened, and Maravic felt a brief moment of abstract good cheer. Fortuna still held enough ethics and civilization to blush when caught at a crime. They weren't dealing with a conscienceless monster.

"What else have you stolen?" Mikhail pressed on relentlessly. "My notes? Van Wyck's notes? Wilson's notes? Bea's entire corpus of works and studies?" His voice grew sharp. "Was it for the *money*, or for the credit of 'discovery?' "

Stasileus, watching as an objective observer, saw the tensions in the room, the emotional net, the histories; he saw the minds of the three as if laid out upon a dissecting stage. He traced the three-way relations of each to each: the people in the room affected themselves as well as the others. He also understood his role as observer, technically a part of the system.

He alone knew what would happen next, and although he didn't understand it, he knew that he dared not avoid it.

"I am no thief," Fortuna said with a straightening and tensing of her shoulders that made it clear she was lying.

"I am the leader of the scientific expedition," Mikhail announced formally. "I'm going to have to impound your tapes." He looked up at Maravic. "Escort her out of here for a few minutes, until I can gather what's needed." His gaze traveled a bit farther, to rest on Stasileus's intent face. "Help her, Stacey."

Stasileus nodded. He understood his own psychological make-up intimately and knew himself powerless to resist an order, or even a suggestion. He foresaw Fortuna's next actions, if not in detail, in outline. He knew what was about to happen.

Maravic understood by Mikhail's forcefulness how important this was to him. She stepped closer to Fortuna, but Fortuna withdrew from her reach and marched direly toward the door.

Stasileus stepped fully into view, his hands

148

loose at his sides. Fortuna, in a quick flash of blazing wrath, pivoted on her forward foot and jammed her tightly clenched fist upward into his face. Her knuckles, aimed by rage and by all the frustration of a lifelong anger, skimmed lightly over his small nose and burst with undiminished force through and into his wide right eye.

For a moment, Fortuna's rage maddened her; she drew her fist back for another blow. Looking up, preparing her aim, she paused. Stasileus's eye was a punctured, burst, dripping ruin. He gazed at her from his other, with no reproach in his mild, only slightly pained expression.

Then his eyelids closed over both eyes, the good and the destroyed, while his whole body shook with agony. He stepped back one step, then two, and fetched up against the bulkhead. With his feet planted, he slid down the wall into a squat, curled tightly against himself. He hugged his knees, bent his head carefully forward onto his chest, and sat motionless.

Maravic and Mikhail, horrified, found their horror echoed in Fortuna's dread-stricken face. The three looked at one another, already beyond thoughts of blame or of retribution. Fortuna sidled into the corridor and ran forward to the control room, calling for Taviella in a voice that terror made small.

Maravic looked at Mikhail, who gritted his teeth and advanced with her to Stasileus's side. Maravic bent forward and placed her hand on Stasileus's elbow.

"Stacey?"

∞

Forward, Taviella handled the controls with more than her usual care. She squinted at the instruments and moved her hands in microscopic arcs. The sound of the struggle back in Fortuna's cabin served not to distract her but to focus her on her need for concentration. On her data display, several series of vectors flashed, depicting quantities and qualities of the ship-surrounding jumpspace sustainment field. Most of her concentration was on the camera display, which showed a camera's-eye view of jumpspace outside: a red, eerily glowing background spangled with hard, black stars.

The fields were tripped; the vectors aligned. The computer, freed now from any distraction, correlated measurements and inverted description matrices with brilliant electronic speed. Ahead of the ship, space was ripped bodily open, the rift forming a giant, gap-toothed maw of blinding darkness. Taviella aimed the ship through the opening, manipulating field constants with her hands and mind.

Gently and smoothly, the giant *Indagator* swept through the gap, sliding into normal space high above Kythe-Correy's brilliant yellow star. The chainplastic hull metal emitted a low, sobbing groan as stresses abated. A slow, spurious rotation accrued to the vessel, as well as a large unbalanced velocity; otherwise, the breakout was smooth.

"Now, Eric." Taviella's hands were busy across her boards. "Go see how Maravic's doing."

"Right." Eric scrambled to free himself from his

straps. He paused to pat Taviella on the back. "Good breakout, Tav."

"Thanks. Now go."

"Right."

∞

Eric was only gone a moment before Fortuna dragged herself into the control room, her normal air of superiority completely gone.

"Captain Taviella?"

Taviella whirled to face her, her instruments forgotten. "What? What's wrong?" Never had she seen such hangdog shame and misery upon a face previously so haughty.

"Stasileus. . . . He's hurt."

So much was said, without words, in Fortuna's face, her miserable expression, the way she held her hands. Taviella leaned forward and spoke into the intercom microphone with cold precision. "Bea Chapman, report to Fortuna DeVries's cabin with medical equipment. Stasileus has been hurt."

Then she damned herself with the harshest words she would allow herself to use: the intercom was still open to all stations.

One by one, voices called in, asking for more information. One by one, Taviella answered them: "We don't know anything yet. Stay put."

∞

By the time, five hours later, when Bea was ready to close up her impromptu surgery on Stasileus, the *Planetslayer* had achieved a smooth, stable orbit about Kythe-Correy. Gerald Wilson stood by Mikhail as the two glumly watched a screen showing them images of their orbital ground-trace. Eric and Remington huddled in the pump room, idly drinking, idly cursing, idly wishing themselves capable of doing something to help. Fortuna moved cautiously around the periphery of any group of people, although she was largely ignored. Had Stasileus been able to watch her, he would have seen her emotional strength recovering, and her ill will, still undaunted, reemerging tentatively. Van Wyck Henson was locked in his stateroom and did not care to be disturbed.

Maravic and Taviella sat side by side on the corridor floor just outside the closed door to the stateroom where Bea worked alone and in silence. Emotionally numb, they waited, too shocked and stunned even to hold hope.

Eventually, Bea emerged, a small, crooked smile on her face. Maravic and Taviella looked up at her, their faces identical images of anxiety and questing doubt.

"He's fine." Bea's voice held a coy hinting tone that belied her comforting words.

"His eye?" Taviella steeled herself to ask.

Bea looked at her and let her face sag down into its accustomed weary lines.

"I had to remove what was left of it, of course. He'll never have use of it again."

"Can—" Taviella had to swallow. "Can it be regrown?"

"Yours could. Mine could." Bea breathed deeply, her fatigue showing. "His? Not possible." She shook her head.

"Blind. . . ."

"In one eye." Bea looked at the two crew members. "There's more." She turned her eyes away. "He has less than six years to live. Maybe less than five." She looked back. "If you love him, make those years count."

"How can that be?" Taviella's voice was little more than a whisper.

"There's a lot we don't understand about the Vernae. But there's a lot we do. They were apparently built — handcrafted, brewed in vats, stitched together like suits of clothes. We've long since lost the technology. You already knew most of this: they were made, built to be slaves of the ancient and unlamented Empire. Slaves: obedient, docile, highly intelligent, yet nonviolent. And they were built with safeguards. One of these was a short life span." Bea laughed, a dark, humorless laugh of near despair. "The oldest Verna on record was forty-one years of age. The mean age of death is thirty-one. More than ninety-seven per cent of them die between the ages of twenty-eight and thirty-four. That's precision engineering, as your young man Eric could tell you."

"By the gods . . ." Taviella swore.

"Yes." Bea looked at her wearily. "By the gods, who permitted such evil to endure for so long."

"His eye?" Maravic asked.

"Oh, that's all taken care of. It's padded and compressed, and bandaged to a fare-thee-well. Later, I'll clean it out again and seal and stabilize the flesh. The pain has been relieved. And he's strong; you probably know how strong he is. He's delicate, and an infection could have done him in, but he's strong and will recover. I'd recommend an eye patch."

Maravic smiled through her tears. "An eye patch. He'll look like a rogue. A cartoon highwayman, a bandit with a knife in his teeth." She began to sob. "He'll look so damned foolish. . . ."

Taviella tried to weep and found that she could not. She searched her mind for thoughts of hatred, but found only a blank emotional void surrounding Fortuna's name and image. She tried to react, and there was no reaction within her.

"The eyes of the Vernae are special. You'll probably have learned about that by now." Bea explained with the tone of a lecturer, letting impersonality help shield these two from the direct effects of their friend's loss. "The eyes are large — almost impossibly large. Fortuna could hardly have missed hitting one. Another feature of the Vernae that is evolutionarily counterproductive." She sighed. "But those eyes are extremely powerful. They have a sensitivity to light and dark, and color, like ours, but also to frequency of observation: a kind of stop-motion-camera effect. Further, they're sensitive to some particular kinds of motion. Certain invertebrates have the same knack. . . . Well, to keep it simple, the eyes are far too complicated to be repaired or regrown. The optic nerve bundle carries a huge volume of information to the brain, preprocessing much of it locally. The eyes, in effect, are brain tissue as much as nerve tissue." She paused and looked to one side. "It could have been his hip. They have real problems with hip dysplasia."

"His eye is gone forever."

"Yes."

"When will he be strong enough to resume normal duties?"

Bea closed her eyes, then opened them. She was obviously deep in the throes of exhaustion. "Tomorrow. Let him sleep. Let me sleep. Tomorrow."

"He'll be out of bed? He'll be okay?"

"Tomorrow."

∞

Everyone slept late the next day. Their orbit slung them around the world once every one hundred seven minutes; below them, day passed into night and again into day. The ship monitored itself, sweeping space for megameters in all directions, alert for any unexpected dangers. The air purifiers hummed, sending warm drafts of air gusting through recessed ducts into the rooms where passengers and crew slept. Artificial gravity plates in the decks held humans and alien to their bunks. The great engines purred imperceptibly, banked down to idle shutdown. And hundreds of thousands of tons of herbicidal viruses in fluid suspension sloshed, very gently, in the ship's vast holding tanks.

It was nearly noon when Taviella called everyone together. Bea entered the crowded lounge last, bringing the wounded Stasileus with her. He watched the humans who watched him and understood that they waited for a sign.

"Hello," he said.

"Stacey?" Mikhail spoke first. "Are you okay?"

Stasileus held one giant hand up near his bandage-swaddled head. He smiled weakly. "I still have one eye to see with. I will be okay."

A faint bit of cheer lightened the mood. Even Fortuna, though responsible for much of their woe, was gingerly accepted again, although she trod carefully. Stasileus seemed to hold no grudge against her and continued to treat her as if the incident had never happened. The mood was darkened again when Van Wyck Henson refused to come out of his stateroom, despite any and all pleadings. He had work to do, he claimed, in his thick, heavily accented voice; he had more important things to do than go for a useless joyride.

By early afternoon, ship's time, everyone had broken out their packs and equipment. It was the work of no more than minutes to fit everyone into isolation suits, after which Mikhail and Maravic ran down the line double-checking seals and valves. Even Stasileus was given an oversized suit. Maravic took extra care to check his fittings.

Then everyone trooped forward through the ship to the airlock, and into the ship's boat. Taviella took the controls and launched the boat away on a gentle spiral toward the planet below.

Her landing was flawless, as she brought the boat down over a range of low, sere hills, brown and forbidding, but alive, covered with a thick, surface-hugging scrub. Once over the hills, she turned the boat toward a nearby seacoast, passed high over a dense wood, and landed gently amid blowing yellow grass speckled with tiny white flowers.

Earlier expeditions had passed this way, but it was still with a thrill that Taviella set foot upon the plain. The unknown could be conquered and made familiar; the explorer could come home again.

The party of nine scientists and crew members had stepped out upon the world of Kythe-Correy, to learn only a few of its many secrets before they went back to space.

10

Always I am haunted by that one grassy
path — it led over a hill, and thence I do not
know. Always I wonder where it had led me
if I went. Never to know. Never to know.
　　　Pappas the Cynic, *Eight Lost Wagers*

Without specifically calling attention to her actions, but also without any particular stealth, Taviella had brought along an automatic pistol from
the ship's locker. As the group of people stood,
blinking, in the golden sunlight of the meadow,
Taviella caught the attention of the members of her
crew, excepting only Stasileus. One by one they
drifted toward her, Eric first, then Remington and
Maravic, until, separate from the scientists, they
held a quiet conclave.

Taviella looked at each of them in turn, measuring them against each other and against herself.
Knee-deep in brilliant yellow grass, they all stood
silently. Taviella spoke first, on a radio band she
had preset for the crew's use only. "Remington?"

"Yes, ma'am?" Remington's thick fists knotted

uncomfortably within the suit, and his expression, behind his wraparound face shield, darkened.

"I want you to take this." Taviella handed him the gun. It shone like new, the grip unworn, the barrel as smooth and clean as if it was fresh from the factory. Yet the pistol had been fired before in anger. Remington reached out and accepted it. The weapon was a hefty responsibility; he felt the weight of duty adding to the weight of the gun, making the burden that much greater.

"Yes, ma'am." He held it awkwardly for a moment, then tucked it away in one of the pockets attached to his suit's right leg.

"Keep an eye on Fortuna." Taviella's voice was controlled and even, yet all three of her crew members felt the power of it. Taviella sighed then and explained at length. "I've been thinking about this. It kept me awake a good part of the night. I don't trust that woman."

"We could have locked her in her cabin aboard the ship, couldn't we have?" Maravic asked plaintively. The sight of the gun awakened unhappy memories in her.

"The ship doesn't really have any locks. It was never built with a ship's brig. She's too clever, especially with technical things, to be trusted with any makeshift lock we could construct. And she might not do more sabotage aboard . . . but then again, she might. It's best to have her here, where we can watch her."

"I'll back Remington up," Eric volunteered, "unless there's something else you'd like me to see to instead."

"No, that'll be fine. But keep half an eye on the others, too."

"I'll be watching Mikhail," Maravic said, a bit too swiftly.

Taviella smiled, honest enjoyment brightening her face. "I'm glad." More earnestly, she added, "Be sure to tell him what's going on. He's their leader, and he has the right to know what precautions we're taking." She smiled, and Maravic was heartened by it. "And there's this, in addition: I trust him."

"What about Bea and Wilson?" Eric asked.

"As I said: keep half an eye on them, and report anything suspicious. Remington, you probably won't need the gun. If you do use it, be certain the use is justified."

"No problem."

"That's all, then."

Remington tromped away, flattening a path through the gleaming grass. Eric looked after him, then, after glancing once more at Taviella, strode off after him.

"Taviella?" Maravic's voice came through Taviella's helmet radio receiver on a different, private frequency.

"Yes?" Taviella fumbled with the selector buttons affixed to the forearms of her suit. "Yes?"

"What about Stacey?"

Taviella shrugged. "We can't all watch everyone. I'll stay with him whenever I can."

"All right." Maravic lifted her gauntleted hand to Taviella's shoulder for a moment, then moved off to join the others.

∞

If Fortuna noticed Remington dogging her steps —
quite likely, for his surveillance was not particularly subtle — she said nothing of it. Alone, out-
numbered, and still substantially shocked by what
she had done, she remained aloof, collecting specimens of insect and plant life. From time to time she
and Gerald Wilson would confer over the dissection
of a flower or stalk of tall grass.

"I'm not a biologist," she said, and somehow
made her acknowledgement of ignorance sound as
if it were a source of pride for her.

"On this planet," Wilson said with a chuckle,
"I'm not either."

"I beg your pardon?"

He straightened and looked her in the eye. "No
one is. And no one ever will be, if this planet is
razed. The structures of life are so varied. . . ." He
sighed. "It probably looks to you as if we're standing in a field of grass, amidst hundreds of small,
white flowers."

"Yes," Fortuna admitted dryly. "It rather does
look that way."

"But this" — Wilson held up a clump of leafy
stalks — "is not a *grass*. Not *per se*." He held it up
for Fortuna to see. "The stems aren't jointed, you
see, and the leaves have palmate venation — the
veins spread out like the fingers of a hand."

Fortuna looked at it, somewhat uninterestedly.
She felt cooped up within her suit, breathing recy-
cled air, while outside a cool, afternoon breeze blew
across a serene meadow. "And the flowers?"

"Well," Wilson said in an academic tone, "they *are* flowers, of course, which is not to say—"

"Never mind." Fortuna laughed. "You're building up a technical case, the finer points of which I am evidently unprepared to enjoy."

"The primary point is that the evolutionary history of all of these structures is different from the ones we're more familiar with." At a loss for words and suddenly overcome with his shyness, he backed away and began striding over the meadow, searching for prizes for his collecting bottles.

∞

Maravic and Mikhail strolled, hand in gloved hand, their boots crunching over the grasses and flower stems. Now and again, Mikhail stopped to pluck a weed or tiny bush, and often he paused to examine plants that were too large to uproot. The meadow, although it was very large and nearly flat, dipped and rose slowly as they walked, until they found that they had wandered quite a distance beyond sight of the others. Shrugging, unworried, comfortable in their quiet companionship, they continued walking. Ahead, a thin stand of tall, slender trees topped a highland, and they headed for it.

Unaccountably, Maravic giggled.

"What?" Mikhail demanded, himself smiling. "Did I just step in something?"

"No," Maravic said, "it isn't anything like that. I just got to thinking . . ."

"Yes?"

"Well, on any other planet, where we weren't sealed into our suits for life-or-death protection, and you and I wandered off on our own for so long a time . . ."

"Yes?" Mikhail still didn't see what she was getting at.

"They might think we were sneaking off for a bit of illicit snuggling."

"Oh." Mikhail looked quickly away, and his grip on Maravic's hand loosened.

After a time, Maravic said, in a very small voice, "I'm sorry. I didn't mean . . ."

Mikhail turned to face her, his expression warm and very tender. "I wasn't offended." He smiled. "And you're right: that's exactly what people would think."

"I never meant—"

"You're a very beautiful woman, Maravic," he said softly to her as he took both of her hands in his. Gingerly, held apart by their encumbering suits of thick, heavy fabric, they embraced for a moment.

Moving apart, the two gazed for a long time at one another. Maravic's soft features and happy blue-gray eyes sparkled; Mikhail's dark eyes gleamed beneath his thick, black brows.

Together, they turned to the fore and walked softly through the tall grasses toward the stand of trees.

"Besides," said Maravic after a while, "there's always later, aboard the ship."

At that, Mikhail laughed aloud, a joyous laugh of love and good cheer. His hand on Maravic's tightened, and they walked together to the top of the slope. Beyond the trees, a shelving series of escarpments fell away to the shore of one of the world's seas. In the distance, a large island lay, now visible as little more than a long, featureless black line on the horizon.

"There's no intelligent life on this world, is there?" Maravic asked at last, her mood sober and quiet.

Mikhail smiled wryly. "None but us. Eight humans and one Verna." His expression leveled. "Why do you ask?"

As an answer, Maravic pointed, and Mikhail followed the gesture. A small troop of wide-eyed creatures had gathered to watch the two intruders. In the shadows beneath the trees, six or seven of the small, nimble-fingered animals watched, and their expressions seemed to Maravic and to Mikhail to be familiar and intelligent.

"Those are — I don't remember the scientific name — some sort of leaping monkeys." Mikhail said. "They're quite agile, and I suppose they *are* 'intelligent,' in the sense that they're clever with their hands."

"Given ten thousand years . . ." Maravic sighed.

The group of simianlike creatures edged forward, moving in small hops, dragging their long tails behind them. Maravic and Mikhail waited silently, until the nearest of the small monkeys came up and felt at their suits with tiny, four-fingered hands. They showed no fear of the humans, although they displayed a sensible alertness.

"But we can't give them ten thousand years, can we?"

164

"No," Mikhail answered sadly.

Slowly, they backed up, soon outdistancing the curious monkeylike animals. After another long glance at the sea, the two humans — aliens on a pleasant, alien world — retraced their steps and headed back to the meadow where the boat waited.

∞

Bea Chapman, while collecting samples of flora and small fauna for eventual dissection, also kept a close eye on Stasileus. His oversized suit helmet revealed most of his head; heavy bandages swaddled his white-furred face. He had already adapted fairly well to the loss of sight in his right eye and had readily retrained himself to walk with a steady balance. While watching him, she discerned something slightly disturbing: he was also watching her.

She looked away. Her thoughts required ordering. Automatically she reached down and captured a small, wriggling animal, a four-legged vertebrate somewhat reminiscent of the common lizards of familiar zoology. It went into her collection bag and through the double flap into the inner partition. A quick whiff of nerve toxins killed it instantly, preserving it for future examination.

I'm willing to kill, she thought absently. *I have no more actual moral strength to oppose killing than do the people who ordered the death of all of this world's life. In killing, there is only the difference of degree, never a difference of kind.*

She preferred to labor under no burdens of hypocrisy or delusion. Life — all life — was precious. The murderer of a lizard could become the slayer of a world.

And Stasileus was still watching her.

She straightened. "Come here." Her words to him were gentle, but she knew, as did he, that they were a command.

Stasileus, huge within his ill-fitting suit, still moved easily through the high grasses, his over-sized boots crushing plants beneath each step.

"Yes?"

"You were watching me?"

"Yes."

"You were . . ." She paused, while she thought. "You were *studying* me." She squinted at him. "You're learning from us, aren't you?"

"Yes."

Bea nodded. "We've needed an alien outlook for quite a long time." She regarded him. "We've only met two other alien races, you know: the Sonallans and the Reynid. But they're both almost exactly like us."

"I am like you, too."

Bea didn't laugh. "I suppose you are. We made you. Our species crafted yours, because we thought we needed servants. It's our own fool luck that we got philosophers instead." Her tone of voice was more bitter than she intended. "What have you learned?"

Stasileus's voice was high and distant; the radio link between them carried his voice to her faithfully, with all of the high, vibrant overtones echoing strangely through his words.

"Humans have come farther than they know. You no longer need the violence that drives you. But you don't know this. You cling to your violence, to your rebellion, to your defiance, and to your anger, as someone will cling to the rung of a ladder at a time when they are afraid to reach up for the next."

"We are afraid?"

Stasileus nodded. "And your fear is completely unnecessary. You lack the will to climb beyond your rage."

"Are we, then, no more than madmen?"

"You are gods."

Bea turned from him and paced slowly away, knowing, somehow, that he would follow in her tracks. About them, the meadow stretched away, the high grass hiding little mysteries, while distance hid great ones. Bea looked up and thought that she saw the serrated lines of distant blue mountains. Overhead, the sky shone a brilliant blue, almost painful to look at.

When the meadow was poisoned by the *Planetslayer*'s viruses, becoming a seething pond of bacterial scum and damp ashes, the mountains and sky would remain untouched. Would the world really be the same?

"We are not gods," Bea finally said, firmly and certainly.

Stasileus could not answer without disagreeing with her, and that was something his obedience kept him from doing. He followed her through the high yellow grass in dignified silence.

"Damn you," Bea said softly, "how can you say

such things about us? Fortuna, who poked out your eye: is she a god? Or Gerald Wilson, who hides all day behind his fear and shyness? Or Van Wyck Henson, that walking stack of little but filth?"

"They are the same," said Stasileus. "They are both gods."

Bea turned her head and shoulders back to look at Stasileus. "Scared ones?" she demanded.

"Yes."

"Even Fortuna?"

"Yes."

"How? How can you say that?"

Stasileus's voice was soft, but it carried a depth of sincerity that Bea seldom heard.

"You are angry with her. Your fury is directed at the woman who hurt someone else. You see in her the mirror of the anger that you know yourself capable of feeling, and you fear for your own control. The knowledge that anyone, anywhere, can fail leaves you more afraid that you, too, might fail. You no longer recognize in yourself the child that once leaped and danced.

"But before your fear there was the Empire of Archive, where greatness was unfettered. They dared. Oh, what they did not dare!"

Bea shuddered as she heard the empire of the insane centuries praised. Those wild people, those maniacs . . . Modern humanity was nothing like that.

"The human race, under the Empire, once leaped and danced," Stasileus continued. "They built a fire so bright it challenged the sun and skies of home. Are you so afraid of being burned by that

168

fire? Its embers glow in you still. Your forefathers laughed, a huge outrageous laugh, utterly defiant of death and failure. They ran and swaggered and copulated; they imbibed strong liquors; they were one with their desires and their lusts.

"But then they fell. Fear slew them. Now, you, their heir, walk where they flew, still hiding from their shadow."

Still walking, still looking away, Bea made no response for a long time. Finally she slowed and turned slowly back. Some of the scientists and crew still stood in the field, near the grounded boat. Others had moved away, out of sight. From her distant vantage point, the people Bea could see looked small and unimportant, as she must certainly have looked to them.

"Would they have killed the life on this world? Would they have taken this world by force?"

"The humans of old?" Stasileus asked. "The bright and burning men and women of the old Empire?"

"Yes."

"They would have," Stasileus said firmly after a second's delay. "They would have scoured this world clean in an instant, and then made it into a garden for their pleasance."

"And the moral doubt that I now feel?"

"It was as alien to them as it is, in deepest truth, to you."

"Can that be?"

"Do you eat meat?"

Bea spun away again, and this time Stasileus did not follow.

∞

Eric passed near Remington, while the two kept watch over Fortuna.

"Not much of a job, eh?"

"No," Remington agreed.

"Um . . . You better tuck that pistol a bit more out of sight."

Remington looked down in surprise, to find that the zipper of his leg pocket had come part way open. He quickly pushed the gun butt back inside. "Good thing that wasn't my main seal."

"Right," Eric drawled.

"Do you think that Fortuna noticed it?"

Fortuna's voice came over the radio link, a great deal of energy in her words. "I'm on the same frequency as you two boys," she snapped. "Since when do you think you need a pistol to guard me?" The thought seemed to irk her.

"Sorry, ma'am." Remington said, and looked at Eric, who looked away in disgust.

"Damn it," Fortuna grumbled, "I made a mistake. I'm not idiotic enough to compound it. I didn't expect to be trusted . . . but putting a guard over me with a pistol is pretty blatantly offensive."

"We have our orders, ma'am," Remington said laconically.

"I'm certain of that. Neither of you would have the wit to arrange it for yourselves."

Simultaneously, Eric and Remington switched their radios over to the crew-only frequency.

"Feisty, isn't she?" Eric mumbled.

"But it was an accident, wasn't it? Stacey's eye?"

170

"Probably. She did steal a lot of Bea's notes, though . . ."

"Yeah, there's that. And our navigation computer programming."

Eric nodded. "Here comes Taviella. We'll be lifting soon. It'll be good to get back to the ship."

∞

Before returning, however, Taviella wanted to look at one more site on the world, to get just a bit more feeling for the world's landscapes. She flew the boat east, until, in only half an hour, the sun had fled behind them from noon to afternoon and sunset. She grounded the boat in a clearing on a high forested mountain ledge, overlooking a vast eastern desert.

One by one, the crew members and scientists piled out of the boat, to lose themselves under the dark, shadowy trees, or among high-grown paths that led beside swift-running streams of cold water. Taviella watched them go.

In the red light of the sunset, she walked uphill, to her right, moving under huge gnarled boughs. The western sky was a furnace of sunset colors, cut off by the high hills between the landing site and the west. Streamers of cloud slowly changed color overhead.

Finally, Taviella found herself on a rocky promontory, looking out over the huge bowl of the night-shadowed desert. Its floor swept away, dropping farther and farther into the distance, forming a funnel of darkness that drained away to her right.

Far, far away, to the left, a mountain jutted up, giving the desert a northern rim; Taviella found herself regarding that mountain, trying to stare a hole through the thickening gloom so that she could fathom its features.

The mountain seemed, in the half-light, to be one giant block of stone, but now weathered and cracked into innumerable fissures. A tumble of boulders had collected at its base, and its summit had split into slabs of stone that would, some day, shear away and crumble down into the desert floor. The darkness deepened, but Taviella still watched, until that mountain became a silhouette against the lighter sky. The air was crystalline, perfectly still; as Taviella's eyes accustomed themselves to the darkness, she found she could still make out the desert floor, dotted with more and more distant clumps of underbrush.

As she watched, a cold, diffuse burst of light blossomed, far below her, far away: a natural discharge of lightning. It looked as if someone had triggered a flashgun against the desert rocks and sand, although from Taviella's vantage, the flash was wan and tiny. After a few minutes, she saw another, more distant, out toward the desert's horizon. It was a nebulous, pale flash, looking almost like a low, glowing fog that appeared and disappeared after only a second.

No thunder accompanied the distant lightning flashes; they bloomed and faded in complete silence, far beneath Taviella's feet as she stood on the ridge. And, silently, they increased in frequency. For long moments they glowed and faded, glowed and faded, casting no illumination, simply shining softly in the darkness of the infinite desert.

Electrical discharges, Taviella thought. *Area lightning. Something normal; something beautiful, but not unique.*

After about an hour, the discharges slowed, then ceased. With leaden feet, Taviella made her way back to the boat.

Soon, when all the others had returned, she flew the boat up into the sky and made a cautious rendezvous with the *Indagator*. The ship received them mechanically.

Then, once out of their decontaminated suits, they made a hasty and cold supper and retired to their staterooms, to study, to read, or to sleep.

11

Disrespect for our institutions must be
tolerated, but need never win our full and
open approval. That something is permitted
need not mean that it is accepted.

Justice Venda, *Collected Casebooks*

At a late hour, when Taviella should have been
expected to be asleep, Van Wyck Henson knocked
solemnly upon her door. Irritated, Taviella put
aside the large drawing pad and her charcoal
pencils, slipped a robe over herself and moved silently to the door on bare feet. Her barbarian heri-
tage still revealed itself, now and again, when
events took her by surprise; she moved with grace
and skill, learned from a childhood training in
woodcraft.

Henson's bloated, stolid form filled the doorway, reminding her bluntly that there were those
who had not learned either grace or dignity from
their home world.

"It's very late, Doctor Henson." Even as she
spoke, Taviella sensed a furtiveness, a reserve, and

a bit of fear in the portly scientist. "What do you want?"

He made as if to push past her into her room, but she stood fast. After a moment, he husked, "I am threatened. Fortuna . . ." He swallowed thickly. "Please let me come in." His eyes flicked from side to side, barely visible behind the thick, darkened lenses that he insisted on wearing.

"Come in." Taviella relented, backing slowly away from the doorway. She retreated to her bunk, while Van Wyck, after securing the door, seated himself heavily on the chair by her desk.

"I have been having second thoughts," Van Wyck explained in his hoarse voice. "I think that perhaps the destruction of this world is not a good idea." He leaned forward, his reeking breath washing over Taviella. "I cannot give you exactly my line of reasoning. I am probably completely wrong. Besides, it is all very com-pli-cat-ed. None of it would make any sense to you."

Taviella shook her head, amused and annoyed as always by Van Wyck's arrogant combination of self-superiority and self-belittlement. "Explain to me everything you can. And who is threatening you?" She leaned forward. "Is Fortuna causing trouble again?"

Van Wyck Henson waved his hands awkwardly in front of him, as if to deny something, but what he was denying was far from clear. "I was led along a wrong path of logic, by the people who said that life was precious." The way he said that last word made it clear that the doctor held little, if anything, to be precious.

175

"They speak of life as something that is a unique principle, as if . . ." He paused, his huge upper body swaying. "As if it were they who were the barbarians, and not we! As if they held to the old and primitive views!" His offense was unmistakable.

Taviella leaned back again, resigning herself to a long exposition.

"The insistence on the difference between life and not-life caused me to think in error," Van Wyck continued. "But I am an educated man and have learned to think along paths that are not instantly obvious. I found another truth, and now I am in danger. For life I do not give a spit." He pursed his lips as if to belie his words, but Taviella's expression of alarm and indignation stopped him in time. He swallowed with great effort and went on.

"Life is not precious: there is too much of it. Life is not a . . . I cannot find the word. Life is not a thing in and of itself. Life is not anything. Life is only a combination of chemicals, do you see?"

Taviella nodded slowly. "All right." Far from convinced herself, she waited.

"Chemicals — that was what made me think." He beamed. "I came up with an answer that I didn't like. It would only confuse you, but I have to try to explain it to you. Do you see?"

"Explain it, then." Taviella's patience was not inexhaustible, and the man's circumlocutions were interminable.

"The chemicals of the virus that we hold in the liquid storage tanks of this ship are made to kill all the plant life of the world below us. The virus attacks only the chlorophores of the alien plants. In a week or maybe a month, plants everywhere are dying." He waved his hands theatrically. "Dying. Crunch, they become brittle and they fall. Other plants burn, and fires sweep across dry plains. Then the animals die, and all is over. But" — he raised one finger direly — "what chemical combinations come of virus with chlorophores? What chemicals arise when this is burned? Is sunlight a factor? No! Sunlight is blocked by clouds of moisture and particles of dust. Temperature drops. Chemicals react more slowly. Good. Do you see?"

"Do you know what would happen?" she asked. "Or are you merely guessing?"

Van Wyck Henson lowered his head, looking sidelong at Taviella. "Do I know? Oh, no, I am too poor a scientist, too ignorant a barbarian savage. I was schooled in a hurry. I don't know."

"Then—"

"I asked Fortuna!" Van Wyck's eyes blazed. "I told her what I thought. I told her that I was having doubts about whether the project should be permitted to continue. And now ... and now ..." He almost sobbed. "Now I am in danger."

"How?" The threat to Taviella's position as captain affronted her. The woman certainly would be brought up on charges when they returned to Marterly, among other things for wounding Stasileus. But if she was planning further mischief, Taviella was prepared to unleash her wrath here and now.

"She told me I should keep silent," Van Wyck said, and then he did begin to sob, blubbering noisily and wetly into his hands.

Taviella, repelled by his ungainly misery, threw him a towel. "Go on."

"She said that if I were to say anything to anyone, I would . . . would . . ."

"Yes?"

"Would die!" he whispered, in a horrid, strangled voice.

"Doctor Henson."

"Yes?" His weeping had ceased, leaving his face smeared and streaked.

"Go back to your quarters. Lock the door. No one will harm you."

"All right. Yes."

"That's not all. I want you to talk to Bea Chapman and Gerald Wilson. They're the two who are most knowledgeable in the subject of the chemistry of life. Tell them everything, and show them any equations or formulae you've developed."

"But my life? Will I be endangered?"

"Not aboard this ship." Taviella's determination and righteousness shone in her face. "I will permit no threats or violence."

"Fortuna is an engineer," Van Wyck Henson said forlornly. "She could strike me down in a hundred ways, and no one would know."

"You've told me. Tomorrow, talk to Gerald and Bea. Tonight, sleep — and lock your door."

"The door? But she knows ways to open it."

"She won't. Try to relax."

Finally, after enduring several more minutes of his self-pitying despair, she was able to persuade him to leave. She locked her own door, stripped off her robe, and withdrew to her drawing pad. As she worked, sketching lightly with the charcoals, the outlines of the mountain and desert she'd seen while on Kythe-Correy grew more and more crisply defined. She wondered, for a while, whether she ought to look in on Fortuna and ask her a few sharp questions. But then she reconsidered: Van Wyck Henson's fears could only be delusions.

∞

To Taviella, the control room the next morning had never looked more comforting or familiar. Maravic sat in the copilot's seat, monitoring the ship's systems, going about her business in her always efficient way. The lights blazed clear and white, and the room gleamed. Bank after bank of indicators blinked or shone steadily, their electronic green glows sending the message that all was well. It was almost possible for Taviella to believe that the mission would soon be over, one way or the other, and that the ship would bear them back to Marterly.

"Systems okay?" she asked, just for an excuse to hear Maravic's cheerful voice.

"Doing fine." Maravic flipped through an inventory of switches, nodded in satisfaction, and entered a notation on a computerized ledger.

"Been up long?"

"Oh, no. I just got here. It seems to me . . ." She stopped herself, for some reason unwilling to continue her thought.

"Yes?" Taviella prompted.

Maravic looked up over her shoulder at her. "I haven't been happier in years and years. Mikhail means so much to me — almost like part of me. And I think he feels something of the same for me. I can share my thoughts with him and know that they're safe. I'm happy when I'm with him." Despite her cheery words, she wasn't smiling.

"Why, that's wonderful. Wonderful for both of you." Taviella's smile was open and honest. "He seems like just about the most sensible of the scientists" — her smile turned wry — "although that's not saying much, is it?"

"Taviella, I'm worried."

"Why?"

"I'm afraid I haven't been paying as much attention as I should." This time she did smile, but only briefly. "I'm never going to forgive Fortuna for what she did to Stacey. And I'm probably never going to be able to stomach that addleheaded Van Wyck Henson. But I'm worried about the mission. I think that someone is out to sabotage it."

"Who?"

"If I knew that . . ." Maravic sighed deeply. "I don't have any proof. I don't think it's Bea. She hates the project from the bottom of her heart, but she's not the sort to do anything about it."

Taviella walked around behind Maravic, then paced back to the doorway. "Could it be Gerald, then?"

"He's about all that's left, isn't he?" Maravic shrugged. "And he's so shy and secretive. He hasn't said five words to me the whole voyage. It's easy for me to mistrust him."

"Maravic . . ."

"Yes?"

"Please forgive me for asking, but . . . Where does Mikhail stand on all of this?"

Maravic frowned, deep in thought. "I think he's on the up-and-up. He's an astronomer and a mathematician, and he really doesn't go in for all of the biochemistry. He likes plants" — she laughed — "the way a gardener does. Do you know, he even has a small garden, back on Marterly? And—"

"And you're in love," Taviella teased happily. "It does show. I think it's beautiful. Do you think you'll want to stay with him?"

"On Marterly?" Maravic made a face. "And give up space travel? The only way they're going to get me to stay on one world for more than a month is to bury me there. And even that might not work."

"Then . . . ?"

"He's thinking of some way to come along with us, for one or two voyages anyway. Long enough for us to learn where we stand, at least."

"Aboard this tub" — Taviella gestured, taking in the whole of the *Indagator* — "there's more than enough room. Aboard the *Coinroader* it would be a tighter squeeze . . . but it could be done."

"Is this ship important to you?"

Taviella spoke instantly. "No. I'd rather have the *Coinroader* and be free. This big, ugly ship is more of a curse than a blessing. The *Coinroader* is sleek and powerful. This is just a . . . a flying nose."

Maravic grinned. "I guess I agree with you." Her grin faded. "But it does represent a source of income that the *Coinroader* doesn't."

"Maravic, do you want the mission to succeed?"

"I don't like failure," Maravic answered after a

181

thoughtful pause. "I don't like the fact that we'd be charged a default penalty. I'd prefer to get it over with and get paid for it."

"What about the moral and ethical aspects of the decision?"

"I'll be honest, Taviella: I don't like it. I'd be happier if we could simply skip on home and report that we couldn't fulfill our part of the mission. But that's not the truth. Moral? What's moral in this case? I say we sterilize the planet and go home."

Taviella placed a hand on Maravic's shoulder. "You may be right. But something's bothering me. Van Wyck Henson came to me last night."

"That's enough to bother anyone," Maravic said with a giggle.

Taviella smiled. "He's quite a character, isn't he?" Her smile faded. "He said that he had new information on the chemical reactions that the virus would produce, and that Fortuna had threatened him. He was afraid to share the details with the others."

"I hope you told him to go straight to Mikhail."

"I told him to go talk to Bea. I didn't think about Mikhail."

"Bea is a good choice, too."

"I hope so."

∞

Mikhail Petrov discovered Eric Fuller and Remington Bose working at their still in the pump room. "Aha!" he called aloud, in a tone of exulting righteousness.

Eric and Remington whipped about, badly startled. Remington almost fumbled his beaker of grain mash, while Eric nearly fell flat on his backside trying to move about in the cramped space between the giant pipes. Both realized immediately that there was no way to hide the incriminating evidence of their still.

"Oh, krat," Remington swore.

"I knew it," Mikhail exulted. "I knew it."

"Look, Mr. Petrov . . ." Eric began.

"I knew there had to be somewhere on this ship that a thirsty man could get a drink." The expression of triumph on his face faded, leaving him once more himself: a mild and polite scientist; an astronomer on leave; a gentleman, if a slightly mischievous one.

"Um . . ." Eric looked at him out of the corner of his eye. "You might have . . ."

"I might have chosen a less melodramatic way of introducing myself?"

"Yeah."

"I'm sorry." Mikhail gestured, arms out, hands open, a disarming and honest admission that he'd meant to startle them, but not to scare them. "You spend so much time in here, it's a wonder that I'm the first to investigate."

"You're the second," Remington said. Satisfied that Mikhail wasn't about to betray them to Taviella, he returned to his brewer's art, pouring the mash into a receiver and carefully testing the temperature. "It'll be ready in half an hour. You care for some?"

"By the gods, yes," Mikhail huffed. "A man

183

could die of thirst on this mission. 'Wine in its skin, and I in mine; the tempest overpasses; the cold winds shall wail . . .' "

" '. . . While I'm by the fireside, licking my wine; drinking the old year; all summer in a pail.' " Remington concluded the quotation. "Written by Achorus, more than seven hundred years ago."

"And true to this day." Mikhail laughed. "Although what he meant by wine was quite different from vacuum-brewed grain mash." He paused for a moment. "Who was the first to discover you?"

Eric answered him, his voice and expression sour. "Stasileus."

"Okay. He found you because he's nosy. Like me, I guess." Mikhail's happy expression faltered. "Look, if you'd like me to go . . ."

"No." Eric shrugged. "You might as well stay. There'll be plenty for all, and you're pretty much okay. If you tell Van Wyck Henson or any of the others about this, though, well, that would be a blasted shame."

"I understand. A private drinking establishment isn't worth much of anything if just anyone can join. I won't give you away."

"Thanks."

"So Stasileus found you, too?"

Remington looked up from his condensers and thermometers. "He found us, but I think we've lost him." He looked back and forth between Eric and Mikhail. "Have you seen how he's changed? It was happening before he lost his eye. He's more and more serious, more somber. He watches us, as if he's on one hilltop and we're on another."

184

Mikhail regarded this complaint seriously. "Eric, do you agree?"

Eric took some time before answering. "I've never been Stacey's best friend. I usually spend most of my time trying to keep away from him. But Remington's right: he's grown more reserved, more attentive. And he's learned an entirely new kind of question to ask."

"What do you mean?"

"Well, he used to ask things like 'Why do people fight wars?' You know, the questions that can't be answered without going into an hour-long discourse. But now . . . now he asks things like 'Why do you mistrust machinery?' "

"He asked you this?"

"Yes. And him and me both engineers! I told him off and took a swat at him that missed. And I came here to sulk with Remington. I got to talking about it, and, well . . ."

"Yes?"

"It's the truth. I do mistrust machines. I like to keep an eye on them, and I believe in preventive maintenance. Machines are bloody complex, you know, and . . ." Eric paused to collect his thoughts. "But all of that adds up to why I'm an engineer, you see. Stacey's question hit it right on the target."

"I see. . . ." murmured Mikhail.

"What did he ask *you*?" Eric said, correctly interpreting Mikhail's comment.

"Well . . . nothing all that important, really. Or, at least, that's what I thought of it at the time. . . ."

"And?"

Mikhail spread his hands. "I didn't dwell on it

right after he asked, but it's been nagging at the back of my mind ever since. He asked me if I was afraid of losing control of the expedition."

"And are you?"

Gazing squarely into Eric's eyes, Mikhail answered honestly. "How could I be? I've never had it. I never wanted it, and never really accepted it."

Not long thereafter the grain mash was ready, brewed to murky perfection. Remington sampled it first, pronounced it deliciously awful, and passed around little cups filled to the brim. Eric and he drank theirs in one or two gulps and exhaled happily. Mikhail sipped his slowly. It burned his throat as it went down: a fiery, chest-warming sensation of liquid vigor.

"Stasileus is learning from you too, then, isn't he?" Remington ventured.

"Yes," Mikhail said. "But I never expected to be learning from him."

∞

In her cluttered, paper-strewn cabin, Bea leaned conspiratorially toward Gerald Wilson. Their talk was hushed, as if even under these secure conditions they dared not risk being overheard.

"So, you're trying to tell me that Van Wyck Henson has new equations that show dangerous combinations of chemicals arising from the mission," Bea said, feeling a mixture of skepticism and hope. "Can you show me these equations?"

Gerald blushed and squeezed more tightly into the corner of the bunk on which he sat. "He . . . he's a very forceful man. He just told me about all of it. He wouldn't agree to show me any equations . . . not on paper."

"But he seemed certain that he was onto something?" Bea leaned farther forward, pursuing Wilson, leaving him no room to squirm away. Her hand landed on some sticky trash, which she dislodged after a bit of shaking.

Wilson looked around the messy room, his gaze passing over open cases and upended books. He spied the cittern balanced precariously atop a high stack of files. He'd seen it before, through her open door, or at times when he visited her cabin, but he'd never dared ask her about it.

"He was. He was sure that the combination of the virus, decaying wood, bacterial growth, and open flame would produce chemical conditions that would ruin the world for our use, forever."

"Forever?"

"Well, he sketched out a breakdown of the ozone layer for me, although he said that it was only a tentative model. He seemed more worried about persistent toxins in the soil, so that we could never grow our own plants here."

"Why won't he talk to me?"

Wilson cringed. "He won't talk to anyone from now on. After he told me his theories and interpretations, he threw me out — physically! He hoisted me by my collar and waist and heaved me out into the corridor! But he was acting in fear; you could easily see how afraid he was."

Bea frowned. "The man has been reclusive and antisocial all along. I don't like him."

"But he's a genius, truly," Wilson insisted. He blushed but continued. "Think what it must have taken him, coming away from an uncivilized planet in his mid-twenties, knowing nothing more than how to rub sticks together for fire . . . and to earn a degree in biochemistry within twelve years."

"He's vigorous enough," Bea agreed. "A shame he neglected his social education in favor of his scientific one."

"Well, to be sure, he's hard to get along with at the best of times. Now, when he's frightened—"

"Frightened? You said that before. Of whom?"

"He won't say, but it's obvious that it's Fortuna. He's convinced that she hurt Stasileus as a warning to him. Ludicrous, I know, but he leaps to conclusions and won't let them go."

"And you were praising his genius," Bea chided.

Wilson cringed, unable to answer.

"Well, we're just going to have to spend some time with our books, then," Bea said at last, "trying to come up with the same answers he did. Do you agree?"

"I think so."

"Very well. Is there anything else?"

Wilson could no longer contain his curiosity. "Could you play some music on your . . . your . . ."

"It's a cittern," she said gently. "A reconstruction of an old, old instrument. I play it at nights, when I can't sleep."

"My cabin is right next to yours, and I've never heard it."

Bea smiled. "It's a soft instrument." She stood, lost her balance for a moment, recovered herself, and reached for the cittern. Two or three books were dislodged from beneath it and fell noisily to the deck.

Adjusting the stringed frame upon her lap, she laid the neck up over her shoulder and idly plucked out a tune. It was a slow, asymmetric dance, with a languorous wandering melody and a repeated bass accompaniment.

After only a minute or so, she set the instrument carelessly aside onto her desk chair, reaching quickly for it as it slid off onto the floor. The noise that it made when it hit was musical and jarring at the same time.

"It's not damaged, is it?" Gerald Wilson asked in a hushed voice.

"It'll be fine," Bea said, letting the instrument lie where it had fallen.

Wilson was so disturbed by the music and by the dropping of the cittern that he had to excuse himself to the privacy of his quarters.

12

Because I am strong, you are strong.
Because I have courage, you are brave. Let
no one speak of my leading you. I *am* you, by
one and by ten and by a hundred. I am you.
                              Apollonia of Archive,
                              Conscription Day Sermon

John Bradley woke with a feeling of reassurance
that came with the reinforcement of one of his
strongest beliefs. He didn't like being threatened.
Individuals might usee force for several reasons:
panic or fear, to protect loved ones, to attain wealth
or power. All of these were motives that Bradley
understood, regardless of whether he approved of
them. Threats, however, were alien to him.

He shook his head and climbed stiffly out of his
soft, narrow bed. Within moments his full vigor
returned, prodded by the rich scent of strong coffee
now being automatically brewed for him by his
kitchen. He dressed swiftly, fastening his clothing
with one hand while flipping through his morning
mail with the other.

The only item of interest was a note from Andreyev, the sculptor, who rather forlornly apologized for yet another delay in the completion of his project. Bradley sighed; he had been saving shelf space for that statue for more than four months. A bronze bust of Apollonia of Archive would be an ideal centerpiece for his living room, the martyr's image framed by two works of surrealistic portraiture. It would certainly be eye-catching.

He lived alone, but entertained small groups whenever he could; he worked to see that his tiny apartment presented interesting visual and aural textures to lure a visitor's senses and imagination. If anyone on Marterly had a better collection of music, he didn't know of it. If anywhere in the Sector a better sound and visual entertainment center could be cobbled together, he hadn't heard of that, either.

This morning, waiting while he decided what kind of breakfast he most felt like eating, he treated himself to a short walking tour of his collections, something he frequently enjoyed doing. His rack upon rack of music cassettes contained marches, folk songs, full-scale operas, and dramatic works. He frowned, momentarily disturbed by a thought he had often had before: lamentably, the arts of music had never managed to keep pace with humanity's other accomplishments.

He idly inserted a sprightly march into the cassette port and listened to it with an expert and critical ear. It seemed more than ever to be a drab, unadventuresome piece, a march indistinguishable from any of a dozen other flavorless and blandly cheerful pieces. Representational art, as well, had failed to make any great strides in many, many years. One theme in sculpture, martyrs, paralleled one theme in music, combative works such as battaglias and marches. He smiled wryly: one composer had even gone so far as to publish an entire sequence of battaglias denoting explosions with jarring instrumental verisimilitude.

Eggs again, then. His kitchen prepared them to his taste and served them to him in a twinkling. As he ate, he pondered the artistic degradation of an age.

Soon his half-hour of morning leisure was done, and he rose, preparatory to leaving. The threatening note that he had sought to ignore came again to the forefront of his thoughts.

Stay home tomorrow, it had warned him. *You are not expected to win your case.* How annoying, how suggestive, and — he admitted to himself — how tempting. He was sadly disappointed in Kelki Hume for sinking to that level, if indeed it was she. Perhaps one of her Treasury Branch cohorts or underlings had sent the threat. In either case, showing the note to Kelki or to the Tribunal would serve little if any purpose: suspicion would fall just as readily upon him as upon her.

Decisions in the courtroom were ideally made by weight of factual information, influenced, perhaps, by style of presentation. Threats had no place in the law.

He stepped up to the door and began to open it. Just then it crashed brutally inward, the door grip bruising his hand as the heavy panel swung rushing past him. Two large people, thick and tall, burst through the doorway, shoving Bradley rudely back into the apartment. The first kept moving, taking Bradley off balance and propelling him to the floor. Even then the hooded assailant did not relent: he wrestled with Bradley, plunging his clothing into disarray and quite taking away both his breath and his ability to fight back. After knocking Bradley about until he was virtually helpless, the intruder shoved a tube toward his face and jetted a stinging spray of liquid into his face. It was cold and blurred his sight for a few seconds.

When he had blinked away the tears, he found that, although he could see, he also could not see. The paradox was breathtaking. Everything about him was distorted, hideously unclear . . . but it was also as clear as ever.

"What have you done to me?" he demanded, rubbing at his eyes. He could see. This was his hand; he could see every detail. Yet . . .

"We've drugged you," answered the one who had lingered behind while closing the door. His voice was suave and polite. "We've sent a chemical into your brain. You won't be able to identify us."

Here the other interrupted pettishly. "Come along, No One. Hurry on. We will be missed."

"Patience, Nobody." He returned his attention to Bradley. "We are No One and Nobody. You can't see our faces or distinguish our voices. We have your brain under our control."

Although both of their faces had been concealed when they burst into the room, neither of them was wearing a mask now. Bradley looked at them, mystified. He could see the two of them clearly and distinctly. He could readily perceive every detail of their faces and features. Yet at the same time he saw nothing. The sensation was nightmarish and upsetting. These two men — he at least thought they were men, but there was no reason they could not have been women — had no faces. At the same time, they most certainly did have faces: he saw their eyes, lips, hair, teeth. . . .

I'm having trouble with their voices, too, although I can hear the words just fine, Bradley thought. He shrugged internally. *I think I'm about to get a headache.* Any thought of resistance on his part was ended by the oversized gun that the second man drew from a small satchel.

"What do you people want?" Bradley asked, a trifle out of sorts. In the background, all but unnoticed, the march played on at a low volume, the brasses muted and woodwinds dimmed, the percussion vainly trying to inspire the limping music to a conclusion.

The one who held him pinned said nothing but moved swiftly, shifting his weight atop him to keep him from rising. The one by the door leaned back and smiled. It was a smile that Bradley would remember, even if it was vague and unrecognizable: wide and very self-assured; the smile of a vain man entertaining guests in his own home.

"You were warned, were you not?"

Bradley sniffed in disdain. "I've been ignoring anonymous notices and threats since before you ever picked up your first firearm, lad. Get your friend off me, would you?"

The other said nothing and tightened his hold.

"The time has come," the languorous man named "No One" said softly, "when you must learn the difference between threats that you can safely ignore, and . . ."

"And what?" Bradley demanded.

The man smiled hugely. "And the other kind."

"If you don't have your friend get off me, and double quick, I'm going to proceed directly from annoyance to anger. And once there . . ."

The intruder's smile widened, although Bradley would have been prepared to swear that it could not have gotten any larger. "Now, Mister Bradley," the voice said, dripping with arrogance. "Are *you* threatening *me*?"

Bradley, finally realizing these people were not going to be intimidated out of existence, fell silent and stopped squirming. With the cessation of his struggles, the other man leaped lithely from atop him, to stand with his partner.

Bradley, released but not freed, looked long and hard at the man's gun. It loomed, weighting down the man's hand, representing a chill metallic icon of instant death. Bradley shuddered.

"The chemical that we've given you has the effect of paralyzing that faculty of your brain that is used to recognize human features, both faces and voices. You don't know who we are. You are unable to tell us from any of the thousands of people you've met during your life. I could be your father . . . or your mother."

But you're not, Bradley thought, and smiled to himself. *You're a man, and I think your friend is a*

195

woman. That's not much data, but it's more than you intended to give me.

"Who are you?" Bradley asked of neither one in particular.

"We certainly would be foolish to tell you," one of them answered.

"What do you want?"

The two looked at each other and smiled, without, however, quite losing their alert surveillance of Bradley. "We don't want anything. Not anything at all."

Bradley nodded and stood, regaining some of his assertiveness. "In that case, having obtained nothing from me, you have what you came for and are quite free to leave."

"But we don't want to leave just yet," the man said, and he laughed.

They were professionals. Bradley knew, with a sudden pang of helpless anger, that they were going to kill him. It was because of his insolence in daring to take on the Treasury Branch in an open lawsuit; it was because he undertook to thwart their vital plans.

He wasn't important to them. He was an attorney who had taken on a case for a group of clients. He didn't even particularly care about the case. In the same way, he realized, these two assassins didn't care about him. They didn't know who he was, what his beliefs, hopes, yearnings, fears, or ambitions were. To them, he was only an obstacle.

"You're going to kill me, aren't you?" he said numbly.

"Yes," the man said, and his expression seemed

to soften. His friend, leaning casually on his shoulder, smiled slowly — a wide, toothy smile of cruel anticipation.

The march on the cassette player ended. In that instant, a glimmer of a plan came into John Bradley's head. He motioned toward the machine with his head and, when the man nodded his consent, strode over to change the tape. Bradley assumed they wouldn't mind having more music, since it would cover the noise of what they probably intended to do next. Without calling any attention to his actions, yet without any giveaway show of stealth, he placed an opera, *Revolutionaries' Common*, in a second port and sped it ahead to the beginning of Act Three. Looking at the timings listed on the cassette case, he nodded and dug around for a march of precisely the correct length.

This music is all very important to me, he thought glumly as he pressed the start switches simultaneously. *It's a part of me. I'm going to miss it terribly.* . . . But that was ridiculous, he realized: once he was dead, he wouldn't miss much of anything at all.

The music of the march swelled, filling the room evenly and smoothly; there was no obvious source for the tones, which, rich and full, rose and fell rhythmically.

"An impressive reproduction system," the assassin said, his eyes mocking.

"I've spent a lot of option cash maintaining it," Bradley said with pride.

"A shame you won't enjoy it much longer."

"How much longer?" Bradley met the man's

gaze. "When do I go to meet the gods?" He gritted his teeth. "How soon do you take me out and shoot me?"

"The timing requires some degree of precision," the man purred, and the one leaning on his shoulder grinned in cruel mirth.

Bradley looked around the apartment, mentally cataloguing his art treasures for perhaps the last time. He already felt strong pangs of regret. His collections weren't the primary things in his life; people were, and the law was. But his arts were his retreat, his sanctuary.

He looked at each item in his collection one more time, in part because he felt he might not see them again, and he wanted to try to remember them, but also because even professional assassins can make mistakes, and some of his displays were large and heavy. . . .

"I should be in court today," Bradley said, still patient with these people who had so misused him. "I have a case to win."

The man grinned a foolish, lopsided grin. "How dedicated you are."

"Yes, I am." Bradley steeled himself; the music was about to change.

"And why?" the assassin asked. "Why do you insist on dedicating yourself to causes that are not your own? Why do you champion others? Why do you care?"

In this moment of heightened tension and nervous preparation, Bradley paused for a long moment and thought about it. *Why? Because only clods and dolts are beyond caring.* Seeking to better the world was his duty, his battle, and he had long since resolved to be a happy warrior.

The march ended, and the playback machine switched from one cassette to the next.

Into the room boomed the loud voice of the actor portraying the rebel Thendall in the opera. The speech was his announcement of the success of his revolution to the doomed house of nobles. The words sounded clear and full, as rich in timbre and as undistorted as if the actor were present in the room with Bradley and the two assassins.

"I have you now! You're mine! Did you think to escape?"

At the first words, the man spun, his pistol out to his side, threatening neither Bradley nor the door. His partner straightened, then quickly sunk to a low, agile crouch, from which he could leap in any direction.

Bradley jumped to one side, deftly lifted a large clear glass globe filled with thousands of tiny, colorful nodules of glass and crystal, and in one continuous motion threw it with all his might at the first man's unguarded shoulder.

The globe shattered against the assassin, who, astonished and chagrined, fell against the door. The gun dropped from his numbed fingers and he, stunned into at least momentary unconsciousness, fell the other way.

His partner, in the same instant, leaped directly for his rebellious captive. Bradley, however, moving faster than most men of his size would be able to, ducked beneath the attack and rolled swiftly over the floor to snatch up a bronze statuette. It was of a nude woman, but the body was stretched into an abstract representation of unnatural slenderness. Bradley grabbed it by the base and swung it like a club.

Thendall's soliloquy reached its triumphant ending, and the music that followed quickly swept up in a harmonious, threatening crescendo into the accompaniment for the war chant of Basil. Thinking about it with a part of his mind, Bradley realized that the music was thoroughly inspiring to him, undoubtedly goading him to a more heroic performance than he normally would have been capable of.

He secured his grasp on the statue and met the man's charge. The assailant raked at Bradley with outspread fingers; Bradley jabbed the statue bluntly into the killer's midriff. He doubled up, and Bradley clubbed him across the back of the neck. The man's arms flailed up in a clawing, killing embrace, and Bradley nearly hit him again before he saw how blank the man's eyes had gone. Now on his knees, the man faltered and fell only inches from Bradley.

Bradley whirled, ready for another assault. But the other intruder, knocked senseless when he fell against the doorjamb, posed no threat. Bradley found a roll of strapping tape and bound their hands behind them.

He looked around the room, then back at the two prostrate assassins. Well, well. That had hardly made any mess at all. One chair had been overturned, and of course the glass globe was shattered, its multicolored contents strewn far and wide. The durable statuette had been scuffed, but not marred.

A moment later the full reaction hit him, and he found that he had to sit down. *Those were professionals! I beat them with a damn fool trick, and they were experts.* He looked at the statue lying on the green-carpeted floor, and he did not try to suppress his shudders.

After a moment he regained enough strength of purpose to phone for the constables. The militia officers would arrive within minutes, but before they could, he made another phone call.

"I need to speak to the scheduling officer for the Court Tribunal, department fifty-four," he said into the phone, his voice now nearly normal.

"Yes, sir. In regard to which case?"

"Gerald Wilson vs. the Concordat of Archive. It was due to be reconvened in" — he glanced at a wall clock — "thirty-five minutes or so."

"Very well. State your business."

Bradley smiled. "I'm the councillor representing Mr. Wilson, and I won't be able to attend this morning's session. I'd like to request a brief postponement. And I can assure you that it's a justified request."

The clerk paused while making notations in the daybook. "Yes. Well, it had better be. Tomorrow at eight?"

"That's fine."

He set the phone down into its cradle. Not too bad. . . . A slight noise alerted him; he whirled. A third man had come into the room, holding a small pistol before him.

The uniformed constables from the militia were polite and well spoken, and quickly recognized that Bradley's tale of threatening intruders was obviously true.

"Where are they now?" asked the sergeant.

"Gone."

The sergeant placed his fists on his hip. "That much, I can see. Who took them?"

"A third man came in, told me to sit down, and dragged them away."

"Did you see where he went with them?"

"No." Bradley shrugged. "I felt that I had been lucky enough to be left alive. At that point, further exertions didn't appeal to me much."

The sergeant looked at him with a peculiar expression. Bradley squinted back at him, trying to decide what about his expression, exactly, it was that he thought peculiar. He gave up in disgust.

"Sir, are you all right?"

"I've been drugged." He gestured toward his face. "They hit me in the eyes with some sort of chemical spray."

"We'll get you to help right away, then," the sergeant said, and he and his men did exactly that, saving further questions for later.

The strange chemicals in his blood, and the discarded and illegal firearm that Bradley could prove was not his, went a long way toward establishing his story.

Bradley was interviewed at a neighborhood medical station by an investigator in charge.

"Never saw them before, eh?" the heavy officer asked. Slab-faced and slab-sided, he was nearly as large as Bradley and more heavily muscled, the result of a strict daily regimen of exercise and training. His face was deeply tanned, and his dirty blond hair was cut close to his long skull.

"Never in my life." He shrugged. "Of course, I have to admit, I didn't really see them this time."

"And they admitted their intent to have you killed?" The officer looked like the sort whose normal duty was breaking up street fights or keeping people away from the scene of an accident. Perhaps, Bradley thought, he had only recently been promoted to the job of investigator. He wasn't wonderful to look at, but Bradley wasn't about to complain. It was good to be able to see and recognize faces again.

"Yes, sir; they said that they were going to kill me."

"In so many words?"

Bradley closed his eyes and tried to remember. "No," he admitted, "but they answered in the affirmative when I posed a direct question. Their intent was completely clear."

"Fine, fine. We'll get it all right down, then . . ." the investigator began, pausing when interrupted by his phone. Both he and another attending officer reached for the phone simultaneously.

Right. Recently promoted, Bradley thought.

The other officer took the phone, then handed it to the investigator. The investigator glared at his subordinate, then turned his full attention to the receiver.

He returned to Bradley with an unhappy expression on his face. "It looks as if your assailants have gotten clean away."

"Do you know who they were?"

The investigator's face hardened. "I haven't any idea, sir, but it sounds like a Judicial Branch caper to me."

"The Crew."

"Yes, sir. Judicial Branch secret police. A bunch of damn bailiffs with unlimited license. Always up to no damn good, harrying people who've done no wrong. If they'd had their way, sir, I doubt we'd even have ever found your body. Begging your pardon, sir."

"How can they do this? How is it justified?"

"You'd know as well as I would, sir. I'd guess you maybe stumbled too close to something. Or . . . gods, sir, I don't know."

Bradley shook his head in bewilderment. The Crew. A nasty lot of extralegal thugs. That altered the complexion of the case. He shrugged; it could have been any number of other groups. As a lawyer, he'd made his share of enemies over the years.

"Well, thank you, officer. If I'm not needed, I think I'll go back on home. That is, if the doctors here will let me leave."

"Will you be wanting support and protection, sir? Where they strike once, they can come back again."

"I think . . . yes. Could you have a patrolman stop by my place at six tomorrow morning?"

"Righty-ho, sir."

"Thank you."

The patrolman would find Bradley's home untenanted and, upon entering, find the bed unslept in. Bradley hadn't walked more than three blocks toward his home when two more Crew agents, dressed for the street, accosted him and forced him into a ground car.

The first thing they did to him was spray another dose of chemicals into his face.

13

This will provide the most explosive environment imaginable.

John Bradley, *The Undealt Hand*

Taviella called the ship's company together in the dining room, late in the ship's afternoon. During the morning, her temper had grown shorter and shorter, until Maravic fancied she could see storm clouds gathering. Now, however, Taviella's mood was businesslike and correct. She'd even gone so far as to suggest to Stasileus to whip up an early meal of his home-world foods, since his last dinner for the group had been well enough received.

Mikhail arrived late, leaving only Van Wyck Henson and Gerald Wilson not in attendance. Taviella was rather surprised at Wilson's absence, but decided not to press the issue.

Carefully working his way around the periphery of the cramped dining lounge, Mikhail smiled a forlorn smile of exhaustion. "Van Wyck Henson refuses to come out of his room," he said. "He insists that there's a plot against his life."

The roomful of crew members and scientists greeted the news with a range of disdainful reactions. Eric snorted aloud, while Remington smiled his broadest smile, a theatrical grin of exaggerated evil, as if to say, "A plot? You bet there is." Bea looked gloomily down at the table; Maravic shook her head pityingly; Fortuna bristled with anger and disdain.

"Doubtless he named me as the chief of the conspirators," Fortuna snapped, holding her head high and her shoulders stiff. "I am tired of being blamed for all that goes wrong here."

Taviella crossed her arms and leaned forward onto the tabletop. "I don't object to Doctor Henson's delusions, because that's precisely what they have to be: delusions of the most scatterbrained type." She regarded Fortuna dolefully. "You, however, have proven your penchant for violence."

On the tabletop, Fortuna's hands clenched. "It was an accident," she breathed heavily. "I never, never intended to harm Stasileus permanently. I am not a gentle soul, and I admit freely that I was trying to punch him in his face." Her face contorted. "But does anyone think that I wanted it to happen the way it did?"

Taviella looked away. "Mikhail? You just came from a meeting with Doctor Henson?"

"Yes."

"Did he ever mention Fortuna's name? Did he accuse her of plotting against him?"

"Not directly. Hers was one name he mentioned, but he accused others as well. It was clear to me that he didn't know, and that he was naming people for imagined reasons, not for material ones."

"Did he explain to you his views on the scientific and technical reasons he believes he has for aborting the mission?"

Mikhail leaned back, bumping his head accidentally against the cramped bulkhead. "He tried to explain it to me, but I didn't get a lot out of it. I'm not a chemist."

"Let's hear from those who are." Taviella looked up and down the table and would have asked Bea to speak next, had she not been interrupted by the simultaneous and equally meek arrivals of Gerald Wilson from the corridor and Stasileus from the galley with dinner.

"Food's on?" Wilson asked appreciatively.

"Loathsome," Bea sniffed.

"I've made wheatcakes and crisp vegetables for you, Professor Chapman," Stasileus said, his high voice echoing in the lounge. As Maravic had supposed, the neat black eye patch he wore only made him look raffish and sardonic, characteristics utterly at odds with his straightforward personality. Taviella couldn't look at him without stifling a shudder.

Wilson soon found a seat to squeeze into, in time to receive a plateful of varicolored and varitextured gels and semiliquids of Verna home-world cooking. There were bread puddings, two soups that thickened into a creamy broth when poured together, and a spicy sorbet glazed with flecks of sugar.

"A very rich array," Maravic complimented Stasileus. "You're spoiling us."

"On my home world, we kept up the practice of cooking, against the day when the masters should return."

"But why play the part of a slave? With the masters gone, shouldn't you have rejoiced in your freedom?"

"We . . . don't think that way."

"Are we your masters?" Mikhail asked. "We don't want to be, you know."

"Every human is the master of every Verna." Stasileus paused and thought about it, his head cocked to one side. "What you choose is not relevant in this matter: I obey, even without commands."

Mikhail nodded. "Then we can only command gently." He shrugged, then asked hesitantly, "Might I have another helping of the soups?"

"Yes." Stasileus moved to obey.

"This leaves us," Taviella said, "with the matter of Doctor Henson's calculations. Bea, Gerald, have either of you been able to come to any conclusions?"

"None whatever," Bea said softly. All about her, tiny morsels of spilled food gave testimony to her carelessness. She leaned forward, planting her elbows on the table. "He tried to explain his views to me, but basically, he's just guessing. He hypothesizes that the virus and the decay products of the virus-infected plants would, when treated with open flame, produce a series of long-lasting toxins. He speculates that these toxins would be persistent enough to make the surface of the world uninhabitable. If he's correct, the entire project would be pointless. Counterproductive, in fact."

"And you disagree?"

Bea looked around the table. "Remember that this is not the first project of this type. The sterilizing of Catalart, where I assisted, worked precisely according to plan. No spurious combinations of chemicals arose."

"Gerald?"

Wilson blushed, but managed to speak. "I have tried to follow his calculations, and I have evidence ... just a little ... that he might be right. I need to follow it through at some length, however."

"I'll want to see your notes," Bea snapped. "I'm getting nowhere at all trying to make sense of Henson's rantings."

"But if you use his ideas as a departure ..." Wilson stammered, then shut himself up in an agony of shy withdrawal.

"You're the biologist." Bea looked at him, and at the way he could not meet her gaze. "You and Henson know the most about this kind of calculation. But I find no evidence to support it."

Taviella looked around the table. "Mikhail, we're going to have to reach a consensus, right here and now. I'm only the bus driver." She smiled, trying to disarm some of the dinner's tensions. "Perhaps you ought to call a vote."

Mikhail sighed deeply. "I'm very much afraid you're right. Gerald? Do we have enough evidence to cancel the project?"

"No." Wilson's eyes were downcast. "But I personally vote against it ... just because I don't think it's right to take chances when the stakes are so precious."

"Fortuna?"

"Proceed with the operation, of course."

"Bea?"

Bea paused for quite some time before answering. "I oppose the project," she said at last. "I have never liked the idea of destroying this wealth of life for no better reason than providing people with living room." She paused again. "But I also have an obligation — and a need — to set aside my personal views in favor of my professional duty. I have one planet on my conscience: an entire planet, irrevocably destroyed. It doesn't harm me to add another to it." She looked up. "And from what I know of them, Henson's calculations seem invalid to me. I vote to proceed with the operation."

"Doctor Henson isn't here," Mikhail observed, "but I suppose that we should mark him down as opposing the procedure." He looked around, seeing all eyes upon him. "That leaves it up to me, doesn't it?"

No one answered. Maravic pushed her chair a bit closer to his, lending him what support she could. Their hands momentarily brushed.

"I . . ." Mikhail began. "I just don't know." He thought for a moment, then smiled. "I hate this kind of decision."

"Would you like a coin to flip?" Eric's rude suggestion was ignored.

"Very well," Mikhail said after a time. "Gerald's and Doctor Henson's objections are slim and assumptive. Our Treasury Branch orders are clear. We've managed to delude ourselves that the value to science of this world's biosphere is something that means something in our deliberations . . . and it does not." He sighed. "I'm not sure that we ever really had any choice at all."

He looked around at all of them one last time before pronouncing his decision.

"We follow the procedures we have been instructed to follow."

"Thank you, Doctor Petrov," Taviella said, her voice subdued.

"Forgive me, rather, I should think," he said, and managed a tremulous smile.

Taviella looked around. "For the record, crew, how do you feel?"

"Finish the job," Maravic said sadly.

"Kill it," agreed Remington.

"Right." Eric's laconic response, uttered sourly and moodily, finished the roll, for Stasileus, who should have spoken next, held his peace.

Taviella looked up at the huge alien, and her eyes met his. An unspoken message passed between them.

I don't want to kill the planet, Taviella realized, consciously aware of the fact for the first time in the voyage. *I don't want to do my duty.*

Stasileus looked carefully at her, almost as if he were reading her mind. She looked up at him and almost pleaded.

I do not want to do this thing.

Looking away, she quickly regained control of herself. "We go ahead with the project, starting tomorrow, unless someone can come up with clear and convincing scientific evidence that we should not."

She and Mikhail both regretted the need for the

decision; she and Mikhail would both be glad for some way to avoid it.

She and Mikhail, Taviella realized finally, were simply the wrong people to have been given such an ugly job.

∞

Dinner broke up soon thereafter, and Stasileus cleaned the lounge and the galley. He spent longer than necessary, cleaning the dinner's utensils by machine and again by hand, his one eye focused through the door and away beyond the bulkhead. He saw the diners leave the lounge, as the scientists and the crew broke up into small groups. Taviella and Maravic and Mikhail drifted forward, to share the bright warmth of the control room. Remington and Eric, each incomplete without the other, huddled in the security of the nest they had made in the pump room. Bea and Gerald stayed in the lounge, immersed in their texts and aided by their computers, struggling to make sense of Van Wyck Henson's claims about a chemical danger. Fortuna repaired to her stateroom and, like Van Wyck Henson in his, hid there in solitude.

Stasileus watched them all, a little bit surprised to see that some of them were watching him back. The tensions, the schemes, all were coming to a head, and as far as he was aware, he alone knew everything. He knew all the schemers, all the victims, all the plots in every detail.

He had set out to learn the ways in which humans thought, and had succeeded all too well.

The night grew late. Stasileus wondered if he were the only one to feel the sense of impending doom. With a shudder, he realized that he was.

∞

Gerald Wilson had risen and gone to his bed. Bea Chapman alone remained in the lounge, scribbling away in her clumsy handwriting, making rings on her papers wherever she set down her coffee mug. Her hair tended to drift into her eyes, and every now and again she batted at it with the back of her hand. Around her, a litter of crumpled and discarded papers defined her throwing range; as Stasileus watched, she tore up another sheet and threw it with all her might at the opposite wall. It bounced airily and rolled into the galley.

"Bea?"

She looked up. "Oh, Stacey. What do you want?"

"Can I help you move your work to your room?"

Bea stared at him, until her shoulders slumped, and she nodded. "I'm in your way, aren't I?"

"I need to clean the table," he said truthfully. But what he said wasn't the whole truth: he did need her out of the way.

"All right. I'll accept your help . . . with thanks. You get the books, if you would, and I'll gather up the papers."

"Shall I also bring the papers you've rolled up and thrown?"

Bea's smile was thin and uneven. "No. Discard them. Destroy them. I will be happier never seeing them again."

"Yes, ma'am." He carefully lifted up the books that lay strewn about the table and followed her to her room.

"Do you think the calculations even exist?" she asked him, looking at him in distraught urgency. "Do you think that Doctor Henson is telling some kind of ghastly lie?"

Stasileus might would have lied himself, using an evasion or a half truth to cover for his own plans. But his obedience, an integral part of him, compelled him to give her the answer she desired.

"Van Wyck Henson was lying. That is all he has ever done."

Blinking, Bea looked up at Stasileus. "Can that be?"

"Van Wyck Henson is a liar. He is a living lie."

"Is he . . ." Bea swallowed. "Is he really a scientist? Is he really a biologist?"

"Yes." Stasileus's voice was high and resonant but firm. "He is one of the very best."

"All right . . ." Bea, diminished next to the giant alien, turned and went into her stateroom. Stasileus didn't know if she would continue searching for equations that didn't exist, or if she would find sleep.

∞

On Invernahaven, with Musele at his side, things had been more certain, and patterns had been more clear.

"Authority reaches backward in a sequence," she explained to him once, as the two sat side by side in a wilderness glade before a high-stacked wood fire. Night had come, but the fire and its smoke distorted the stars until only the brightest few hung in the branches of the trees overhead. The wood smoke was resinous and sharp, smelling strongly of the wood's fast-burning, explosive sap. Before them the fire snapped loudly, throwing hot flakes of wood high into the air.

"Every sequence has an origin," Stasileus responded, the knowledge fresh in his head from his mathematics studies.

"All authority derives from the person of the Emperor," she said.

Stasileus waited, knowing that he was being tested. He knew that the Emperor was gone, strangled to death by the warrior-hero Basil. Did this mean that there was no longer any authority?

"I don't understand," he said at last.

Musele spoke patiently; young Stasileus worshiped her, then, more than ever. He loved the play of the firelight, reflecting tiny highlights up and down her breast and flank; he loved her high, musical voice; he loved her dark, dark eyes. She was his authoritar, and she governed him, and for that reason also he loved her.

"Law comes from the Emperor, who made the suns and the gods, and who cast himself in the form of a man for our enlightenment. When he was slain in revolt, his law did not cease to apply."

"Law works in sequence," Stasileus said, thinking swiftly. "With the Emperor gone, someone else holds his authority."

"Some one or several individuals may hold his law. Law is a sequence: a Sultan may name several

216

Viceroys, each of whom might appoint many Legates. If a Viceroy is slain, his Legates continue to hold his authority until they are relieved of this responsibility by their Sultan."

"The Emperor is gone and we are alone," Stasileus said, finally catching on, "but our law is still his law."

"Yes." Musele leaned closer to him, her body pressing against his in a loving embrace. "Tomorrow we select our authoritar, to hold the law for us all, everywhere on this world. But we are only poor Legates choosing one of our number to lead us until a Viceroy or a Sultan shall appear."

Then, before she engaged him in the opening sexual rituals, she sighed, very sadly. "Legates? We are only slaves, choosing a slave to direct us. We should pity him, even as we follow him."

The next morning, refreshed, the two of them walked back to the city, passing through the high boulevards and over low, multi-arched bridges until they arrived at a main artery leading to the city's center. All of the Vernae of the city, perhaps all of the Vernae of the planet, walked toward the central plaza where the drama would unfold. Stasileus soon found himself hip to hip and shoulder to shoulder with more strong and tall Vernae than he had ever known existed. The solidity of their ranks gave him pride: slaves they may be, but they were slaves that had strength of arm and back. They were good slaves.

He stood in the center of a solid mass of varicolored Vernae: there were whites, blacks, and every shade of brown from the lightest of sandy tans to the deepest earthy tones of dark mud. The warrior-hero Basil was said to have been a white; Stasileus looked at the sea of beings of all colors, surprised to see how many whites like himself there were. Musele might still be near him, although in the press he could not see her, nor hear her voice. Everyone was talking, all at once, including himself: he spoke to a crippled gray male whose back had been injured in a fall. Because of this injury, the bent elder couldn't see over the heads of those before him, and he was grateful to Stasileus for his description of the spectacle.

Soon, a hush fell over the crowd. The Vernae stood and breathed in unnatural, still silence. Upon a high stage, one was led forward by another. The one in the lead, a lean, tall, light brown female, swept her arm around in a gesture that encompassed the whole of the crowd. She then indicated the one she led, a sturdy, dark brown male. "This is Corydon." Her high, echoing voice rang out over the square, so that all could hear it clearly. "Command him to command you."

"Command us!" Their voices burst out, the three sharp syllables crisp and loud in the sunlit air. Then silence.

Corydon nodded, accepting this new order. "Disperse," he shouted. "Go back to your tasks."

And the ceremony was over.

Stasileus walked away from the square, searching for Musele. The streaming throng hindered his search, and it was only that night, arriving back at the home he shared with her, that he found her.

"What have you learned?" she asked.

218

"That command is a task."

"What else?"

"That no command may be refused."

"Sleep now."

Stasileus slept.

∞

Stasileus awoke, aboard the *Indagator*, aware of what actions he would have to take. The variables had all fallen into place. The plan, conceived long ago, was ready to be put into effect.

He rose from his seat in the lounge, surprised that he had actually slept. He shook his huge head, hoping he would not be too late. Slowly he crept through the silent ship, through the corridors lit as brightly at night as they were in the daytime, but corridors so much more quiet. He passed the closed door behind which Taviella slept, unaware of his presence. He stealthily moved past Maravic's door, and Bea's, and Fortuna's.

At the forward airlock, he settled down to wait. The ship's time was four in the morning, an arbitrary and artificial delineation of time, but the one by which the crew and passengers had agreed to abide. No one would be abroad at this hour who was not considering mischief.

Stasileus was not free. All law derived from the Emperor. In his absence, however, the slaves who toiled without direction needed to operate by some sort of consensus. One of them must command another to take control.

Taviella was in the lead, but was not the leader.

She was unaware of her own mind: she had made a decision and been unaware of it. She had ordered Stasileus to free her from completing the mission.

Soberly, sensibly, Stasileus thought the matter through, knowing that his choice was not free. Mikhail, too, was in the lead, and he, too, had made a decision. But his authority was less than Taviella's, and his honest determination to see the ugly mission through was second to hers in importance.

Stasileus waited. Before long, he saw Gerald Wilson walking down the corridor toward him. Stasileus faded back into the cross-corridor and made himself unseen. Wilson, looking about himself in a melodramatic attempt at stealth, busied himself with the forward airlock.

Stasileus came silently up behind him and spoke in a very quiet voice.

"Mr. Wilson?"

Wilson spun around in alarm, his startled eyes horribly wide. His mouth worked, opening and closing, but no words came out. He leaned back against the airlock door and fought to control his breath.

"You startled me, Stacey," he said at last.

"If you were to open the airlock door, an alarm would sound."

Wilson looked from side to side, as if seeking an escape. "I . . . I wasn't going to open the airlock door."

Stasileus proceeded relentlessly. "I will go to the control room and disable the alarm. You will need to make your preparations aboard the ship's boat."

Wilson goggled at the alien, his eyes blinking in alarm. "I . . . I . . . I don't know what you're talking about."

Stasileus continued in a calm tone. "You will need to arrange an ejection charge on the door, and you'll need to disable several other safety components. I can help you. I have access to the control room, and I am an engineer."

Wilson lowered his voice and moved near Stasileus in trembling urgency. "Are you going to help me?"

"Yes."

"You aren't going to stop me?"

"No."

"And you won't tell anyone? You won't give me away?"

"Not unless you make that necessary."

Wilson's breathing was still frenzied. "Do you agree with what I intend to do?"

"Yes." Stasileus looked solemnly into Wilson's eyes. "In order to save the world of Kythe-Correy, Van Wyck Henson must die."

Wilson swallowed, and his hands shook. "And you're going to . . ."

"I'm going to help you kill him."

Wilson looked at Stasileus for a long time, then shuddered. "Let's hurry, then. I don't want to get caught."

Stasileus nodded. "No. That would serve no purpose."

14

It is very heavy, this life, and too much
for one to lift. It is very cold, this loneliness,
and too much for one to endure. It is very
dark, this nightly mystery, and too much for
one to solve.

Achorus,
The Skeleton and the Chaffinch

Stasileus's hands at the controls sent commands
flying from the control room to the lifeboat's onboard computer. The green and yellow lights of the
instrument panels brought reflected highlights to
his thick white fur. His good eye squinted in concentration. An automatic landing sequence needed
to be installed in the lifeboat, as well as several
other autonomic routines. In addition to technical
accuracy, secrecy was of paramount importance;
for him to be caught now would mean no less than
his destruction.

Forward, at the lifeboat, Gerald Wilson made
his preparations in strained silence. His forehead
grew clammy with sweat, which he wiped away

with the back of his hand. The thought of discovery sent pangs of fear through him, and despite his sweat, he shivered. But his job was soon done. He closed the airlock and walked softly back through the ship to wait for Stasileus outside the door to the control room.

Stasileus emerged after only a moment. "All is ready. The lifeboat will eject in five minutes. Did you prepare everything correctly?"

Wilson shuddered in horror, but lifted his head. He was determined; he would see this through. "Yes. Everything's set." He smiled, a thin, nervous smile. "I guess this is the last anyone will ever see of Van Wyck Henson."

Stasileus regarded him studiously for a moment. Which of them had aided the other's plan? Who was the master and who the assistant?

A deeper problem tormented his mind, a question he knew, now, to be central to the obedience of his species. He had learned the ways of his human masters; he had learned the elaborate involutions of human thought. He had learned, at last, that they thought and believed on different levels, in different ways. He had learned how people delude themselves; how they rationalized; how they lived in a dream-world partly of their own creation.

He was built to obey, and to obey even without commands. But how was he to obey when his masters' wishes and commands were different?

He rested his huge hand on Wilson's shoulder. "We have done the right thing, no matter what happens next." Wilson smiled weakly at him, and the two went quietly back to their staterooms.

The rest of the five minutes elapsed amid the silence of the ship in its orbit. Far below it, the planet turned, daylight arriving over the mountains and deserts, night falling upon the single vast azure sea.

The lifeboat, driven by the instructions placed in it by the *Indagator*'s computer, powered itself and launched away into the star-flecked sky. Turning over in flight, it accelerated swiftly toward the planet's surface. Kythe-Correy's gravity tugged at it, adding to its impetus, bringing it deeper and deeper into the atmosphere.

Aboard the *Indagator*, several status lights on the main control room instrument panel began to change color. At the same time, the main computer, working in accordance with Stasileus's orders, erased a substantial portion of its memory, including an account of all control-room activity for the past ten minutes. Another section of indicators began to glow a dull orange, signaling an abnormal situation, but no alarms were sounded. The forward airlock sealed itself, again automatically, with a snap and a hiss.

∞

An instant after the thump and clank of the departing lifeboat, Taviella sat bolt upright in her bunk, grabbing wildly for her night robe. For a moment she wondered what had awakened her, yet even as she thought, her hands dressed her and her feet hurried her through her door toward the control room. No one else was out at this hour, nor should they be. But ahead of her, Remington's door opened swiftly, and he nearly collided with her as he emerged. His hair was tousled and disorderly, but his eyes were wide awake.

"Shifting cargo?" he asked in a crisp voice.

"Lifeboat launch," Taviella answered, her own voice controlled, yet somewhat tight.

The two turned as one and hastened to the control room. Remington burst through the door first and plopped himself loosely down into the copilot's couch. Taviella, a split-second behind him, threw herself into the pilot's seat, her eyes scanning the instruments quickly and skillfully. The indicators announcing the lifeboat launch caught her eye first, then the controls showing the abnormal computer activity. She tried to call up an account of all computer activity for the past hour, and was distressed to discover a ten-minute gap in the file.

Remington, meanwhile, got quickly on the intercom and awoke Maravic, Eric, and Stasileus.

"Emergency stations, crew," he snapped. "Maravic, you're needed here." So far, he'd refrained from sounding a general alarm; the passengers might well have no idea of anything unusual happening. Without looking at Taviella, he asked, "Shall I wake the scientists?"

Taviella bit her lip. "Yes," she said at last, "but have them stay in their quarters. And try to reassure them."

"Hmph," Remington retorted. "Is anyone going to reassure me? What's going on?"

"I don't know."

That simple admission from Taviella did precisely the opposite of reassuring Remington. He flipped the intercom to general address. "Okay, everybody," he said in a soft, professional voice, "we have a little problem, and I want you all to stay where you are so the crew can work on it. It's nothing serious, and we'll all be better off if you don't try to ask us about it on your intercom stations." He felt helpless and clumsy in the emergency, and his words sounded thick and inarticulate to him. He closed off the intercom station, noting with no surprise that two stateroom's intercom signals were flashing: Bea's and Fortuna's.

Well, I'm not going to answer them, he thought, and quickly got up out of the seat as Maravic came into the room. Maravic, he noticed with approval, was wide awake and in control of herself. She'd taken the time to slip into her jumpsuit, but hadn't paused either to fasten it all the way or to draw on her boots. Barefoot and bareheaded, she ignored him, moving swiftly past him to drop into the seat he'd just vacated. Eric was right behind her, barechested, shoeless, his hair tousled but his eyes fully awake.

Stasileus followed, not too closely, not too distantly, and stood out of the way. No one even noticed that he was there.

"Status?" Maravic asked Taviella.

"Secure."

Maravic looked down at her control board and fiddled for a second with her instruments. "Eric? Engines?"

"Fine," Eric reported from his own engine control panel. He sounded as if the whole alert was a waste of his time, and that an engine alert just might be something less likely than a meteorite strike or stellar flare. He sounded as if he was bored already and only wanted to get back to his bunk. "Hell, Stacey could have handled this," he added, "without even getting in the way."

"Remington?" Maravic looked up, noticing him for the first time. "What are you doing here?"

"I was just leaving," Remington said hurriedly, and went off to his own station in the pump room.

Maravic's voice, slightly amused, yet seriously concerned, followed him to the intercom station there. "Is everything okay?"

"Fluid cargo stable," he answered tonelessly.

Taviella, in the intervening moments, had given up on trying to restore the computer memory, and had focused the reach and range of the gravitic radar. One of the ship's lifeboats had indeed been launched and was now heading toward a landing on Kythe-Correy.

"Maravic, see if you can raise the lifeboat. Find out who's taken it."

"Check."

"Remington, see to the passengers. Find out who's missing."

"Right."

She ran back over her displays, trying to gauge whether or not the lifeboat was on a piloted flight. It seemed to be. Its landing approach was sure and steady. A quick glance at the instruments controlling the main repulsors showed that the boat was well out of range of their manipulative override.

Remington's voice came back on line a few moments later. "Mikhail, Fortuna, Bea, and Wilson are all here. Henson doesn't answer."

"Hold on . . ." A passenger's enjoyment of privacy didn't extend to circumstances as important as these; Taviella hit a sequence of keystrokes that unlocked and opened the door to Van Wyck Henson's stateroom.

Remington's next report came from inside that room. "Nobody here."

"Get everybody to the lounge. Tell them Doctor Henson is gone. Canvass them for ideas and opinions. We'll be along soon."

"Right."

"Taviella?"

"Yes, Maravic?"

"No radio response from the boat. Whoever's aboard isn't answering. But . . ."

"Yes?"

"Henson doesn't know how to pilot a boat," Maravic said unhappily.

Taviella drew a breath. "If he's smart enough not to touch any of the controls, the boat will land itself."

"Will he be that smart?"

"We'll have to wait and see."

But even as she watched, the boat turned over again, and she read on her screen the minute indications of its gravitic engine decelerating it for terminal approach. The radar showed it settling down to the planet's surface with a relative velocity of less than five meters per second.

"Boat's down," Taviella said softly.

"Radio beacon on."

"Any messages?"

"Just the beacon."

"Damn it!" Taviella thumped the arm of her command couch with her fist. "What kind of game is he playing?"

Maravic thought for a second. "His taking of the lifeboat should have sounded alarms."

"There's been ten minutes of control-room computer use erased."

"Could Henson have done that?"

Taviella looked at Maravic. "No. But Fortuna could have."

Maravic swallowed. "Right."

"Wait here. Get the ship's boat ready for launch. I'm going to have a quick talk with the passengers, then Eric and Remington and I are going down to the landing site."

"Check."

∞

Remington stood leaning against the wall, surveying the four remaining passengers with icy aloofness. Eric and Stasileus stood by the other corridor entrance to the lounge, equally alert. Fortuna sat forward, her elbows on the table, her expression challenging and surly. Bea and Mikhail sat back, perplexed and visibly concerned; Mikhail felt quite helpless and very much at a loss for suggestions. Wilson sat hunched forward, as if trying to hide within the circle of his arms and shoulders.

Taviella arrived in the lounge at a walk and carefully looked over the six humans and one Verna who looked up to greet her. As she entered, Remington nodded at her and left the room. Taviella looked around. "Okay guys, what's the consensus?"

"We don't know," Mikhail said unhappily. "This comes as much a surprise to us as it does to you."

"Why would he just leave like this? Why would he steal a lifeboat?"

Bea looked up and met her gaze. "We never believed he would have." She slumped back again in her chair. "I suppose this proves something about us. About us all."

"What?" Taviella's tone was tense and snappish, almost sarcastic, but she sincerely did want to know what Bea meant.

"We've all been so untrusting of each other." Bea looked around. "Even before the word of plots or intrigues. There just isn't any trust aboard this ship, and never has been. It makes me unhappy, and yet I've been the cause of part of it."

"Bea," Taviella spoke softly, "can you tell us what you know?"

"About Van Wyck Henson? Nothing. I've spoken ten words of personal conversation with him during the entire voyage."

"Fortuna?" Taviella prompted.

Fortuna's face and expression worked around, as if she were preparing to explode in rage; instead, she stiffened her jaw and spoke in a low, tight voice. "I don't know anything about this. Nothing at all. I was asleep."

"The computer was partially erased," Taviella said, eyeing Fortuna warily.

"Do you accuse me of erasing it?"

Taviella shrugged. "No. Not yet. But you did crack the operating system earlier, and—"

"Yes, I did!" Fortuna's voice was shrill and unpleasant. "I took a copy of it, and you can charge me with theft if you like. But I never interfered with ship's operations. Never."

Remington returned at that point, forestalling Taviella's response. "I've searched the ship carefully. One environment suit is missing. Henson's room is a pigsty, but it looks like that's the way he left it. Nothing else has been taken."

"Very well," Taviella said. "Stasileus, you and Maravic are in charge. Remington, you and Eric come with me. We're taking a trip downstairs."

The four human crew members hurried out, leaving Stasileus to watch over the scientists. Mikhail stretched and went into the galley to make coffee and tea, which Stasileus helped him serve. Bea and Fortuna sat motionless and silent, and Gerald Wilson sat huddled in misery, unable to meet Stasileus's gaze.

∞

The ship's boat was slightly larger than the lifeboats. Taviella and her two crewmen hastened inside and double-checked the telemetry link with Maravic. Then Taviella launched the boat free and headed toward the planet.

From below, the beacon continued blazing the location of the downed lifeboat, repeating a brief mayday and identification code at high intensity. She homed on it, bringing the boat down through the thick layers of atmosphere, cleaving the blue sky of Kythe-Correy. Over mountains, plains, rivers, and hills she flew, losing altitude steadily. The signal fell below the horizon, then came up again swiftly; Taviella neared the source of the signal, then brought the boat to a slow drift at an altitude of two hundred meters.

She halted it and hovered: in the middle of a broad, sloping, upland meadow, the lifeboat lay on its side. It had apparently landed without being damaged, but the door to the passenger compartment was open.

"Suits on, guys. We're going to have to go and have a look."

"Right," Eric grumbled. "You want one of us to wait here?"

"Yes. You stay. And I'll have this with me." Taviella held up her pistol for them to see, then set it aside. "Take the controls."

"Right."

She and Remington struggled into the tight-fitting environment suits, and Taviella tucked the pistol into one outer pocket.

"Drop us."

Eric wordlessly obeyed, lowering the boat to the surface of the meadow with a steady hand. The boat grounded some fifty meters from the lifeboat. Taviella first, then Remington, cycled through the tiny airlock. They emerged onto a smooth, grassy slope, where tall clumps of yellow weeds came up to the middle of their calves.

"Doctor Henson? Are you there?" Taviella's radio call went unanswered.

"No radio traffic whatever," Eric said, "other than the beacon."

"You've got a stronger transmitter; you call for him."

"All frequencies. Hello. Doctor Henson? Answer, please."

No response came.

Taviella approached the silent lifeboat with all of the stealth and observation that her youth on an untamed world had taught her. Her neck was supple, and her arms and shoulders were loose and ready. Automatically she observed the low grass, pressed down by the bulk of the lifeboat. Her training returned to her easily now, and she bent low to inspect the grass for indications of Van Wyck Henson's passage, while still maintaining most of her alertness ahead and to each side.

Her senses spread out from her, in a widening circle of awareness. She sensed Remington walking behind her, to the left, slightly away from the lifeboat. She felt the wind outside, moving slowly over the outside of her suit, and stirring the grasses in vast yellow waves. She neared the open airlock door, looked carefully at the grass and ground, then stepped inside.

After cycling through the lock, she inspected the small craft from stem to stern in one quick sweep. Doctor Henson was definitely not aboard, and there was no place he could conceivably have hidden.

She stepped forward to the instrument panel. The lifeboat was operational and capable of flying upward into orbit again. She flipped the transmit switch on the radio. "Maravic? Eric? The lifeboat's empty."

"Where in the name of five red hells does he think he's going to go?" Eric said. "This entire planet is poisonous."

"There are supplies here . . . but he didn't take any with him."

Maravic's voice came over the link, filtered by distance and retransmission. "There's no sign of him from here. Only military ships have the scanning capability to track one man from orbit."

"I'm going back outside," Taviella said. She passed through the doorway again and stooped to examine the grass. "I can't see any trace of his passage."

Remington started to move closer, but Taviella waved him back. "Let me look around and see if I can find his trail."

"Looking for bent blades of grass or something equally obscure?" he asked.

Taviella had to smile. "Obscure? Where I grew up, a bent blade of grass might make the difference between eating and going hungry." She laughed, a tight, nervous little laugh. "Or between life and death." She searched more widely, still finding no traces of Van Wyck Henson's track.

"Henson grew up on the same planet that you did," Eric suggested. His voice came clearly over the radio link in Taviella's helmet. "Maybe he knows enough to avoid leaving any marks."

Taviella shrugged. "Hiding your trail is always harder than following someone else's . . . but you're right. I could do it, so I have to assume that he can."

"What?" Remington asked, incredulous. "You mean someone that big could move through this grass without leaving any traces?"

"I suppose that sounds very barbaric to you, Remington."

"That's . . . That's not what I meant. . . ." Remington stammered.

Taviella laughed. "It sounds barbaric to me, too. But that's the way I grew up. And if there's a path here, I can't find it."

"Any chance he never walked away from the boat?" Eric suggested.

"What do you mean?"

"Suppose that both airlock doors opened at the same time, while he was at, say, fifty kilometers altitude."

"He'd be sucked right out through the lock," Remington said. "Why in the world would he want to do that?"

"Could the lifeboat have been rigged that way?" Eric persisted.

From orbit, Maravic's voice answered his question. "It could have been. Taviella, can you dump the lifeboat's computer to me?"

"Will do." Taviella passed once more inside the cramped lifeboat and keyed a series of instructions to the small onboard computer.

"Did you get it?" she asked.

"Blank," Maravic answered. "It seems to have erased itself, too. Someone is obviously intent on keeping us baffled. Who could that be other than Fortuna?"

"I don't know," Taviella admitted in frustration. "Anyway, the door couldn't have opened during the flight. Eric?"

"Yeah?"

"There's still normal air pressure in here. The doors couldn't have blown."

"Check the tanks," Eric suggested. "See if the pressure's been restored."

Taviella did; the tanks were fully stocked.

"So he's alive," she said.

"And down here," Eric grumbled.

"Somewhere," Remington agreed.

∞

There was nothing more to be learned from examining the site of the downed lifeboat. Taviella insisted that it be left where it was, in case Van Wyck Henson could not be located. It would offer him a cache of food and water, and a place where he could breathe withouthaving to stay inside his environment suit.

"He obviously doesn't want to be found," she observed, "but we can't just strand him here without any hope of survival."

"I don't see any particular reason why not," Eric complained.

Taviella answered him gently. "We're not that kind of people, Eric."

"You might not be." But he knew she was right, and said nothing further.

They flew a series of spirals out from the lifeboat's landing position, dropping low to investigate copses of woods or outcrops of rock where Van

Wyck Henson might be hiding. They uncovered no trace of him.

Four hours later, tired and disappointed, they returned to orbit and docked with the *Indagator*.

∞

After another three hours of searching from orbit, hoping for some contact with Van Wyck Henson, Taviella gathered the crew and passengers together in the lounge.

"We've had no radio contact with Doctor Henson. But there are other ways of signaling us." She counted off the points on her fingers. "He could build a fire, and we'd be able to see the smoke. He could contact us with his suit radio, or with the lifeboat radio. At just the right time of day, he could signal us with a mirror, sending a primitive heliograph message. That time of day is just past, and he's now down there for the night. Against the night side of the planet, any fire he might build will show clearly, and so I propose to wait until dawn. If we haven't spotted him and if he hasn't answered us, we have no choice but to leave orbit and head back to Marterly."

"Marterly?" Wilson sputtered, then shrank into himself in embarrassment.

Taviella breathed deeply in and out. "I probably should be enraged. I probably should be furious with all of you. But I'm not. Van Wyck Henson may be a barbarous thug, he may even be insane, but he's a man, alone on a poisonous world. He may be hurt. He may be dying. Or . . . he may be hiding from us, laughing up his sleeve that he's managed to stymie us. I don't know. But he's had one certain effect on the mission: we're turning around and heading back for Marterly."

"The mission, of course, would have to be cancelled," Mikhail agreed. "No matter what the cost, we are not about to go and drop rocks on an inhabited world."

"That's right." Taviella's voice was firm. "Anyone . . . even Doctor Henson . . . deserves better than that. Unless we find him within the next fifteen hours, the operation is cancelled, and we're going back."

"Marterly has one or two scout craft on permanent assignment," Mikhail said. "They'd be able to find him. It'll take us one week to get home, and the scout less than one week to come back here. I assume the lifeboat has air and water for one person for two weeks."

Taviella smiled. "For a lot longer than that."

"He'll come back to it, then."

"I hope so."

∞

The fifteen hours passed without any sign or signal from Van Wyck Henson. Taviella, with Maravic's full agreement, refused to presume that he was dead. Quite the opposite, they concluded that he had lived and was hiding from them deliberately. But they agreed that they had no moral choice in the matter.

Slowly, under Taviella's guidance, the great

ship *Indagator* climbed away from the world and sun, moving away toward the stars.

Once more the engines boomed and energies were projected, rupturing the continuum of space. Glaring and red, jumpspace swallowed them up. Kythe-Correy was left behind, and Marterly awaited them.

The mission had failed, and Van Wyck Henson had caused the failure.

15

You killed me, but I am here still. Death
is not so large a place.
Apollonia of Archive, *Final Sermon*

John Bradley awakened in the midst of comfortable surroundings. He lay as if at ease upon the
deep cushions of a long settee, in a high-ceilinged
room decorated in subtly blended shades of yellow.
Orange-yellow sunlight streamed through thickly
tinted windows; the ceiling of the room had been
painted a soft pastel yellow. Several other items of
furniture helped fill the room's emptiness: some
deep armchairs, a large wooden table, an ornamen-
tal bookcase lined with antique-style volumes. Two
closed doors led from the room.

Bradley remembered nothing. He looked about
in astonishment and tried to reconstruct the past.
No recollection came to him of how he could possibly have come to have been asleep in this room. The
last thing he remembered . . .

The last thing he remembered was being captured in the street.

I think I'm in trouble. . . . He looked about for his watch, which he always took off before retiring, and discovered it to be fastened to his wrist. He had been asleep fully dressed. The lateness of the hour shocked him. It was shortly past one o'clock in the afternoon. He had missed his court appearance, again, and his case had undoubtedly been thrown out because of his absence. A perfect record of attendance had been ruined, due to those obnoxious and interfering Crew agents.

"Where in the pluperfect subjunctive am I?" He looked around and around the room in growing confusion. "Damn it, drugged again."

He shook his head and strode swiftly toward the nearer of the two doors. Perhaps a phone call would bring help.

He pulled open the door and halted in amused perplexity. It led only to a shallow water closet, currently quite bare. He marched diagonally across the room to the other door and opened it cautiously. He caught a glimpse of a long hallway with a window at its end, just before the two people standing outside the doorway halted him and shoved him rudely back into the yellow room.

"A moment of your time," said the one in the lead, speaking with a sarcastically exaggerated politeness. Bradley looked at him, squinted, shook his head, and squinted again. His eyes had been interfered with again; he couldn't make out the face.

"My associate and I feel that it is best if you do not leave until you have been given a fuller understanding of what we want from you." The man's words were urbane, but Bradley could easily sense his sadistic triumph at having a helpless captive under his control.

"We've drugged you anew," he explained. "You have, at our insistence, missed not merely one day of court, but two. I think that this quite firmly settles the matter, and the Justices will have no choice but to interpret your absence as a sign of your bad faith. You have lost, Mister Bradley. Face up to it. You have lost."

Bradley frowned. "I don't accept your word for my defeat. I may, in fact, be defeated, but I'll find that out for myself."

"We have what we want. There is no reason for us to harm you. But this should serve as a warning to you: never dispute our authority again!" The threat in his voice was impossible to mistake.

"Why should I not?" Bradley asked in some heat. "I have an oath to fulfill, and a case to plead. Why are you afraid to let this case be heard? Whom do you serve?"

The man silenced Bradley by hitting him full in the face. "We are afraid of nothing. We are operatives of the Crew."

"I knew you had to be." Bradley shook his head and bent forward to try to fix the man's features in his mind. He saw every detail of the chin and nose clearly, and yet found that he could not name the color of his hair, or even make a fair guess at his hair's length. The man was a will-o-wisp, a phantom whose wavering outlines and cloudy features were beyond his ability to pin down.

"We are in league with the Crew," the man said softly.

Bradley thought about that. *In league? But not members per se?*

"Say no more than you must," hissed his companion. Bradley looked at the other's vague form and found himself still vaguely convinced, as he had been yesterday, that it was that of a woman.

"There is little danger to us." The man laughed, a noise that was jarring and unnatural to Bradley in its disguised and cloudy tones, as heard by his drugged ears.

"I can't identify you, that's for sure," Bradley grumbled. "I can see you, but I can't seem to perceive you. I find it highly annoying."

"Not as annoying as it would be to us if we were forced to kill you."

Bradley snorted. "You'd have done it by now. Not even the Crew can afford to go too far."

"Do you think not?" The man bent close to Bradley and breathed softly in his face. "We can kill you without compunction. Your death would be a complication, one we would far, far rather avoid. But we can kill you, remember that. There are those who feel that we ought to have killed you already." He paused. "What do you know of the Crew?"

Bradley humored the questioner, finding no point in incurring his wrath by not answering. "They serve the Justice Branch as a cadre of enforcers and bailiffs, and they deliver subpoenas. They maintain courtroom security. They oversee the administration of prison planets. They're the court's muscle."

"But they are slightly more than all that, aren't they?" taunted the man.

243

"There are rumors of the Crew acting as a body of secret policemen." Bradley shrugged. "Until yesterday, I personally discounted these rumors."

"But they are the truth." The man paused, as if for once uncertain. "We are also able to act on our own, for purposes such as we might see fit."

"So it seems."

The other one spoke. "For the gods' sake, No One, stop giving away information. This one is not important enough to waste so many words upon."

"Perhaps you are right, Nobody. Councillor Bradley, I bid you sit and relax in this room, which will be your home away from home for the next eight days. Meals will be brought to you upon occasion, on no regularly occurring schedule. You have exhibited a tendency to escape, and we shall not encourage you in it."

"Wait. . . ." Bradley muttered. "One more question, please."

"Yes?"

"Why?"

"Why? You wonder at our concern for the case involving the future of Kythe-Correy? You don't see the relevance?"

"No, I don't."

"You don't see the ways that wealth could come to this pathetic backwater subsector? You discount the power of incoming money to drive men to actions not typically thought of as legal?"

"Well . . . obviously . . ."

"You simply hadn't thought about it?"

"That's right."

"That is for the best. Once more must I caution

you: never dispute our authority again!" The man and his partner left the room without another word, and Bradley knew that the door was well locked behind them.

Zealots, he grumbled to himself. *Spare me.* They had described him as having a tendency to escape; he'd bloody well demonstrate it for them — and the sooner the better.

He went to the window and looked out. They were in a part of Marterly City reserved for reconstructions of antiquities. That explained the centuries-old opulence of the building on a world that was younger than the architectural style. He was held captive in a museum. Beyond the garden and grounds, and beyond the high fence surrounding the house, a fully modern city awaited him, and the distant past held no appeal for him any longer. Not while his future and his city waited to be met.

He smiled, quietly amused with himself. He had been kidnapped and drugged, yet he had not yet reached the end of his patience.

Crossing the room, he bent over a heavy wooden table. Straightening, he lifted it laboriously before him and walked slowly with it to the window. He rested it on the floor for a moment, catching his breath; then, with all of the force of his arms, shoulders, back, and legs, he heaved the table through the window. Orange-tinted glass sprayed outward in a glittering shower of tumbling shards. The table caught on the carved paneling surrounding the window frame and tore away, flipping end over end as it fell to the green garden below.

Bradley then edged his body out through the

window as quickly as he could, scarcely mindful of the jagged edges of broken glass. Instead of climbing down, the direction most obvious, he clambered hurriedly up. Thick vines had been trained to grow along the house's side, reaching all the way to curl over the lip of the roof. Bradley didn't plan to climb quite all the way to the rooftop — the Crew agents would likely have aircars at their command, and he didn't like the idea of being so vulnerably exposed. But the window was built out from the wall in a small cupola, itself sheltered by a slight overhang of the roof, and it was in this small space that Bradley sought to hide himself.

As he had expected, the door into the room opened within seconds, and footfalls and voices echoed for a moment in the room. He had climbed almost to safety and required only another moment or two to be out of sight from both above and below. He smiled to himself as he heard the Crew agents in the room checking the door of the water closet. A good thing: hiding there had been his first plan.

"The garden!"

"Head him off!"

"Damn it! I told you we should have killed him!"

Bradley raised an eyebrow at that and whistled soundlessly in the shadows of his sanctuary. *The Crew employs hotheaded assassins.*

The room cleared out in only moments, and Bradley relaxed atop the cramped roof of the window cupola. Was his plan actually going to work? He edged back and forth until he found a position that was almost comfortable and peered carefully out. Crew agents thrashed through the overgrown garden, raising a cloud of dust and chaff in the warm, still air. That, too, was good: hiding himself in the garden had been his second plan.

After no more than fifteen minutes, the agents sounded an all clear and retreated back into the house. Five minutes after that, fearing discovery, they fled in two large aircars. Bradley estimated that there had been no more than five of them.

He emerged and climbed down, his feet moving carefully through the knotted tracework of the vines. At the bottom, a gravel path led around the house to the front gardens. Moving cautiously, Bradley made for the nearest exit.

The afternoon was warm and balmy, and the flowers and high hedges of the garden sent up a sunny scent of spring. He hastened along the walkway and passed through a high metal gate that had been left unlocked.

The streets were his, and he wasted no time in traversing them, taking left and right turns mostly at random. Before long he saw a phone kiosk and called for the Constabulary.

Only a few minutes had elapsed before the Militia gravity sled dropped out of the sky, and fifteen heavily armed and armored soldiers clattered out. One large man approached Bradley and stopped in astonishment.

"You again? What kind of escape artist are you?"

That made Bradley think, and he realized that he was rather proud of himself.

"Have we met before, Inspector?"

"Don't you recognize me?" The man seemed astonished at that, and Bradley found himself squinting, trying to place him. An Inspector in the Militia Constabulary, and apparently a big, bluff man. But beyond that, Bradley could see nothing.

Bradley smiled. "No, and for a very good reason. I've been drugged."

"Again? Damn!"

"Yes, indeed. I still can't see faces."

"Damn." The inspector's voice was sharp and unexpectedly angry. "Where is it you were held?"

"Just back there . . ." Bradley gestured over his shoulder, then blinked. The houses all looked the same, and he could not, try as he might, recollect the turns he had taken in his flight.

"I'm sorry," he said at last. "All I can tell you is that it was a large house inside a garden wall, and that one west-facing window is broken."

"Oh, is that all?" The inspector laughed without mirth. "Come into the sled with us, and we'll spot it from the air."

The interior of the gravity sled was cramped, even though the soldiers were careful to make extra room for him. The forward compartment was partitioned off from the troop section by a tiny doorway. Bradley leaned through the opening and tried to help guide the pilot. The inspector, hunching forward in the copilot's seat, coaxed information from Bradley.

"From aloft, knowing how long you were running before you phoned us, we'll spot that window and double quick."

"Thank you, sir."

"You don't recognize me, you say? We met only yesterday. . . . Well, tell me about the drugs they gave you."

"I don't know the names of the drugs. They must have hit me with the same chemical as yesterday. I can't recognize faces. Or streets, it seems."

The inspector swore. "I know the stuff. Garbage. It's damn unhealthy for you. The second exposure increases the risk, too. We'll have you to a medical lab right quick after we've hit the house you were kept in."

"Thank you."

"Don't thank me," the man said unhappily. "This has been a big failure on my part. Those sons of—" He controlled himself. "Those extralegal adventurers snatched you right outside my medical depot yesterday, almost as a snub at my authority. Well, I haven't got much authority on a Sector Capital world, and I know it, but I don't like having people kidnapped whom I promised to safeguard."

The car ran swiftly up and down the north-south net of streets, until the broken window in an upper floor showed, gaping, the house where Bradley had stayed a short time. From the outside it seemed smaller than Bradley's impression of it would have indicated, the gardens more tightly enclosed within the high wall. The sight of the broken-backed table lying legs-up in a flower bed was proof enough, however, and the vehicle dropped heavily to the ground, scarring the grass and causing the high trees to whip as if in a miniature gale. The soldiers darted out and crashed through windows and doors alike, seeking to flush out the kidnappers. It was to no avail: the house was long since vacated.

"Was it the Crew again?" the inspector asked.

"Was it the Crew last time? There wasn't any clear evidence then. But there was this time. I think they were the same two people. They called each other No One and Nobody."

Soon a corporal came up to report that the place was deserted.

"Sorry, sir," the inspector apologized. "It looks like they got free again."

Bradley grinned. "I had hoped that you would catch No One. But Nobody got away." He felt unpleasantly dizzy, and wondered why the inspector had failed to laugh.

The inspector looked at him sidelong. "Are you all right, Mr. Bradley?"

"Oh, perfectly fine," Bradley said, just before he passed out.

∞

From his hospital bed, Bradley phoned the Court Clerk's office. "Hello. This is Councillor Bradley, in the case of Gerald Wilson versus the Concordat of Archive. I'm calling to ask for a postponement—"

"Again?"

"I'm afraid so. But I do have what I think the Tribunal will see as a valid excuse for my absence."

"Let me check, Councillor." The clerk vanished for a few moments, then returned to the phone. "Councillor Bradley?"

"Yes?"

"Your case was dismissed today when you failed to appear. And let me tell you, sir, that Justice Venda was very happy to throw it out. He seemed positively overjoyed."

"How nice for him," Bradley said with a sigh, and hung up.

He lay against the stiff, cold sheets and closed his eyes. The myriad of scents and sounds of the hospital merged into a soft background sensation, and he found himself drowsing.

Sometime later he was awakened by a gentle hand on his shoulder. Bradley was glad to be able to recognize Kelki Hume; he had begun to dread going through the rest of his life without ever seeing a familiar face.

"Good afternoon, Ms. Hume."

"Good evening, Mr. Bradley," Hume said with a chuckle. "It's well past eight o'clock."

"I heard about the dismissal of the case." He shook his head sadly. "Congratulations, anyway."

Hume sat herself on the edge of his bed. "That's a bit premature. I asked that the case be reopened because of the extraordinary circumstances surrounding your abduction. And for another reason."

Bradley's heart beat a bit faster. "What?"

"The *Planetslayer* has come home. They failed in their mission. The Tribunal is going to demand to speak with the passengers and crew."

"Kythe-Correy. It lives?"

Hume reached down and patted him on the shoulder. "Yes." She smiled wickedly. "For now. The legal issues have yet to be settled."

"You're willing to fight this one in open court?"

"I am now, and always have been."

"Will you tell me why?"

She smiled, her eyes alight. "Does Treasury tell Commerce?"

"I didn't think so."

She laughed. "It's very straightforward: we need to know if we can get away with planet-forming projects on a large scale. Because, Mr. Bradley, we're not about to stop. There's a great deal of wealth locked up in this Sector, and in several others, and the Treasury Branch wants it unlocked."

"The legal question is just a test?"

"Of legality." She looked at him, mirth in her eyes. "The Treasury Branch isn't the sort of organization that goes in for hiring kidnappers. We're too straitlaced for that, you know. But it's far more than just a test. We're trying to get a feel for the depth of opposition. And we're also trying to stir up a little support."

"Someone sent those kidnappers after me on your behalf."

"Do you think that's why they were sent?"

"Why else?" He spread his hands helplessly. "Some anonymous benefactor of your position sent that team to waylay me. What else can I conclude? Even my kidnappers spoke of the economic benefits that their masters would recognize if the jump routes through Kythe-Correy were installed."

Straightening, Hume looked down at him. "A hell of a lot of people will be making money when that jump route goes through. It cuts three whole weeks off of the transit time of this Sector. The entire Concordat will be enriched."

"The Treasury Branch most of all," Bradley reminded her.

"Perhaps," Hume admitted.

"It might be some private industrialist, seeking personal advantage. . . ." Bradley suggested, intending to refute his own suggestion instantly.

"Or it might be a patriot, working illicitly for the good of all." Hume took his hand. "In any case, I will not benefit from lawbreakers' actions. The case is reopened. The court date is three days from now." She smiled at him. "I hope you'll be able to attend."

"I wouldn't miss it for the world," Bradley said sincerely.

16

You lose. You always lose. There is no
victory; there is only defeat and failure. You
can't lift this weight; you can't see in this
darkness.

Trinopus, *Three Lesser Paradoxes*

With Eric's help, Taviella had turned the ship's
lounge into an informal hearing room. Fortuna,
fidgeting and flighty, sat in one chair in the corner
by the door to the galley; Maravic, Taviella, and
Mikhail sat as a tribunal facing her. The large, two-
part dining table had been folded up against the
walls, so that the floor of the lounge was bare: it
was the largest open area aboard the ship, leaving
Fortuna isolated and forlorn.

There was no hope for secrecy aboard a ship
whose tight-knit society, even ruptured the way
the *Indagator*'s had been, was composed of nine
individuals living alone and isolated from the rest
of the universe. Taviella permitted the rest of the
crew and passengers to watch and listen from the
three doorways into the lounge. Eric and Reming-

ton hunkered low, watching with grim amusement from the aft doorway; Bea and Gerald stood stiffly in the forward one. Stasileus filled the doorway to the galley, watching with his one huge eye.

Bea looked at him, struck suddenly by an errant perception: not only had the Verna lost weight, but his eye was becoming sunken. She frowned and looked more carefully. Stasileus was definitely ailing; a matted line of crust surrounded his one good eye, and he seemed to be having difficulty focusing. Furthermore, his ears drooped, an indication of unhappiness in most sharp-eared animals. Bea wondered about this, but said nothing.

Taviella finished arranging her sight-and-sound recording device and spoke aloud.

"Day three hundred one, year eleven hundred nine. Treasury Branch tanker *Indagator*. Taviella-i-Tel in command. Preliminary investigation into the disappearance of passenger Doctor Van Wyck Henson. Hearing convened." She looked one way at Maravic, then the other at Mikhail. "Maravic Slijvos, ship's First Mate, and Mikhail Petrov, expedition team leader, members of the tribunal."

"Get it over with, you idiot," Fortuna sneered. "You haven't got an ounce of proof against me. I haven't done a thing. Not a damn thing." She stuck out her jaw. "Let's stop wasting time."

"We have nothing but time, here in jumpspace," Mikhail said reasonably. "Might as well go through this while our memories are fresh."

"You pathetic weakling," Fortuna snapped. "You've been out to get me since we started." Her voice changed, suddenly becoming syrupy. "But then, maybe you have something to gain by persecuting me."

Mikhail looked down at his hands upon his lap and made no response.

"Fortuna, you are compelled to answer these questions." Taviella spoke formally and clearly. "You are being recorded, and devices later will examine the record for the truth or falsehood of your answers."

"Hmm? No voice-stress analyzers aboard ship?" Fortuna clucked her tongue in mock dismay. "Bad planning, Taviella."

"Did you make an illegal copy of the computer's navigational operating system by tapping into portions of main memory forbidden to you?"

Fortuna made a little frown of distaste. "Yes."

"What was your intention? What were you going to do with it?"

"Sell it, of course. If nowhere else, to Perrin University, where the purchasing office is just a bit desperate for low-cost software."

"Did you have anything to do with the disappearance of Van Wyck Henson?"

"Straight to the point, eh, child?" Fortuna's attitude had changed from vitriolic to flippant.

"Answer the question."

"No, I did not."

"Did you arrange for the computer to erase portions of the log memory?"

"By no means."

"Did you arrange for the ship's lifeboat to be launched?"

"No."

Taviella leaned forward in her chair. "Fortuna, the evidence is against you. You have the technical knowledge. You have all of the necessary skills, and you've shown yourself to be untrustworthy. You injured my assistant engineer; although we'll consider that an unpremeditated act for now, we can't ignore the fact that it happened. At any rate, in the matter at hand you're our only suspect."

"Nonsense!" Fortuna laughed. "Eric or Remington could have done it just as easily as I. Even poor one-eyed Stacey could have." She turned to him. "Couldn't you have, Stacey?"

Stasileus shivered slightly and answered her. "Yes. I could have."

"There. You see?"

Stasileus continued, speaking in a high, tremulous voice. "But you needed to get caught."

No one spoke for a long moment. Then Taviella and Fortuna, at the same time, exclaimed slowly, "What?"

"Fortuna's personality revolves around her guilt," Stasileus said. "Her need for expiation works against her need for acceptance. The aberration has two solutions: either she could habitually confess to wrongs that she has not committed, or she could commit wrongs in such a way as to be caught."

"You're insane!" Fortuna hissed. But the ghastly expression on her face was mingled with a peculiar hurt look that told Maravic, watching closely, that Stasileus had been directly on target.

Stasileus looked into her eyes for a long, long moment before he answered her.

"Yes, Fortuna. I am insane." A spasm of tremors shook his body, and his eye closed painfully.

Maravic frowned and leaped from her chair to aid him. Taviella, equally distressed, spoke hastily into the recorder. "The hearing is recessed." She switched it off and joined Maravic at Stasileus's side.

∞

"May I visit him?" Gerald Wilson asked Bea, who stood watch at Stasileus's stateroom. The room had become, temporarily, a sickroom, for there was no question now about Stasileus's health. He was seriously ill. His ribs showed through his skin, and his fur had dulled from its normal gleaming ice-white to the flat, lusterless color of bone. His eye had sunk even farther into his skull and was surrounded by peeling black crusts. His mouth was parched, and his lips cracked, while his tiny black nose ran continually, a clear, watery discharge. And he trembled constantly, a body-wracking shivering unrelated to fever or chills. This had Bea worried more than any of the other dire symptoms.

"Yes, you may. But be careful of what you say. I have a suspicion about what has happened, and it involves cruelty to him."

"Do you want to come in with me?"

"No. I've got to run a few more blood sample tests. His illness may have a physiological basis, although I doubt it."

"Oh." Wilson paused. "Am I safe going in with him?"

"Safe?" Bea laughed. "Are you afraid he's going to leap up and bite you?"

Wilson blushed deeply and bent his head.

"Go ahead in," Bea said with a smile. "Try to keep his spirits up."

"All right." Wilson squeezed gingerly through the doorway and regarded Stasileus on the bunk. After checking to see that the door was tightly shut, he approached the ailing Verna.

"Stacey? How do you feel?"

"I learned too much. I cannot disobey; I cannot obey."

Wilson leaned closer to him. "I can simplify your decision."

Stasileus trembled and said nothing.

"You have to obey orders?" Wilson whispered.

"Yes."

"Here is an order. It is a life-and-death command. I order you to say nothing, ever, to anyone about what we did when we launched the lifeboat."

"I understand." His tremors grew more violent; spasms and shudders shook his entire body.

"So that's it, then. You won't tell." Wilson felt a sudden fear. "You won't tell, will you?"

"I'm not able to tell."

"Good. Um . . . why not?"

"Taviella doesn't want to know."

"Are you crazy?" Wilson hissed. "She wants like hell to find out!"

Stasileus answered him weakly, his body shivering uncontrollably. "She wants to find out, but she does not want to know."

Wilson would have asked further questions,

but was interrupted when the door opened and Bea intruded.

"How is everything?" She edged past Wilson and looked critically at Stasileus. "He's worse!" She whirled to face Wilson. "What did you say to him?"

"Nothing! I told him that we were all pulling for him, and that . . ."

Bea, bending to minister to Stasileus, wasn't listening. Wilson, wide-eyed and fearful, crept out into the corridor and was gone.

"Stacey?"

"Yes, Bea?"

"Look at me."

"Yes, Bea."

Although he had tried to hide it, it was painfully obvious. Stasileus's remaining eye was blind. Bea examined it carefully, inserting a thin, flat probe between his eye and the socket. She pushed and pulled, gently edging the eye to one side and then the other, examining the peripheral muscles, unhappy with what she saw.

"Are you suffering from conflicting orders?"

"Yes."

"But it's more than that, isn't it?"

"Yes."

Bea thought for a few minutes, and the silence was broken only by the hushed whirring of air through the overhead ducts.

"Ordinarily, when you or another of your species suffers from a conflict of orders, what do you do?"

"Nothing."

Bea smiled. "Precisely nothing?"

260

"There is a tendency toward mental collapse and inertia."

"You sit on the floor and shiver like a whipped child," Bea corrected him. "I've seen it happen. You're trembling now."

Stasileus made no denial of the obvious fact.

"Do you have any medical knowledge relating to these symptoms in members of your species?" Bea's question was hurried, impatient.

"No."

"Well, I have some. More than anyone else of my species . . . but still quite an insignificant portion of knowledge." She began to pace, trying to ignore his trembling. "I believe that you are caught in a premature aging crisis, brought on by your conflicting needs to obey."

Again, Stasileus had nothing to say.

Bea turned to him and approached him closely. She sat on the edge of his bunk, leaning over him like a parent over a sick child; like a god peering into the face of the dying, making a final judgment.

"Stasileus, you have been right in every one of your estimations of us. You pinpointed Fortuna. Hell, you pinpointed me, in that meadow back on Kythe-Correy. Now, can you be as wise and helpful in your own assistance?"

"No."

"No?" Bea mocked him with the word; she made it into a scourge. "You saw fit to give us wisdom that we didn't know we knew. But now you refuse to succor yourself." She paused and looked at him, pathetic and shivering under his bed wraps. She took his hand and gripped it tightly.

"We're not through needing you. Did you know that?"

Stasileus turned his blind face to her. "Thank you."

"Sleep now."

Stasileus dropped away into a dark and dreamless of sleep, hearing not Bea's voice, but the voice of his Musele.

∞

Finding Taviella alone in the control room, Bea entered boldly. Taviella looked up, eager for news.

"You're killing your Verna," Bea pronounced.

Taviella blinked in dismay. "I am?"

Bea relented. "But you don't know it. It's not your fault."

"Tell me everything."

Bea seated herself gingerly on the arm of the copilot's couch. She stretched her neck in weariness. "The Vernae were made by our ancestors. Made to be slaves, sex toys, whipping posts, objects to be used and thrown away. Made to be used up. And there's nothing that a Verna can do that a robot couldn't have been fashioned to do better. The engineers of old Archive were good enough, mighty enough, to make a comic-looking slave, a jester: the Verna.

"But they built too well — and in doing so, they erred. The Empire made a lot of errors, and we're still paying for them. They made their Vernae with quick, inquisitive minds." She looked at Taviella. "Have you ever noticed that one of the most common things Stasileus says is 'I don't understand'? It means that he doesn't but he wants to. He wants to know things; he wants to learn."

A silence passed, leaving Taviella and Bea each momentarily alone with her thoughts.

The Empire produced such beauty, Taviella mused. *Why must all of it have been twisted?*

Bea's thoughts were equally glum. *We set out to murder a planet. Instead, we discover truths about ourselves we'd rather have forgotten.*

"A versatile slave," Bea went on at last, "needs to be able to anticipate orders. During the time of the Empire, when education would have been prohibited to them, the Vernae doubtless still showed native cleverness. This would have been dismissed as intuition. But in fact it was the working of minds fully as intelligent as ours trying to deduce the order in what looked like a very chaotic universe.

"And Stasileus was educated. He was given the tools of mathematics and the scientific approach, coupled with the practical technology of engineering. He was given the tools to make sense of it all. Small wonder he turned his observational talents upon us, the most interesting figures around him.

"He learned what makes us think the way we do: he learned what we are and why we are that way. But what we are isn't very nice."

Taviella nodded in agreement. "Someone murdered Van Wyck Henson. That's not very nice at all. Please tell me how I'm hurting Stacey, and I'll stop."

"Stacey learned to understand what it is we want. And what you want is directly countered by

263

the orders he's been given by someone else. You've never gone to Stacey and said 'Tell me all you know about Van Wyck Henson's disappearance.' If you do, he'll die within minutes."

Taviella closed her eyes.

"But he's ahead of you," Bea said, pressing on. "He knows that you want to know. His entire behavioral identity is based on obedience. He told us that. 'I obey, even without commands,' he says. He knows that you want to know, and that knowledge, conflicting with the orders given to him, whether by Fortuna or by someone else, has generated a paradox in his mind — a trap from which he cannot escape."

"What can we do to save him?"

"Are you willing to let Henson's murderer go free, in order to save Stacey?"

Taviella paused. "I . . . I don't know. But I'd certainly be willing to say so to Stacey, if it would help him."

"No." Bea smiled thinly. "You can't lie to him any more. He knows too much."

"Does he know how much we all love him?"

"Oh, yes. He's aware of that."

∞

Mikhail sat with Maravic, sorting through their plans for the future in the way that children will sift through bright scraps of paper and trash, trying to fit together the prettiest pieces into a fragmentary picture. Aware that they were playing, aware that the game might engender the reality, they sat side by side in two chairs in the lounge, dreaming happily.

"Aboard this ship or aboard your *Coinroader*, I'll go with you if I may." Mikhail's voice was tender and somewhat jolly. "I've given it quite some thought — indeed, I've thought about it more than anything else during the past nine days. The university owes me a leave of absence. And if I make a vacation of it, that's nothing to them. A working vacation is even better."

Maravic, practical even when daydreaming, took mind of the technical details. "With the university subsidy on fuel that you could get for us, we'll be able to make detours toward interesting astronomical objects." She leaned closer and nudged him confidentially. "And we've done that ourselves, once or twice, just for the sightseeing. I could tell you tales. . . ."

"I want to go where you go, Maravic."

"And I want to be with you, Mikhail. The search for profit is neverending, like the search for knowledge. The search for companionship . . ."

"It's a better search than most," he agreed, smiling happily.

"What about the Kythe-Correy project?"

Mikhail snapped his fingers. "That for it. I was never the leader of this ill-assorted pack of world-wreckers. I got the assignment by luck of the draw, and should have refused it then."

"Then you wouldn't have met me," Maravic reminded him.

"Eh? Well . . ." He laughed. "Things worked out the way they should have, then. But no more: I won't again participate in sterilizing a world that wealthy."

"Wealthy?"

"In biological diversity."

"And Van Wyck . . ."

Mikhail sighed. "He's probably no more than part of the biological diversity by now: I very much doubt that he's alive."

"They'll find him from orbit," Maravic reassured him. "If he was smart enough to stay near the lifeboat, he'll have food for months. If not, I suppose a man can live in an environment suit for two weeks."

Mikhail made a face. "A devil of a fate."

"Better than dying."

"I'm not too sure."

After a bit they brightened and began again putting their lives together.

∞

Gerald Wilson found an opportunity for one more secret conference with Stasileus.

"Stacey? It's me. Gerald Wilson."

"I know you."

"I've learned what is happening to you. Please. I don't want your death on my hands. Tell them. Tell them everything."

"Tell them yourself."

"I don't have the courage."

Stasileus looked up at him with his one blind eye. "You had the courage to come along on this mission, knowing that Van Wyck Henson would not return. You had the courage to play the necessary part. You are not without courage."

"But I am," Wilson said softly. "I'm the worst coward who ever crawled." He looked at Stasileus's unseeing face. "Tell them. Save yourself. Please!"

"I cannot. I may not."

"Why?"

"Taviella doesn't want me to."

There seemed nothing more to say. Wilson sat, holding Stasileus's hand. His compassion was not merely feigned. He cared.

It was his caring that had gotten him into trouble in the first place.

∞

After a while, Taviella eased into the room.

"How is he?" she whispered.

"I think . . ." Wilson shrugged in helplessness.

Taviella grimaced. "Stacey?"

"Yes?"

Stasileus's voice was weaker than ever before. His lungs were partly filled with fluids.

"Gerald," she said, without taking her gaze from the stricken Verna, "will you leave us?"

"Yes." Wilson silently exited the room, leaving Taviella alone with her friend.

"Stacey?"

"Yes?"

"Don't say anything you don't want to. Don't hurt yourself. But please talk to me. If you can, please tell me what's hurting you."

Stasileus shivered, his trembling increasing

until his entire body was wracked. A tight, high-pitched groan escaped his lips, the first sound of pain Taviella had ever heard from him. It was too much.

"Stop!" She sat beside him on the bunk and lay her upper body across his, warming him, shaken by his shudders. She hugged him tightly. Over and over she repeated to him that he was loved, loved by her and by Maravic, loved even by Remington and Eric.

"You're one of the crew, Stacey. We treasure you."

His spasms subsided. Taviella, her cheeks tear-streaked, broke her embrace and pulled away, bending over Stasileus's shivering form.

"Don't give away anyone's secrets," she urged him in a comforting whisper. "Don't say anything you don't want to. Just tell me what's bothering you. Just talk to me. Tell me what's making you hurt."

Stasileus collapsed, rolling himself up into a tight ball of misery. He didn't groan this time, but his silence was even more ominous.

Taviella leaped up and darted for the exit, shouting as she threw open the door. "Bea! I think—" She didn't have time to finish the message. Bea had been standing right outside the room, waiting for Taviella to finish. She pushed past Gerald Wilson, who had also stayed just outside, waiting to find out what Stasileus might say.

Rushing to Stasileus's side, Bea knelt and felt at the stricken Verna's head and wrist. From the medical bag that she'd left by his side she pulled a hypodermic, took a quick measurement, and injected him with a sedative. Taviella followed her back into the room and watched silently.

"That's to sedate him," she muttered. She prepared a second injection and applied it. "And that," she announced, breathing heavily, "should stabilize him. He won't die . . . not just yet."

Gerald Wilson, standing in the doorway, cleared his throat discreetly. Taviella and Bea ignored him.

Closing his eyes, mustering his courage, Wilson spoke.

"Taviella?"

"Yes?"

"I think it's time I cleared up some matters of confusion."

17

Citizens shall behave with honor toward
one another; justice shall be dispensed from
every man's own heart; my rule should be
unnecessary and my guidance should soon
fade.

*Proclamation Number Seven
of Arcadian I, Emperor of Archive*

Taviella looked blankly at Wilson. "What do you
mean?"

He swallowed heavily. "Not here." He darted a
glance at Bea, who still knelt by Stasileus's bed.

"Come with me, then." To Bea, she muttered
what encouragement she could. "Take care of him,
Doctor Chapman. Please keep him alive."

"I will." Bea never turned to look up; her attention was fixed on Stasileus.

Taviella escorted Wilson to her stateroom. She
gestured him inside, then shut and locked the door.
He slumped to a seat on the chair at her desk; she
crossed the small room and sat on the lower bunk.

"You know something?"

Wilson hung his head miserably. "I know everything. I planned it from the beginning . . . so carefully." He grinned, a horrible, humorless rictus. "And it worked. If I were to keep my silence, no one would ever know." He looked up at Taviella, his face utterly forlorn. "But Stasileus would die. He might die anyway. And then . . ."

"Then you'd have two murders on your hands," Taviella said matter-of-factly. "You killed Doctor Henson, didn't you?"

Wilson faced the floor. "Yes." Again he smiled, an unwilling and unhappy smile. "And no."

"Explain, please."

"I am Van Wyck Henson."

Taviella registered shock and slow, resistant comprehension. "You . . . ?"

"I played the part. I wore an inflatable stomach, makeup . . ." His face worked in anxious misery. He looked as if he didn't know whether to laugh or to cry, but it was certain that once he started doing either, he wouldn't be able to stop.

"Okay." Taviella breathed in deeply. "Tell me everything."

Wilson swallowed and cleared his throat. The hoarse, wet sound of it convinced Taviella in a way that no words ever could have: it was Van Wyck Henson's throat, preparing to spit. Wilson, unaware of the effect the sound had on Taviella, coughed again, fighting to control his emotions.

"Life is different from nonlife. We have the skill, in our chemistry, to synthesize virtually all the components of life. We can synthesize an entire array of chlorophylls, from chlorophyll itself to any of twenty-nine similar molecules. We can synthesize tiny, hard-shelled viruslike things that are *almost* alive. And we can take things that *are* alive and distort them to suit our purposes, almost at will. But we can't synthesize life." Wilson paused, and Taviella thought he was taking quite a while to get to the point. But she let him continue without interruption.

"The old Empire could, though. We know that they had the skill, but that they didn't use it widely. We don't know why. They were also ahead of us in the skill of altering life. They built the Vernae, using animals and men for source DNA. The creation of that obedient and brilliant race took them hundreds of years; the job is still probably not completed to the satisfaction of the original plan.

"They also did things — horrible things — to themselves. To us. We are no longer the race that evolved so many millions of years ago on Archive — if we did indeed originate there. There's some reason to believe that we did not. Did you . . . Did you know that there's a tiny complex of genes in one of the loci of your DNA that prohibits you from killing yourself?"

Taviella blinked. "What do you mean?"

Wilson smiled weakly. "Directly. You could not take up a knife and destroy yourself with it. You couldn't put your gun to the front of your head and pull the trigger. It's a freedom that's lost to us."

"But people do sacrifice themselves," Taviella objected.

"Yes. In war, and in acts of heroism. Very different from self-destruction out of despair. The normal suicide rate for the human race should be one hundred and fifty per million population. That's what we'd expect it to be, *a priori*, based on our not terribly advanced understanding of the human mind. That's the rate for the Reynid and the Sonallans, and they're virtually as human as we are. But our rate is less than one per ten million."

"Why?"

"We have been tampered with. Someone, long ago, long dead, felt that despair was something we ought to be compelled to live with. It seems foolish and abstract, but that's one slight element of freedom that's been denied us.

"The point," Wilson continued, "is that life is something that we cannot create, only alter. And once it's altered, we can't restore it back to what it was before we changed it. We've been altered and will never again be *ourselves*, only something that someone wanted us to be. We don't even know what primeval humankind looked like: were we shorter, squatter, uglier? We were probably all of that and worse.

"One of the first goals of science is to aid us in knowing ourselves. If we were able to trace our own evolution, our self-knowledge would be substantially richer. Now, with what we've been left, we're rootless. We have no archaeological record, no prehuman or protohuman artifacts. We don't even know how long ago the race developed the knowledge of nuclear energy, let alone truly primitive discoveries like the wheel and axle, or storage of water.

"Worlds left untouched, worlds like Catalart

and Kythe-Correy promise — promised — such hope for pure research into the way life follows its own patterns. Did you know that the simplest things, the most completely trivial things, can tell entire volumes about the way life works? One example: when some trees put out branches, and the branches put out smaller limbs, which divide into twigs, there is a continuously preserved angle of branching. The largest branches might spring out at thirty-six degrees, plus or minus a fraction, from the vertical trunk. The same angle applies to the limbs growing away from the branches, and the smallest twigs as they split off from their parent limbs. Trees are highly geometrical. . . .

"Is this pattern continued on Kythe-Correy? Is this a pattern that is inherent in plant growth, as some people believe — or is it an artifact of some tree-engineer of the Empire, who determined that trees ought to grow geometrically?" Wilson looked down at the floor. "This must all seem abstract and foolish to you."

"Gerald," Taviella said quietly, "I'm a business-woman. I'm here for the money. But that doesn't mean I'm blind to the beauty of science. It also doesn't mean that I like the idea of destroying Kythe-Correy."

Wilson lifted his hands in eloquent appeal. "What can Kythe-Correy tell us about ourselves? What secrets died with Catalart? Do you know how many worlds we have — used to have — with truly indigenous life? Twelve! Archive; Bealisworld; Kythe-Correy; Lumanoma; Catalart. . . . But no longer."

274

Taviella frowned. "There are other worlds . . . hundreds of worlds . . . with native life."

"No. They were seeded from Archive. Although there are many who disagree and want to suspect an earlier radiation of species through space, by an earlier human agency." He shook his head. "Do you see how much we've lost? Can you see why I had to try to stop you from killing Kythe-Correy? We don't even know how old we are!

"I worked with friends. We stole a lot of money — I won't tell you how, although I guess I'll end up making a full confession later, to the authorities on Marterly. And we also did a lot of legitimate fundraising. You can do astonishing things in that field once you have only a little seed money. We hired a law team and sent them to the Subsector Supreme Judiciary on Marterly. Their job was to defend the world of Kythe-Correy through legal advocacy. But we knew we were too late; we knew that the case couldn't be decided before a pilot and crew was dragooned into service for the mission. And, indeed, once our legal challenge became known, the Treasury Branch masters of the project moved into top speed and impressed the first crew they could."

Taviella eyed him sidelong. "We weren't Sargent's first choice?"

Wilson couldn't meet her gaze. His hands drooped at his sides. "You weren't really a choice at all. He took what he could get. He'd have preferred military pilots, lent him by the Navy. But to obtain Navy aid would have taken him too much time. He got his crew as fast as possible, by pulling Commerce Branch strings."

"Go on with your story," Taviella muttered through tight-clenched teeth. She shook her head; to relax herself, she pulled both feet up onto the bunk and reached for her drawing pad and charcoal sticks. While Wilson explained his actions, she sketched him, beginning in rough outline, then filling in his agile, energetic features.

"We created Van Wyck Henson. One of our team forged his papers, crediting him with a Doctorate at the DuPres Academy of Sciences. But, you know, there isn't any such place. The 'Academy of Sciences' is no more than a storefront business that we purchased, off away on Tulfred's World. One of our members keeps it running, selling clothing, paying the rent and taxes . . . and answering queries about the Academy's credentials. And about Doctor Henson's. None of this would have stood any careful examination: Doctor Henson would have been discovered as a fraud soon after our return to Marterly. But he served his purpose: he aborted the mission. Now if only the delay has been sufficient . . ."

Taviella looked at him over the top of her drawing pad. "How did you manage to keep two identities running simultaneously aboard the ship?"

Wilson swallowed. "That wasn't easy. . . . I spent a lot of time crawling through the overhead air ducts between Van Wyck's room and my own. And it took time to put on his makeup. You'd have laughed, had you ever seen the operation: inflatable stomach, padded thighs, padded shoulders and arms. . . . The beard had to be glued on carefully, to withstand close inspection. I used eye drops to cause my eyes to look inflamed, and if you think his garbage breath smelled bad, you should have tried tasting the pills that gave it to me. And the restoratives tasted very nearly as bad. . . . He was a synthetic man, fated to die on Kythe-Correy. I had to arrange it so that you'd look for him, not find him, and assume he was still alive. That last was important. I know your breed: no spacer will ever knowingly cause the death of a passenger."

"That's right," Taviella agreed seriously. "With Van Wyck assumed to be on the planet, there was no way we could go ahead with the bombardment."

"So one night," Wilson said, "I sneaked out to the lifeboat hatch, made a few arrangements, and—"

Taviella appeared to be concentrating on her drawing, but her attention was fixed on Wilson. "Who helped you? Who got into the control room and erased the computer's memory log?"

Wilson blushed. "The same one who arranged the lifeboat's airlock doors to cycle automatically, as if someone had gone out onto the planet's surface. I couldn't have taken either of those actions myself. I hoped you wouldn't notice; I hoped that everyone would simply leap to the conclusion that Van Wyck was marooned below, and that the inconsistencies would be overlooked."

"Who helped you?" Taviella waited a moment. "Was it Fortuna?"

"Stasileus."

Taviella's hands froze. Then, slowly, she began again to sketch. "Stacey? Gerald, if you ordered him to help you, and he obeyed because he had no choice—"

"No! It wasn't like that at all! He volunteered to help. And the worst thing is that I never even knew why. I don't know yet!"

"Very well." Setting aside her sketch, Taviella gestured for Wilson to get to his feet. "We're going to Van Wyck's room first, where you're going to show me your disguise apparatus."

"All right."

Behind, on the bunk, her sketch lay face up: it had started as a drawing of Gerald Wilson, but now the features were the pudgy, bearded ones of Van Wyck Henson.

∞

"I smuggled these aboard in Van Wyck's computer terminal. It's actually hollow: just a keyboard and screen." He held up the limp bulk of Van Wyck Henson's inflatable stomach, his dark glasses, and his detachable beard.

Taviella looked around the room. She stood atop the lower bunk and steadied herself by gripping the upper. The ceiling ventilator grille was within easy reach. She pushed it lightly, and it popped loose with a gritty metallic rattle. Looking inside, she saw that there was room for someone of her build or of Wilson's to crawl through. She smiled: Van Wyck Henson would have been stuck in the grilleway like a large cork in a small bottle.

"Why did Stasileus help you?"

"I told you: I don't know. He surprised me while I was messing with the lifeboat. I thought that my entire project was ruined, and that I had been caught. Instead, he told me that he was going to help me. You can imagine how flustered I was. I still don't know why."

Taviella poked her head up into the crawlspace and looked both ways. The shadowy ducts extended off into darkness. Just out of reach, the missing EVA suit lay on the floor of the duct, where Gerald Wilson had carefully hidden it.

"I know why." She climbed back down and brushed her hands together to clean them. "He has to obey, even without commands."

Wilson frowned. "Just seeing me, and knowing I couldn't do it by myself, compelled him to help me?"

Taviella looked down. "That's part of it."

"What else?" Wilson honestly wanted to know.

"He knew that I detested this project." Her voice grew harsh. "I detested Sargent, this ugly, murderous ship, and the entire compulsory, insensitive system that forced me to take a mission this cruel." After taking a long, deep breath to calm herself, she concluded. "Stasileus helped you, because doing that would free me from finishing the job I so much hated."

"He did that for you?"

"Out of his love for me."

Wilson smiled weakly. "He also placed most of the suspicion squarely on Fortuna's head."

Taviella nodded. "Precisely what she wanted, I think. She enjoys playing the martyr."

"Now what?"

"That depends."

"On whether Stasileus lives or dies?"

Taviella met his gaze and nodded solemnly. "That's right."

∞

By the time the *Indagator* neared Marterly, prepared for breakout into normal space, Bea had managed to ensure Stasileus's survival. He was weakened, though, and would never recover his full vitality, although he would remain stronger even than Remington, the strongest of the human crew.

Bea confided in Taviella, giving her Stasileus's most private secret. "He has, perhaps, two years to live. Maybe more. Maybe less."

Taviella, stricken, closed her eyes. "Why?"

"The crisis weakened him. He was unable to resolve the paradox of his conflicting orders, and that brought on a premature aging crisis composed of a reinforcing sequence of physical shocks. It had roughly the effect of aging him by three years. Age-related processes have begun in his body, deteriorative events that will, eventually, kill him."

"His eyesight?"

Bea smiled. "Recovered in his one eye. Well, mostly recovered." She shrugged. "We're not completely sure how those oversized, oversensitive eyes work. I can't tell how much acuity is lost. He can read perfectly well, recognize faces at normal distances, and duck out of the way when I throw food at him."

"Why would you do that?"

Bea looked at Taviella, her smile fading to a

280

sullen frown. "Because that superbly insightful and intelligent so-and-so has been psychoanalyzing me to a fare-thee-well! He's dissecting me like an insect on a scale, showing me things inside myself I never knew existed. And he isn't making it painless!"

Taviella spread her hands. "Once he started studying us, we were all doomed. He'll come to me next, doubtless."

"Don't admit anything. Don't let him guess your secrets. Make him respect you."

"That will be difficult."

"Why?"

"Because," Taviella said, "*I* respect *him*. If he wants to understand me, how can I tell him not to?"

Bea looked at her, an unhappy grimace on her nearsighted face. "You're just no damn fun at all."

"Sorry." Taviella was smiling, but she meant her apology sincerely.

"Hmm. Did you ever learn what Gerald Wilson had to suggest?"

"Yes."

"What was it?"

"Oh, nothing of any significance," Taviella lied.

∞

Mikhail, Maravic, Taviella, and the still-weak Stasileus gathered in the privacy of the control room to discuss their plans.

"We have to agree, now, what we're going to tell Sargent and his Treasury Branch investigators." Taviella looked at her three friends.

"Is there anything remaining that you haven't told us?" Mikhail asked. Maravic, looking up at Taviella, asked the same question with her eyes.

"Nothing. You know the truth."

"If we continue the charade, maintain the fiction that Van Wyck Henson is stranded on Kythe-Correy . . ." Mikhail made some calculations in his head. "It will delay the sterilization project for at least two months. The military scout ship will quarter the planet, and not find him, of course. But they won't be able to presume him dead until all reasonable hope is gone."

"None of the food from the downed lifeboat will be used," Maravic pointed out. "And they'll know that he can't eat the native life. Two months is an extreme estimate of his survivability."

"That gives Gerald Wilson and his friends time enough to go ahead with the legal challenge. His plan will have succeeded." Taviella looked around her at her friends. "Van Wyck Henson was a real person, as far as we're concerned. And his disappearance saves the world of Kythe-Correy. If the legal battle succeeds, the world might live. The trade is fair."

Stasileus spoke then, slowly, his voice as high as ever, but more hollow. "Will you continue to allow suspicion to be placed on Fortuna? Mikhail, will you cover for Doctor Henson's false credentials? Taviella, can you delay Mr. Hens Sargent from hurrying the project through?"

Maravic laughed, a happy, chuckling sound of pure mirth. "Stacey, you've seen human beings when they're being obstructive, have you not?"

Stasileus cocked his head to one side and peered at her with an expression of confusion. "Yes."

"Well you haven't seen *anything* to compare with the obstructions that Taviella and I can throw at Mr. Sargent. You see, we can do something that you can't — and bless you for your disability."

"What is that?"

"Indeed," Mikhail murmured. "What is this ability that we have?"

"Disobedience." Maravic hugged him, then reached out and included Taviella and Stasileus in her embrace. "Civil disobedience."

"We're with you," Taviella agreed.

"I certainly am." Mikhail sighed. "Although it plays havoc with my sense of professional ethics."

"But you're going to sign aboard the *Coinroader* as scientific auxiliary crew, aren't you?" Taviella asked. "You'll be cross-assigned to the Commerce Branch, and that means you'll be, in part at least, a merchant."

"Well, yes . . ."

Taviella laughed out loud. "You'll learn, soon enough. Merchants have no sense of ethics at all."

Maravic, grinning wolfishly, agreed. Mikhail, thinking about it later, was uncertain of whether he was dismayed or appreciative.

And Stasileus watched them all, even when participating in their councils. He watched them, and he learned.

∞

The ship broke through the jumpspace barrier and slowly, lazily spiraled in toward the shining blue world of Marterly. Fortuna and Bea could not help but be aware that the crew of the *Indagator* had come to some sort of secret agreement with Mikhail Petrov and Gerald Wilson. Fortuna resented being left out, while Bea, seeming more self-composed than ever before during the voyage, let it neither irk nor puzzle her. She thought she trusted Taviella, but she knew she trusted Stasileus.

Eric and Remington, let into the periphery of the secret, grinned wide, idiot grins and spent as much time as possible away from the scientists' presence. Mikhail would be joining them aboard the *Coinroader*, a new key element in the battle of the sexes, however enamored he might be of Maravic. Things had seldom looked so promising.

∞

Treasury Legate Hens Sargent fumed with anger as he greeted Taviella, Maravic, and Mikhail. He glared at each of them in turn as they explained the need for them to have returned in failure. Then he held up a hand and halted Taviella's narrative.

"I'll accept the rest of your report in writing." He beetled his brows and spoke in a grumbling, breathy tone of extreme irritation. "Our reserve fleet has dispatched a destroyer to search Kythe-Correy for Doctor Henson."

Maravic looked at Mikhail in amused surprise: a destroyer? Quite a large ship to send on a search-and-rescue mission. Mikhail pressed her hand.

"There's something else," Taviella said firmly, "that isn't yet in my report. I thought it best to tell

284

you personally, first. The *Indagator* isn't safe to be flown. My engineers tell me that it was pressurized with contaminated fuel. Until the reactor's been flushed and the tanks washed out, that ship is unsafe. I intend to log that in at the spaceport's central flight control office, but I thought I'd give you the chance to pull the ship off line voluntarily first."

Sargent blinked in amazement. "Contaminated fuel? That's highly unlikely. Are you sure?"

"Sure?" Taviella asked airily. "Far from it. I'm no engineer. But in my mind, without an engine overhaul that ship doesn't fly."

"This is a petty form of childish revenge!" Sargent glared at her. "That ship is in perfect operating condition! You're lying!"

"I gave you your chance. The portmaster will pull the ship off the flying line within two days of my giving him my report. I don't care what your record looks like, but you—"

"I know when to give in to blackmail," Sargent fumed. "You want your *Coinroader* back, with no strings attached."

"That's right." Taviella smiled at him. "Cargo intact, ship untouched, and Commerce Branch license reinstated."

"You'll get it."

"Now."

Sargent glowered at her, then shouted for Roxolane. After a moment, he shouted again. The Verna did not appear, and he had to prepare, sign, and seal the papers himself. Despite an extreme fit of poor temper, he fulfilled Taviella's demands to the letter.

"Is that all of it, then?" Maravic asked. "We can leave?"

"Not just yet." Sargent glowered at her. To Taviella he handed one more set of orders. "You're wanted to testify at the Tribunal that's looking into the legality of this matter."

"You said we'd be free to go," Taviella protested.

"This has nothing to do with Treasury and Commerce Branch squabbling," he answered harshly. "This is a Judicial Branch inquiry. Don't skip out on it, on your peril."

"We'll be there." Taviella glumly closed the door to Sargent's office and walked with her dejected crew along the corridor.

"He lied to us," Maravic said at last. "He told us we'd be back in space without any controls. And now we find ourselves on trial."

"Sargent lied to us." Taviella looked down at the floor. "But I lied to him, also. I've already been to the portmaster, where I registered the *Indagator* as unsafe."

Blinking, Maravic hurriedly thought that one over. "We'll want to leave as soon as possible after the Tribunal's sitting. We'll want to be out of here *real* fast."

"We will be." Taviella looked at her. "You and Mikhail get ready aboard the ship, and have Eric prepare the engines for takeoff. Sargent might find some way to rescind his permit to depart once he learns that I've condemned the *Indagator*."

"Right," Maravic said. To Mikhail, she smiled. "Didn't I say that the Commerce Branch was an exciting place to live?"

"Very right! And you'll have to teach me all about merchanting," Mikhail agreed. "Although elements of it seem refreshingly similar to managing a university department."

"You've used blackmail also?"

"In my time, when it seemed necessary."

"It's settled, then," Taviella announced. "We leave right away after the hearing."

18

We keep trying, I think, only because we must. It isn't in us to quit. Perhaps one day we'll get it right, but even then we'll be unable to rest.

Szentellos, *Regrets*

Roxolane stood holding Stasileus tightly, the two savoring the furry, living warmth of one another. They gripped each other tightly, chest to chest and cheek to cheek.

"You've been horribly hurt," Roxolane said with a shudder.

"I've been destroyed . . . and remade," Stasileus answered.

"You've gone on; you've become a leader."

"No. I have simply learned too much. I will not live to return to my people."

"You've become a thinker, and an authoritar. You are now so very different from me."

Stasileus hugged Roxolane more tightly. "No. I am not a warrior-hero reborn. I am not unlike you. I am only foolish Stasileus. I have learned what humans are, but in doing so I lost my belief in what I am. I will die soon, content to help Taviella run her small ship."

"Will your knowledge then become lost?" She tried to ask the question calmly, but she could not conceal her fear.

Squeezing her with all his loving might, and squeezed by her in return, he leaned on her shoulder and said, very softly, "Knowledge is never lost. I have made a record, and it will be sent to my home world. The knowledge of human minds is a dangerous knowledge for our kind, just as humans are dangerous to us. But my knowledge, my new science, shall not be lost. In time and with effort, it can be made useful to us. It must be studied and understood. We must learn how to stand beside these humans. Trust and life and knowledge and love must never be forgotten."

∞

The atmosphere of the reconvened Tribunal was vastly different from its earlier form. John Bradley looked about the courtroom crowded with merchants, scientists, Treasury Branch officials, and one personable alien whose presence constituted a crowd in itself.

He had never seen a Verna before, although he knew there were some on the planet. Stasileus looked big and formidable, yet weak and vulnerable at the same time. His great height and powerfully muscled arms contrasted strangely with the meek expression on his blunt, round face. And the

289

patch over his ruined eye made him look utterly comic to Bradley, in an endearing, almost pathetic way.

Justices Goto, Venda, and Lindstrom seemed basically at ease, despite the large turnout. But Bradley looked carefully at each of them in turn and saw that Justices Venda and Lindstrom were hiding signs of nervous tension. Justice Goto, as always, was relaxed and happy.

And Councillor Hume, Bradley noted, was already on her feet in anticipation of the afternoon's circus. An OIS news camera had been allowed into the courtroom, over Venda's doubtless strident objections: Hume had the public forum she'd been desirous of.

"The court will come to order," Justice Hamilton Venda said, not loudly. Instantly the crowd of merchants and other onlookers dropped into their seats and took up a tense silence.

"Councillor Hume, are you ready?"

"Yes, sir."

"And Councillor Bradley. Are you in fact present today?"

Bradley rose and smiled. "I'm all here, thank you, sir."

Venda looked carefully at Bradley before moving along. "We're going to be taking a closer look at the mission of the *Indagator* and why it failed. It is Councillor Hume's contention that this will have a bearing on the legal aspect of such missions in the future." Justice Venda paused, looked around the room and said, very low and very firmly, "This is a court of law, and all relevant evidence is admissible. Nevertheless, we shall not tolerate any deviance from the proper formats and procedures. There will be no run-on responses, and no talking back to the interviewers. Decorum will be upheld. Do you understand?"

"Yes, sir," Hume responded.

"Yes, sir," Bradley said, his voice low and clear.

Justice Lindstrom had some words to add. "No decision will be permitted out of this courtroom that serves to weaken the legitimacy or the functioning of the Concordat of Archive. I want everyone to understand that that aspect of the law comes first." She looked firmly at Bradley and at Hume. "You may now begin."

Kelki Hume strode forward and called for the testimony of Taviella-i-Tel. Nervous but hiding it well, she came forth and stood at attention facing the Tribunal.

"Tell us about your mission, Taviella," Hume asked, matter-of-factly.

Quickly and perfunctorily Taviella sketched in the major outline of the mission as it had been planned. She described the orbital mechanics and the collision dynamics that would have been involved in sterilizing the world.

Throughout her monologue, Hume nodded, accepting her descriptions.

"Were you capable of completing the mission?"

"Yes, ma'am."

"Why didn't you?"

Taviella paused and looked to Maravic for help. She had sworn to assist Gerald Wilson, but she hadn't imagined that would extend to lying in a court of law. Swallowing, she told the truth as she had seen it at the time. "When Doctor Van Wyck Henson disappeared, we didn't dare continue with the mission."

"And of Doctor Van Wyck Henson no trace was ever found?"

"I understand that a Navy destroyer is currently searching the world of Kythe-Correy. We searched before we came back, but couldn't find him."

"Thank you. That will be all." Hume stood back to let Taviella pass. A sharp word from Justice Venda, however, recalled Taviella to the floor.

"One moment."

"Yes, sir?" Taviella faced the bench.

"Who was on duty when Doctor Henson disappeared?" Venda asked.

Taviella blinked. "No one, sir. We were all in our bunks."

"How did Henson disappear?"

Taviella had already gone over this, but she repeated the information. "He stole a lifeboat."

"Despite all safeguards?"

"The safeguards were overcome." Now Justice Venda was getting into new territory.

"How?"

"Through access to the ship's computer, which controls all of the ship's airlocks and EVA ports."

"So someone among your crew helped Doctor Henson by overriding the computer for him?"

"Or else he did it himself, sir," Taviella responded, standing up to Venda's hectoring as well as she could without sounding bluff or rebellious.

"Did he have the science background to work the computer?"

"I don't know."

"But others aboard did."

Taviella faced him squarely. "Yes, sir."

"Who?"

"Myself." Taviella shrugged and went on. "Maravic, Stacey, Remington, Eric—"

"Stacey?"

"The Verna. Stasileus."

Venda snorted derisively. "Go on."

"Any of the crew, sir. Of the passengers, I don't know for sure. Certainly Mikhail and Fortuna."

"Very well. That's all for now. Councillor Bradley, you may proceed."

John Bradley watched Justice Venda with increasing unease. The man's voice and bearing were ringing strident alarm bells in Bradley's mind. He found it altogether annoying, and couldn't discern why. His own cross-examination of Taviella was brusque and unproductive.

"Why did you spare the world?" he asked when he was about finished.

Taviella spread her hands. "A man was stranded there, and we couldn't possibly have gone ahead with the mission."

"Before that, however: did your team have second thoughts?"

"Yes, sir."

"Why?"

Looking at the floor, Taviella answered in a soft voice. "It is a very pretty world, sir."

"All right. Please step down."

The other human crew members were interviewed in sequence.

"State your name, please," Justice Lindstrom asked, eyeing Maravic challengingly.

"Maravic Slijvos."

"What can you add to what Taviella has already told us?"

"Not a great deal, ma'am. I want to point out, though, that all of our decisions were made according to Commerce Branch Detached Merchants' Guidelines."

"By the book?" Justice Lindstrom said wryly.

"All the way. We knew there'd be a hearing."

Justice Lindstrom leaned forward over the bench and peered at Maravic. "You did, did you?" She leaned back. "Why did you know there would be a hearing?"

"I've been in the Commerce Branch for quite a while, ma'am. There's always a hearing. If some board or committee isn't asking why things went wrong, then they're trying to discover why things went right."

"You've participated in this kind of board or committee?"

"All too often," Maravic sighed. A light ripple of laughter coursed around the hearing room.

Lindstrom, flushing slightly, rested her elbows on the bench before her. "Step down."

"Thank you, ma'am," Maravic said, and made her exit.

Chief Engineer Eric Fuller was called next.

"What do you know about this matter?" Justice Venda asked.

"Nothing," Eric said, his voice loud and flat.

"Nothing whatever?"

"I'm just an engineer."

"Step down, please."

Cargo Chief Remington Bose was no more help.

"What was your job aboard this mission?" Lindstrom asked.

"I didn't have a job aboard this mission."

"No job."

"No, ma'am."

"Why were you along?"

"No reason, I guess."

"Weren't you in charge of dumping the liquid cargo on the planet?"

"Yeah," Remington drawled, "but that never did get done."

"It was to be your job, wasn't it?"

"Ma'am, I don't get paid for things that are 'to be' done, just for things I do. On this voyage, I didn't do a thing. I'm sorry."

"Stand down," Lindstrom said in disgust.

Mikhail Petrov was next. Justice Goto stirred himself to ask the questions.

"Did you have any doubts as to the validity of this mission on scientific grounds?"

"Yes."

"Explain, please." Justice Goto watched with hooded eyes, obviously intent on Petrov's words.

"We almost decided, aboard the ship, not to continue with the mission — before Doctor Henson's disappearance. Several times we came close to putting the matter to a vote, and once, at least, Taviella said that she would be willing to abide by the decision of the majority. We finally did vote, and the consensus was to continue with the mission. But we had severe regrets and doubts."

"The planet is beautiful — isn't that what Taviella said?"

"Yes, sir. But its beauty, to me, was in the treasure of scientific knowledge that it represented. The world needed — needs — to be preserved for that reason, more than for any other."

"I see."

Bradley watched the witnesses, but he watched Justices Venda and Lindstrom too, and knew that something was horribly wrong. He wanted nothing more than for this insane hearing to be over soon.

"Only one more witness is left to call. Stasileus?" Justice Venda tripped up slightly over the name. "Stasileus? Please come and stand before the bench."

"He's in ill health," Taviella said. "Can questions be put to him on paper, please?"

Justices Venda and Lindstrom peered at her in a puzzled, irritated way, then both looked at Stasileus. He in fact did look slightly gaunt, and his one eye seemed watery. Justice Venda snorted. "He looks healthy enough to answer a few questions."

"Sir, he's not. Please, sir—"

"Stasileus," Venda ordered, "come down here."

"Yes, sir," Stasileus piped, his voice high and eager to please. He trudged the breadth of the courtroom and came to a stop before the bench, his eyes on a level with the Justices' faces.

"What do you know about this matter?"

Stasileus turned slowly about and smiled a

faint, sad smile of farewell to Taviella. She was on her feet in the next instant. "No! Don't make him tell!"

The room fell into an uproar as Mikhail and Maravic pulled Taviella back. Taviella reached out, her hands uselessly grasping for Stasileus. Moments later, silence reasserted itself.

"Stasileus," Justice Venda demanded again. "What do you know about this matter?"

Beginning, just slightly, to tremble, Stasileus said softly, "Everything, sir."

"Tell me."

Stasileus bent his head, and his body started to shake. "The planet of Kythe-Correy is worth more than my life is, sir."

"What do you mean?" Justice Venda leaned forward over the bench and laid a sharp hand on Stasileus's shoulder. "Tell us all you know."

John Bradley had seen enough. "Stop it, sir. This isn't right. He's not well."

"Don't interfere, Councillor."

"Sir, he's not capable of going on!"

"Don't dispute my authority again, Councillor!"

Bradley staggered back, his mouth wide open. "You . . . You . . ." Something clicked inside his head, and he recognized Justices Venda and Lindstrom as the two who had held him, under the names No One and Nobody, in a museum house in the city.

"One minute," he said, very firmly, and stepped up to the bench. The last vestiges of patience fled from him, and he boiled over into an extremely dangerous mood. "Wait a minute, friend. I know you. I know you now."

"What are you talking about?" Venda snapped, his eyes flashing wide. Beside him, Justice Lindstrom stood, preparing to flee.

Bradley turned and addressed Justice Goto. "These are the two who kidnapped me. They held me, they threatened my life, and they sought to interfere with the due proceedings of justice."

"You're mad," Venda shrieked.

"You're damn right I'm mad!" Bradley bellowed, and began to climb over the bench to get at his tormentors.

"Now, now, Councillor Bradley," Justice Goto said, not loudly.

Bradley, completely lost now to his anger, stood atop the bench and dropped heavily down onto the other side, catching Justice Venda in an unbreakable grasp.

"You held me. You threatened me. You drugged me." He pulled Venda close. "You've got some explaining to do."

"Impossible," Venda croaked. "You couldn't have recognized me. . . ."

"Councillor Bradley," Justice Goto said, very, very softly, "let the man go." His robed hand came up from beneath the bench holding a pocket stunner. "If you don't want to sleep through the rest of this most interesting session, I'd suggest you find a seat. Hmm?" He raised his eyebrows politely. With his free hand he pressed the button that summoned the court bailiffs. "But, Justice Venda," he continued smoothly, "won't you tell me *why* Mister Bradley couldn't have recognized you?"

"He can't prove anything!" Venda shouted.

"Oh, I disagree," Justice Goto said. "It shouldn't take more than a few minutes for the conflicting accusations to sort themselves out."

"Sir?" Stasileus's soft voice cut through the shouting inside the courtroom as if by magic.

"Yes?" Justice Goto looked curiously at the tall alien.

"I have extensively studied the human mind. No human can ever lie to me. Councillor Bradley's allegations against Justices Venda and Lindstrom are true."

Justice Goto lifted an eyebrow. "Indeed? I'll take that into account. . . ." He looked dubiously back and forth between his two fellow Justices and Stasileus.

Five armed bailiffs entered the room in a file. Immediately, Justice Venda sought to give them directions. "Have this man" — he indicated Bradley — "taken away and held incommunicado. Have him—"

"No," Justice Goto said softly. "That wouldn't do." He eyed Venda sidelong. "Not after his accusations of you."

"You can't just let him go!" Venda objected.

"Why not? Where's he going to go?"

"Nowhere, sir," Bradley said with glee. "I'm not going anywhere at all."

Venda looked at him in despair. "How could you have remembered?"

"You shouldn't have reminded me."

The bailiffs, under conflicting orders, settled for quieting the courtroom and hustling everyone back to their seats. When that was done, they stood by, waiting for instructions. Justice Goto waved them away, and they reluctantly withdrew.

"Stasileus?" Justice Goto asked quietly. "Can you talk?"

"He'll die!" Taviella shouted.

"But I will talk," Stasileus said, his voice very low. "I am already broken. I'm pulled a dozen different directions all at once. I hurt inside. I am dying." He looked around the room, spending extra time gazing at Taviella, Maravic, and Mikhail.

"Do you wish to be excused, Stasileus?" Justice Goto asked.

"Because of the unfortunate life on the world of Kythe-Correy, all of this has transpired, in riot and in deceit, and death is the result." Trembling now uncontrollably, Stasileus staggered back toward Taviella. "You are a wondrous race, O humans! I wish that I had never come to understand you."

By the time Bea reached his side, he was dead where he stood.

"The court will recess until tomorrow morning," Justice Goto said into the rising hubbub of concerned voices. His smile was thin and wan. He caught Councillor Bradley's eye and gestured him to join him for a private conference.

∞

John Bradley spoke with Mikhail Petrov, after all had been said and done.

"Justice Venda was merely operating to protect the laws," Bradley explained glumly.

"By breaking them?"

"He didn't like allowing anyone to bring suit against the government. Not even with the government's consent."

"How bloody foolish."

"It's more than that. He saw the court's job as being to do what's right for those under his jurisdiction. Kythe-Correy's death would strengthen the Concordat, both locally and overall. He never understood that Kelki Hume was working for the same ends, and every bit as sneakily."

"But why involve the Crew? Why use illegal means?"

"I don't think he saw them as illegal. In his view, a secret police organization is like any other military formation: a force to be used in emergencies."

"Why did he get involved personally?"

"Oh, that's easy: he's a bit of a sadist."

"He'll have twenty years to reconsider his wisdom. He's been sentenced to a penal colony on another world."

Bradley nodded. "A stiff penalty, but a fair one. How is Taviella taking her loss?"

"Poorly. She blames herself, although she's furious at Venda. He might have a warm reception waiting for him in twenty years."

Bradley smiled. "And I just might be part of that reception."

The two paused and looked up into the starry night.

"Nothing was settled, was it?"

"Kythe-Correy will have another hearing. Justice Goto has promised that no mission to kill it will leave until the decision is permanent."

"There's no guarantee of how his new Tribunal will decide."

"There never is."

∞

Dark fur moved quietly in the darkness. Roxolane stood on a hill above the spaceport and looked up into the sky full of stars. She watched the small, moving glow of the *Coinroader* soar silently up and away. Silently, in the darkness, she waved her blunt, four-fingered hand.

Fantasy adventure from

NEW INFINITIES™
PRODUCTIONS, INC.

GORD THE ROGUE™ Books by Gary Gygax
$3.95 each

Sea of Death
Night Arrant
City of Hawks
Come Endless Darkness
Dance of Demons

The Legend Trilogy by David Gemmell

Against the Horde $3.95
Waylander $3.50
The King Beyond the Gate $3.50

Skraelings by Carl Sherrell $2.95
The Last Knight of Albion by Peter Hanratty $3.50
The Book of Mordred by Peter Hanratty $3.50